PR 9272.9 .T7

Tracy, Robert Archer

The sword of Nemesis

DEC 1981

APR '76

MAY '86

FEB '82

KALAMAZOO VALLEY
COMMUNITY COLLEGE
LIBRARY

25965

THE SWORD OF NEMESIS

AMS PRESS
NEW YORK

THE SWORD OF NEMESIS

BY

R. ARCHER TRACY, M.D.

THE NEALE PUBLISHING COMPANY
440 FOURTH AVENUE, NEW YORK
MCMXIX

25965

Library of Congress Cataloging in Publication Data

Tracy, Robert Archer, 1878-
   The sword of Nemesis.

   Reprint of the 1919 ed. published by Neale Pub.
Co., New York.
   I. Title.
PZ3.T67428Sw7   [PR9272.9.T7]   823   73-18609
ISBN 0-404-11419-9

Trim size of AMS edition of this book is 5 x 6 7/8.
Original edition is 5 x 7 1/2.

Reprinted from the edition of 1919, New York
First AMS edition published in 1975
Manufactured in the United States of America

AMS PRESS INC.
NEW YORK, N.Y.

DEDICATION

TO MY AFFECTIONATE WIFE
JOSEPHINE BESSIE

THE SWORD OF NEMESIS

CHAPTER I

> Music and pomp their mingling spirit shed
> Around me; beauties in their cloud-like robes
> Shine forth a scenic paradise, it glares
> Intoxicant through the reeling sense
> Of flushed enjoyment.
>
> *Montgomery.*

> All are but parts of one stupendous whole,
> Whose body nature is and God the soul
> That, changed through all, and yet in all the same,
> Great in the Earth as in the ethereal frame,
> Warms in the sun, refreshes in the breeze,
> Glows in the stars, and blossoms in the trees;
> Lives through all life, extends through all extent.
>
> *Pope.*

THE verses just quoted were recited in a spirited and earnest tone by the younger of two men who were enjoying a cool and refreshing evening walk in the environment of the Amershams' plantation. This burst of eloquent poetry was drawn forth by a magnificent scene, worthy the brush of Raphael or Michaelangelo, which presented itself to the view of the two men as they stood on an eminence overlooking the town of P. No sound fell upon the ear. Even the merry little crickets had ceased for a while their monotonous music; the workmen had laid down their tools, and the clang of machinery was hushed.

Extending as far as the eye could reach were delightful canefields, robed in their vernal beauty, presenting in the distance a most picturesque appearance. There were to be seen innumerable tropical trees, whose rich foliage, blending harmoniously, formed a complete sea of verdure, enhancing the already charming scene. The landscape below was dotted here and there with houses of all sizes and descriptions, standing in the midst of smiling vegetation. Several schooners and sloops were riding at anchor in the harbor below, while out on the sea fishermen's cables glided gaily along. In the west the rose-colored tints that the sun had left behind kept the eyes spellbound and the mind wondering whether the finger of some fairy queen had not produced the rich beauty of the illuminated sky. The sapphire ocean wore an aspect that baffles description as the multicolored hues of the radiant skies gilded its surface.

Forming a stately background to this enchanting view, was a rugged chain of mountains whose azure hue fascinated the eye, while a number of tall slender palm trees on their lower heights contributed to the general beauty of the scene.

"Yes, excellent, by Jove!" exclaimed the elder man, taking the sweet-smelling Virginian cigar from his mouth. "It must have been such a scene as this which inspired Dr. Faber to write;

> 'And oh! what then must thou be like
>   Eternal loveliness.'"

Soon the two men turned to retrace their steps homewards.

Oscar Lindsay, for that was the name of the elder gentleman, was about forty years of age—a tall and stately man. He possessed a well-formed head, upon which grew a luxuriant mass of hair, slightly silvered here and there. His prominent brow was traversed with lines of thought, and under his shady eyebrows shone out two brilliant orbs that captivated all upon whom they alighted, and seemed to pierce the very soul. The nose was slightly hooked and set off the thoughtful and clean-shaven face to good advantage; the corners of the lips betrayed a somewhat cynical tendency. He had a walking-cane in his hand, with which he playfully knocked off the blossoms of several wild plants that bordered the road.

Lindsay was an eminent lawyer, highly esteemed in the community in which he lived. His companion was a young man of not more than twenty-three. Like Lindsay, he possessed a splendid head, whose classic shape argued intellectual worth. His forehad was as high as it was broad, and his merry eyes, indicating a joyous disposition, sparkled with the brilliancy of youth. A well-formed Roman nose blended harmoniously with delicately formed lips, slightly curved, over which fell a handsome mustache. His prominent masculine chin was closely shaven and strongly marked by a dimple. His complexion was rather dark, but argued vigorous health. In short, Hugh Highfield was a very handsome man. He was the only son of the late Cecil Highfield of the island of Trinidad. He had studied at Codrington College, Barbados, and had gone to spend a few months with his friend, Lindsay, who had also been a sincere friend of his father.

"Would you mind going through the Amershams' estate?" enquired Lindsay of his companion when they were about a half-mile distant from home. "It may be somewhat further, but you will be amply repaid for the delay by the pleasure you will experience in having a look at the works of the plantation. There remain still the relics of the barbarous cattle-mill, which has had to bow and retire before the advent of the superior machinery that has been the result of a later invention, in addition to other curiosities, which I am sure will interest you."

"Certainly," replied the other, "these curiosities are always of interest and you can afford me no greater pleasure, my dear Lindsay, than to point out some of those links which constitute part of the chain of progressive development. I do not think you ought to term the cattle-mill 'barbarous'; it met the exigencies of the times and was as useful in the good old days as your colossal machinery is to-day. Do you despise the stone-axe because it has been succeeded by wrought steel? Ah, ungrateful beings that we are!"

"Never mind, my dear boy," returned Lindsay with a smile, at the same time patting Hugh on the shoulder. "I never meant to reflect on the memory of our simian ancestors. I forgot that the intellect must operate in conformity with its stage of development and—"

"Away with your balderdash, man! Now I see your ironical drift. You mean once more to fire your unrelenting shafts at the theory of evolution; but you may depend upon it that your arrows will meet the fate of Acestes when he would strike the stars."

"Ha! ha! ha!" laughed the lawyer, and the cigar, which was almost spent, fell from his lips to the ground. "What are we coming to when parsons are believing in the gospel of Darwin and Wallace!"

After having spent a short time in visiting the works of the Amershams' plantation, they continued their journey homeward, where soon afterward they were discussing the merits of tea and toast.

CHAPTER II

> There are more things in heaven and earth, Horatio,
> Than are dreamt of in your philosophy.
>
> *Shakespeare.*

ELMSDALE Cottage was one of those stately buildings on which the eye delights to gaze, and furnished a most welcome scene for esthetic minds. It was situated on a very healthy and airy spot in the suburbs of the town. At the eastern side of the building there was a balcony, which gave an excellent view of the environment. From that point one could see in the distance rich emerald fields of lime trees gently waving to and fro, as the sweet zephyrs played among their foliage.

Far away the lofty chimney of the Cordelia estate poured out volumes of thick black smoke, and the gigantic arms of the old windmill afforded some pleasure to the eyes, as the fans were whirled around by the strong winds that usually prevailed about that hilly quarter.

Around Elmsdale Cottage there were tastily planted numbers of cactus and oleander trees, with lime trees interspersed. These all formed a fence, which was not altogether devoid of a certain picturesqueness. The lawn was extensive and beautifully laid out with sod; while in the centre of the grounds was a large basin in which a colony of goldfish darted to and fro in the pellucid water. Water lilies,—beautiful in their rich luxuriance,—covered the entire surface of the pond. There was an elaborate fountain rising about six to eight feet above the basin, and out of the gaping mouth of a hideous lion's head issued continually streams of water, which fell upon flower beds that rivalled those of the most elegant English homes.

Not far distant from the fountain and near the border of the grounds was a pond that contained some young turtles. Very near to this spot stood a large tamarind tree that had braved the storms of perhaps a couple of centuries. It afforded an excellent shade, and was a special resort of the inmates of Elmsdale during the distressingly hot days. A little menagerie was kept under the balcony, where were birds of every hue in cages,—from the interesting little humming bird to the troublesome macaw,—and where the wood-dove's plaintive cooing mingled with the weird unearthly sound of the horned owl. There was Jack the monkey, with his amusing antics and begging gestures, as his visitors tantalized him with a morsel of bread; and Polly, seated upon the house-top was none the less anxious to make herself observed as she reiterated in intelligible tones her last lesson. There were rabbits running up and down in their neat and well-kept cages, and even the amusing little squirrel was not absent from this extensive collection. Suffice it to say, it would be difficult to mention all the pets of this miniature zoo of Elmsdale, which amused in no small degree its visitors.

Water lemons and convolvulus vine, thickly entwined upon specially constructed arbours, ran up the pillars that sustained the buildings, and reached out to the sides of the balcony. The odor from the lovely jasmine that surrounded the cottage filled the outer asmosphere and perfumed the interior of the house. The happy owner of this mansion was a mulatto, but he showed few of the facial characteristics of his Ethiopian parentage. He had a lofty forehead, well-formed nose, and splendidly chiselled chin. He was the natural son of Percy Woodhouse, a rich proprietor.

The old sire was one of those extreme radicals who were wont to be masters of their own opinions. He sprang from a respectable Devon family, and had received his early training at a London boarding-school, whence he went to Oxford to study theology. After he had worn the sacerdotal robes for some time, he was troubled with doubts raised by the profound problems of natural and revealed religion, and at length found himself no longer able to remain identified with the church. His parents endeavoured to convince their son of his grave error. Arguments were useless. The prodigal would not return; and when those whom he loved best united to persecute him for his apostasy, he took to flight, turned his steps westward, and found a home in the island of Montserrat.

Here Woodhouse worked hard until he became one of the potent sugar princes of the West Indies, and accumulated considerable wealth. He was attracted by the eldest daughter of one of his slaves and secured for her a better education than usually fell to the lot of such girls in those days of terror. This attachment proved unfortunate. Percy Woodhouse, the ex-clergyman, was not proof against one of the worst of social crimes that prevailed then, and the sable Mollie Saunders fell a victim to the passions of her benefactor.

Burleigh Woodhouse, the present proprietor of Elmsdale, was the offspring of this illicit union. After several years of concubinage, the elder Woodhouse repaired the wrong by marrying Mollie. Burleigh received a thorough education on the Continent. When his father died he inherited five or six of the most flourishing plantations in the island, together with over seventy thousand pounds sterling.

It was a fine evening when Burleigh,—who was sitting in a lounging chair on the balcony of his princely dwelling, enjoying the rich odour of jasmine and geranium which rose upon the wind,—heard a tap at the door. The servant ushered in two gentlemen, with whom the reader is already acquainted.

"Hello, Sultan!" ejaculated Lindsay in excellent spirits, after his usual manner. "Enjoying yourself amidst the flowers, I suppose."

"Yes, old fellow," was the reply; "nothing better. A splendid panacea for much of the ill that flesh is heir to."

"Very true," chimed in young Highfield. "I am myself passionately fond of flowers. They have taught me many beautiful lessons, and their sweet fragrance has often, in combination with music, lulled my spirit to sleep when overwhelmed with deep sorrow."

At this moment Mrs. Woodhouse appeared on the scene. After the usual civilities had been passed, she took a seat on a sofa near her husband and joined in the general conversation. She was a swarthy woman of dignified appearance. Her features were delicate and refined, her eyes black and velvety, and as she laughed and displayed a set of pearly white teeth, one would have remarked that it was such countenances the ancient Greeks and Romans loved to give to their goddesses. Her language was perfect, and her accent not local, having evidently been acquired on the Continent.

"Well, gentlemen," she said, "I sincerely hope nothing will intervene to prevent your honouring us with your presence at the ball!"

"We certainly trust not," answered Lindsay, "since I should like to give my young guest an idea of what a ball at Elmsdale is like."

"I should indeed enjoy being present," said Hugh, "since Lindsay informs me that it is expected to eclipse all previous records."

"Yes," put in Mrs. Woodhouse; "my husband, you know, adheres to his old motto, '*Dum vivimus vivamus,*' and very rightly believes that the shining shekel does no good when hoarded up in dusky coffers. We hope to give you something to think of with pleasure in connection with your visit to our little island."

"I am most gratified to find that you are among those who indulge in a legitimate enjoyment of the good things of life. I am sure that if God intended us to be anchorites he would have fashioned this world after another sort. I am myself a great believer in the beneficence of God and his purpose in all his creation to secure the happiness of his creatures. When my heart is overburdened by the weight of pressing circumstances, I always find wonderful relief in the sweet melody of the birds around, or in the rich music of the wanton winds, in the fragrance of the lily that perfumes the vale, or in the gay murmuring of some little brook."

An amusing and interesting *tête-à-tête* continued for some time, when Lindsay suggested that the company should take a walk through the grounds. All chimed in with the suggestion, and a full half-hour was pleasantly spent amidst the most charming scenes, while fair Cynthia looked down with her most bewitching smiles. When the party separated, the town clock struck the hour of nine.

As Lindsay and Hugh strolled onward, the former remarked:

"It is an unseasonable hour to make further calls, but I should like to introduce you to one of my warm friends whose generosity I am sure will excuse the lateness of our visit."

Hugh consented to the proposal. He was young, and youthful minds are always ready for adventure. Furthermore, Hugh Highfield was at any time ready to part company with his Butler or Paley for what he called "a stroll" on any night. This seems strange for a student in divinity, but the blood courses warmly in youthful veins and the spirit of adventure will not even be subdued by theology or grave philosophy.

Lindsay and Hugh had now reached the bottom of a hill and were wending their way through a narrow pass that opened into the main road of one of young Woodhouse's plantations. Hugh's eyes fell in an instant on a small rude hut covered with some wild grass.

"Does any human being live there?" he inquired of his companion.

"Certainly, and we are going there," replied Lindsay with a smile.

"What friend of yours can be content to make a home of such a miserable hovel? You're only joking."

"No, I'm not. We shall see presently."

They discovered on nearer approach that the door of this primitive home was closed. It was, indeed, a miserable-looking place. The hut was built of sticks plastered with mud; the covering consisted of "cane trash,"—a material that is used mostly by West Indian labourers who are not in a position to buy shingles or corrugated iron. From innumerable crevices the moonlight streamed in.

The intruders peeped in through one of the gaping apertures of the room and saw seated at a shabby-looking table an old negro who perhaps might have been about sixty-five or seventy years of age. There was something impressive about his features, which were rendered venerable by the long, flowing white beard that fell down upon his bosom. Upon the table before him was a transparent basin of water, over which he bent his hoary head and muttered something in the form of a prayer. He paused for some moments, then in a clear tone murmured:

"Some one disturbs my path."

"What in the name of heaven can this infernal nonsense mean? Is this what you have brought me here for, Oscar?"

Before Lindsay had time to reply, Hugh, with the intrepidity and daring of youth, was in the act of forcing an entrance.

"Be quiet, man," cautioned Lindsay under his breath. "This is the renowned Professor Zac. Wait a moment, and you shall hear his divinations."

Hugh desisted from his rash attempt at intruding into the sanctum of the Professor, and was about to make a remark, when in an intelligible and eloquent tone the Professor surprised them with the following burst of oratory:

"When black clouds cover the sun at midday, then the sorrows of Elmsdale shall begin, and when the white dove no longer sits upon the wall, then the dark lantern will shine to drag the fox from his hole, the bones from the earth, and give back honour and virtue to Elmsdale."

"Shades of Cicero! You scarce could surpass that most excellent orator!" whispered Highfield ironically.

"The man's a monomaniac, or has gone stark mad. Nevertheless, he must have some amount of intelligence, as is clearly shown by his speech."

"If he is mad, there is clearly method is his madness."

"Whence did he receive his education?"

"Oh, he received the first principles of elementary education from his benevolent master, old Woodhouse, to whom he was always much attached, and has always since possessed an ardent desire for knowledge, though he sometimes exhibits an eccentricity akin to madness. He is much respected by his class, and is considered an oracle."

"And despite this craving for knowledge, do you mean to say that he still retains the superstitious beliefs in the worship of demons,—and in Obi-ism,—peculiar to his race."

"Ah! there you make a mistake, my good Hugh; and you are indeed singular. To be candid, there is no worship of Obi in what you saw the old Magus perform. From time immemorial men of all races have tried to arrogate to themselves a certain Superhuman power of peering into the future and the unknown, and their various modes of divination are classified under a variety of names. The ancient Greeks, Romans, Arabs, and even the Anglo-Saxons, resorted to several of these superstitious methods for advice in love, war, commerce, and domestic affairs. It would be futile to try to enumerate these mystic arts, but I can name for you a few of the scientific terms used in that connection. There is the science of Astrology,—almost exploded though still tenaciously clung to by the followers of Islam,—Necromancy, Axinomancy, Botonomancy of the Greeks; Bellomancy of the Arabs, Crystallomancy,

Hydronomancy, and so on. I believe the last form is that adopted by the Professor for unveiling the future. Here it is generally believed that sorcery is peculiarly a Negro art, and the unfortunate darky has often to hang down his head at the charge of being a representative of a race peculiarly noted for its superstitions."

Hugh bent his head dreamily and mused awhile after the very interesting information supplied by his friend; then, suddenly collecting himself, he asked:

"But why does the black man still cherish persistently his superstitious nonsense, when there is hardly a remnant left among Europeans?"

"I am not at all certain of that. Roger Bacon, Albertus Magnus, and Pope Sylvester were certainly Europeans, and do we not find the seed which they sowed taking deeper root every day amongst us? I am sanguine that when education,—I mean true education,—shall have raised fully the human mind and intellect, the fallacies of superstition will be abandoned."

"Perhaps so,—time will tell."

By this time the Professor had risen from his seat, and advancing toward the door, he repeated the same words with which he had before astonished the unwelcome eavesdroppers. In a moment he was face to face with the "Buckras," as he designated his erstwhile masters.

"And is that you, Mahs Ossie?" ejaculated the sage.

"Yes, Professor, it is I who have come to pay you a short visit."

"Very well, sir; glad to see you. Will you come in and take a seat in the mansion?"

The Professor's eyes sparkled with immense delight as he turned to Hugh and greeted him with a cordial, "How d' ye do?" The young student was surprised to hear the old man speak of his miserable hovel as being a mansion, and this confirmed his opinion that he was a monomaniac.

"What have you been prophesying to-day, Zac?" asked Lindsay of the Professor.

"Oh, serious things, Mahs Ossie,"—shaking his head at the same time with a melancholy air. "I see there is something grave going to happen to Mahs Burleigh, and there will be a big stir at Elmsdale before long."

"Will you not enlighten me, dear Zac, as to the time when this is to happen, so that I may be present to rescue my friend?"

"I cannot assist you so far; my light is a little dim; but murder,—red, bloody, murder,—is at hand."

Hugh, who had all the while remained silent, now chimed in:

"Well, my dear Professor, since you are such a prophet, will you tell me whether I shall be successful in my profession, sir? I intend to be a parson."

"A parson, sir?"

"Yes, certainly, sir."

"Why, you will be most successful. I see it in your eyes. You will preach few sermons of your own, and bury many dead; and you know the price of putting a piece of played-out clay under the ground is splendid in these hard times."

"I am surprised at you. You are a strange one indeed. I don't want you to tell me about my mercenary gains in the church. I want to know if I will win many souls."

"Then, sir, you had better turn back. Competition will be too much for you."

"No; I shall not turn back from the plough, Professor. One of my principal aims will be to establish institutions propagating Christianity and inculcating the principles of virtue and happiness in every home."

"Ah, my good Mr. Parson; and how many churches will you build?"

"As many as are necessary."

"And how many shops for the sale of strong drink?"

"Why, you are raving, Professor! Rum shops are not in my line."

"Certainly, sir, I heard you say that you wanted to get up institutions for making people happy, and I assure you, sir, that though I read my Bible often, and hear Peggy and Nancy sing Psalms every night, I never remember the church door till I get down half of Allan's Old Tom. Why, it's then I feel happy and ready to sing for joy, and off I go to the nearest house of worship to join in the 'O, be joyful.'"

These ludicrous remarks from old Zac quite seized the young student, and he turned away with a curious smile playing on his face. He felt now, more than ever, that the Professor did not possess *Mens sana in corpore sano*. Meanwhile Lindsay, who was always ready to humour a joke, broke forth.

"By all means, Professor, I see no harm in one grog shop among the churches."

"Give me five, Mahs Ossie," said Zac, his face lit up with joy. "You're just the man for me. I always knew you to sympathize with a poor man; you know what he needs to keep body as well as soul."

"Let us leave the old crank, Oscar," urged Hugh, turning to the lawyer.

"The old crank!" suddenly reiterated the Professor. "You come to intrude upon me and then call me a crank to boot. You fancy yourself a king of the world because you're going to build your churches, but I am just as much a man as you. There, look!" Then, turning, he said: "Come here, my poor Pompey," addressing his dog.

Immediately a large, fierce-looking dog, which was lying a few yards off with his snout buried in the earth, came bounding to his feet, wagging his tail. The Professor gently patted the dog.

"My faithful friend," said he, "you are intelligent enough to wear a wig and gown, but your bark is too honest to make you famous in them."

"Why, you have come in for your share, Lindsay," said Hugh, turning toward the man of law, who was laughing with all his might.

"We have been well entertained during our visit, my dear Zac," said Lindsay to the Professor; "but we must now leave you."

"Well, Mahs Ossie, the best of friends must part, as the monkey said when he lost his tail. Good-bye." And he clutched the lawyer's hands with enthusiasm. Then, casting a spiteful glance at Hugh, he thundered vociferously: "For your rudeness, sir, I hope you may bury few worn-out carcasses and preach your own sermons."

"O Professor Zac," said Hugh, trying to suppress a laugh, "you need not be angry with me. I never meant to offend you. I am awfully sorry I have aroused your anger, and I beg your forgiveness."

"I am always ready to forgive a man, and especially a parson. I absolve you and wish you success in your undertaking."

"Then good-bye, Professor."

"Good-bye, Parson. I hope we will meet again as better friends." Then, turning toward Lindsay, Zac uttered in a clear, solemn and deliberate tone: "Remember the prophecy of Elmsdale!"

CHAPTER III

> Twine the young glowing wreath;
>   But pour not your spirit in the song
>   Which through the skies, deep azure floats along
> Like Summer's quickening breath!
>   The ground is hollow in the path of mirth
>   O! far too daring seems the joy of Earth
> So darkly pressed and girded in by death.
>
> *Mrs. Hemans.*

ELMSDALE Cottage buzzed like a beehive.

It was the evening of the ball, and everything had been arranged in grand style for the occasion. The servants in uniform flitted about like fireflies. Carriages with their gay occupants appeared in rapid succession. The grand hall of Elmsdale was lighted with numerous candelabra, the rays of which fell on the rich attire of the guests, which was displayed with royal grace. Tasty decorations were to be seen on every side. The dainty fingers of Mrs. Woodhouse had woven flowers into garlands with a dexterity which commanded the attention and admiration of all. Crowds of loiterers and curious sightseers gathered around Elmsdale to hear what they were frequently treated to,—the sweet, mellifluous and soul-stirring music, discoursed by a noted string band from a neighboring colony.

Woodhouse was in the gayest of moods, induced no doubt by the copious draughts of champagne that he had been imbibing since the dawn of the memorable day. The élite of society was well represented at the gathering, and there were present members of the liberal professions. The Hon. Lodric Gordon, the Commissioner, was the first to claim the hand of the hostess of Elmsdale for a waltz, and indeed so gracefully did she dance that there were many applicants afterward for the hand of the charming hostess. But the request of most of the dancers was declined. McIntyre, a relative of Woodhouse, was among the disappointed ones, and he retired sullenly to a corner.

Highfield was lucky enough to secure Mrs. Woodhouse's hand when he courteously sued for it. He was by no means a dancer, but his partner's brillancy hid his defects.

It was midnight, and in the refreshment room, where the lights were burning low and the tables groaning under the weight of delicious viands, sat Oscar Lindsay and his friend Woodhouse, engaged in an interesting conversation, and discussing the merits of a bottle of Dawson's Whiskey.

"By all that's good and great," ejaculated Lindsay, "I forgot to give you the joke of our adventures with Professor Zac some evenings ago, and of the original reception he extended to poor Hugh."

"Oh, you mean Zac, my best man, my faithful and sincere servant," interrupted Woodhouse with enthusiasm. "He is somewhat strange and fitful at times, but he is a good and clever old chap and means no harm to any one."

"How can he mean no harm when he literally cursed Hugh, and would not be appeased until an ample apology had been made?"

"Poor, eccentric, harmless fool!" said Lindsay, as he lay back in his chair and laughed outright.

"But we found him prophesying some fatal things in

connection with Elmsdale, and you are naturally not excluded."

"Ah,—pshaw! pshaw!"

And a suggestion was made to have another draught of the exciting beverage.

"And what did the old mad-cap say?" enquired Woodhouse laughlingly. "Is Jove going to thunder his heaviest bolts upon my unoffending head?"

Mrs. Woodhouse had entered the room in search of her husband. She overheard the last words that fell from his lips, for they had been spoken with great emphasis. She cast an enquiring, or rather a suspicious, glance at Lindsay, then at her husband. Woodhouse, as if to relieve her of her embarrassment, spoke.

"My darling, Zac has been prophesying something unpleasant of our home, which I have just heard."

"Oh, what is it, Burleigh? Tell me,—do not hesitate. I begin already to dread. Zac has many times foretold things that happened in every detail."

And the frail woman stood and trembled from head to foot.

"Alas! this is quite womanlike, my sweet. Your poor sex will ever believe the greatest improbabilities."

"O God, preserve us!" prayed the excited woman, bending on her knees. "Burleigh! Burleigh! I have of late been dreaming some most frightful dreams. You may call me superstitious, but I have a curious foreboding of ill."

"Hence the melancholic air you sometimes assume."

"I did not for a moment think you noticed anything strange in my appearance, but since I have betrayed myself, I must confess to you that my dreams have created in me a very nervous fear."

"My poor darling," said Woodhouse, casting an eye

of tender concern toward his wife, "I hope your spirits will soon regain their usual buoyancy; in fact, if your melancholia be not drowned in to-night's merriment, then I shall seek a more efficacious antidote for you. What do you think, Oscar?"

Lindsay, who had sat pensive, overhearing the conversation, spoke with a sympathetic ring in his voice.

"I am sorry, but I must justly claim to myself a thousand anathemas for having introduced the serpent's fangs amongst the roses; and you, too, are certainly not free from blame, Woodhouse, since you know the superstitious tendencies of your wife."

At that moment a little boy entered the room. He might have been about six years of age, and his features gave one the impression that he would develop into a handsome and intelligent man.

"Come here, Carl," called Mrs. Woodhouse, for it was none other than her own child, who had come to find out if Mother's skirt had been monopolized by any intruder.

"Have you missed Mother?" she asked, clasping her child in her arms and smothering with kisses.

"Oh, yes, I have; but I guessed you were somewhere with Father."

"And if I were to die, what would you do?"

"I think I would die, too," was the reply.

"And suppose Father died," put in Woodhouse; "would you miss him?"

"Do not speak so, dear Father. You are strong and not going to die now. God would not take such a dear father from Mother and me so soon, and before I become a man."

The tender expression of the child produced a spontaneous flow of sympathy between Woodhouse and his

THE SWORD OF NEMESIS 27

wife. They eyed each other warmly and their hearts were overflowing with love. For a moment they concentrated their gaze upon the link that seemed to bind them closer and closer, and thought that in him they possessed a veritable jewel.

Lindsay had joined the dancing party and was flitting away gaily with Maud Fairley, the beautiful daughter of the Rev. Mr. Fairley, to whom, as Mrs. Grundy delighted to say, the lawyer had been paying his attention. Hugh had immensely enjoyed himself in whirling around several handsome and fashionable young ladies, and having now retired to the corner where McIntyre sat, opened up a conversation.

"Well, Mr. McIntyre," said he, "what do you think of this display? Grand, isn't it?"

"Yes," replied McIntyre; "Burleigh has won the palm this time for his nonsensical display; there is no doubt that he spends his money lavishly. There is no doubt, too, that a fool and his money soon part, and his case will be another illustration of this truism. I am really at a loss to imagine why my cousin will go to such extremes. By the bye,—I congratulate you on your success, Mr. Highfield, in gaining so nice a partner in the dance."

This little remark was made in a somewhat taunting tone; but Hugh paid little attention to it.

"Your cousin," he observed, "is a socialist of the most advanced type, and finds enjoyment for himself by securing enjoyment for others. This is a praiseworthy feature of his disposition, and speaks volumes for the excellence of his mind."

"I do not see any excellence there. I see stupidity all through, and am not afraid to say it. If I had my cousin's wealth, I am sure I would know how to spend it, without bringing the world to gaze upon me as some curious feature of a pleasure-show."

Hugh was struck by these uncharitable remarks coming from the lips of so near a relative of Woodhouse. He could read insincerity and deceit in the man's eyes and in the tone of his voice. The company of McIntyre now proved extremely distasteful to him, and he quitted his side, a deep feeling of abhorrence rising in his breast.

Not long after that McIntyre himself arose. He was going out of the room when he was met by Woodhouse.

"Hope you have been enjoying yourself, cousin George," said Woodhouse, his eyes beaming with pleasure, as he patted his cousin on the shoulder.

"I have, my good Burleigh, been enjoying myself to such an extent that I am afraid I have intruded too much on the limits of nature. I feel unwell and must retire for the benefit of my health."

So saying, McIntyre strolled onward; but Burleigh held him back and told him he would be happy to place at his disposal the contents of his medicine chest, which was kept downstairs. No eye fell on the two as they went out. Neither Edith Woodhouse nor her child was present to see the lithe form of the beloved husband and father speed down on an errand of love,—that of administering to the suffering of another,—and wherever they were at this moment, little did they dream that they would never again behold in this life the breathing frame of him in whom all their affection was centered.

CHAPTER IV

La mort n'appartient qu'à Dieu! De quel droit les hommes touchent-ils à cette chose inconnue?
Victor Hugo.

NEXT morning the following sensational paragraph appeared in the columns of the leading paper of the Island:

A terrible blow had fallen on Elmsdale. The princely home of our well-known and respected townsman, Burleigh Woodhouse, has been suddenly thrown into mourning. There was a brilliant ball at Elmsdale Cottage last night, at which gathered most of the leaders of society, and while they were in the height of enjoyment, Mr. Woodhouse seems to have met his death by some means which is yet to be explained. There are, however, evidences which point to the probability of suicide, and seem to preclude the idea of foul play. The revolver that performed the deadly act of blowing out the brains was found beside the body.

Mr. Woodhouse seemed to be at the zenith of his prosperity, and his name has been one of the most honored and respected in the community. It has been asserted that domestic troubles were at the bottom of the tragedy. We shall be able to give our readers further details later on. The inquest will be held at 9 a. m. to-day.

Hugh was walking through the garden that surrounded Lindsay's residence when he heard the newsboy at the gate calling out in an unusually stentorian voice for some one to take the paper for Mr. Lindsay. Hugh quickly advanced, and took the closed sheet from the boy, remarking at the same time:

"You're very early this morning, Jimmy. How's that?"

"Oh, sir," replied the boy, "all the early birds had to get up earlier from dere nest dis morning. De suicide, sir,—de suicide."

"Suicide? Hello! who has done such a foolish thing?" enquired Hugh, as he opened the paper with nervous hands.

The boy had not time to reply before Hugh's eyes fell upon the conspicuous "American" heading which contained the account of the tragedy.

"Good Lord, deliver us!" was the exclamation that fell from his lips. "Can this be possible? How will Oscar receive this terrible bit of news?" Hugh stood for some time as if transfixed to the earth; beads of perspiration standing on his face, although the morning was as cool as it could possibly be,—in the tropics, in the middle of June.

He could not continue to read the account, and with his legs trembling nervously and scarcely able to support him, he went up-stairs to impart the news to Lindsay. The latter was lying in bed.

"Sad news, Oscar!" said Hugh with tremulous lips; and although he was fond of fun and always ready to crack a joke,—often at the expense of truth,—it was evident that his demeanour on this occasion savoured of anything else but fun. His eyes looked sad, and the pallor that fell on his cheeks told that something serious had occurred.

In a moment Lindsay was in possession of the fact of the tragedy, and the emotion and poignant sorrow that immediately unnerved him can be better explained than described.

"Suicide!" cried he frantically. "Who ever said 'suicide'? Why, I would rather believe that the moon is made of green cheese than to harbour for a moment the thought that Burleigh Woodhouse committed suicide! He was too noble and Christian a man to have so precipitatedly ushered himself into the presence of his Creator. But how is it possible that it is only now I hear of this through the newspaper? Confound that coxcomb Burton! Since he remained for some time after we left, it is natural that he must know all about this calamity. He might have passed this way and given us the information."

Lindsay was subject to occasional fits of temper, and he stamped his feet and bit his lips, while a piteous expression clouded his face.

"Compose yourself, my dear Lindsay," begged Hugh, who was himself much pained. "The thing is already done, and there is no use crying over spilt milk. I myself am of the opinion that Woodhouse has been murdered. We must, therefore, turn our attention toward unravelling the mystery and affording the helpless widow our assistance."

"Ah, I told you Zac's divining powers were not to be despised! He surely predicted this thing, and although you laughed at him for his predictions, the awful reality that now faces us must invest them with some importance. I certainly thought the man a raving fool, but now another problem presents itself for a careful solution. Verily the philosophy of human existence is both mysterious and complex."

The conversation continued some moments longer, during which the friends commented on the curious statement of the newspaper, that is, that the evidence which pointed to the conclusion that suicide was committed were sufficiently strong to preclude the idea of foul play.

They could not understand what this evidence could

be, and began to conjecture fanciful things. Again, the paper was stupid to talk about "domestic troubles." Were not the deceased and his wife the best of friends to the last? Woodhouse was rich and did not want money, so they thought this statement was nothing more than the imagination of some alarming reporter.

A servant at the door just then announced that some one wished to see Mr. Lindsay. A description was asked of the person, and it answered to that of Professor Zac.

The old soothsayer was cordially invited to enter and await Lindsay in his study. The Professor gazed ardently at the cases of dusty volumes, which perhaps had never been handled since the day they first adorned the library. There were bookcases made of rosewood and mahogany which contained a beautiful collection of works on Science, Theology, Law, and Medicine. The curious Professor could not withstand the temptation of handling the volumes, bent as he was upon cramming in his brain all that it could possibly take in within the space of a few minutes. He did not remain long in this pleasant diversion, for Lindsay soon appeared on the scene with Hugh at his heels.

The old man looked much out of sorts at the interruption, but tried to put the best face upon it. He greeted the gentlemen with a very polite, "How d' ye do?" Then shaking his head mournfully, he began:

"Well, Mahs Ossie, old Massa is gone forever."

Before the last words died from his lips a river of tears gushed from his eyes; the reservoir of pent-up emotion burst with violent force and Zac sobbed as bitterly as a child. When his grief had somewhat subsided he said, continuing his report:

"It was just a quarter past two in the morning, and

a little after you and Mr. Highfield took home Miss Maud, that we missed Mahs Burleigh, and could not find him anywhere about the house. The Missis began to be very troubled about him and sent the servants with lanterns to search around the house and the garden. I did my best and bawled out as much as I could, but poor old Massa could not hear. We were just giving up the search as a bad job, when Tommy Blackburn tumbled on something under a lime tree, and as he looked carefully with his lantern, what do you think he saw but the dead body of the dear old Massa, steeped in blood and with a revolver close by. He bawled aloud, and everybody went to see what had happened. Madame also went, and when she saw what it was, she gave such a scream as I never before heard. I tell you, sirs, I am now sixty-nine years, six months, and two days in this sinful life, and may God keep me from ever hearing such a sound again! The echo is even now in my ears, and makes me feel most miserable. The poor creature fell down senseless upon her husband's corpse. We took her up, carried her to the house, and placed her in a bed where the little boy was sleeping. Of course there wasn't any more dancing,—everything was topsy-turvey. I went to call Mr. McIntyre to set things in order. He complained of a bad headache, and said it was through feeling ill that he had to leave the ball-room; but as it was such a serious matter, he must go out."

"Did he show any emotion when you imparted the sad intelligence to him?" interrupted Hugh.

"Oh, yes, sir; the poor chap bawled like a bull, although I did not see any water from his eyes. He was very kind, and for the first time since I knew him he offered me a glass of brandy and soda. Yes, he gave me brandy and soda this morning. I was cold, sirs, and I tell you I swallowed it with pleasure. But tell me why you want to know if Mr. McIntyre looked sad?"

"Oh, nothing much, Zac."

And Hugh shook his head as if some important thoughts were passing through his brain.

"Did any one say he heard the report of the pistol?" he continued.

"Not a soul, sir," was the reply, followed by a muttered: "Ah, you are young, but you have an old head on your shoulders."

Neither Lindsay nor Hugh heard the last expression of the Professor, and though they implored him to repeat it, he refused to do so, continuing his sorrowful tale thus:

"When Mr. McIntyre arrived at Elmsdale he began to put everything straight. Before the police came he examined the corpse, and found in a pocket old Massa's will and another letter, which he opened and read."

The two gentlemen were astonished at this statement. They eyed each other keenly, and there were some strange associations at work within their minds. A few moments having elapsed, Hugh broke the silence with the following query:

"Is it not a contravention of the laws of the colony to have so much to do with a corpse before the Coroner's investigation?"

"I should think so," exclaimed Lindsay, with an air of concern. "Matters are wearing a curious appearance, and the newspaper comment can somewhat be accounted for. Did Mr. McIntyre read the will?"

"No; he merely looked at it, then put it back where he found it."

"And the letter?"

THE SWORD OF NEMESIS 35

"Oh, I saw him read that, and Tommy Blackburn and I were there at the time."

"So the inquest will be at nine o'clock, you say?"

"Yes, sir."

Lindsay took out his watch and looked at it. It said half-past seven.

"Come on, Hugh," he cried. "It will take us a full half-hour to get over to Elmsdale."

At this moment Hugh was making some notes in his pocketbook, which although he did not appreciate it at the time, subsequently proved to be of great value.

In a short time Lindsay, Hugh, and the Professor were on their way to Elmsdale at Jehu speed.

CHAPTER V

Scorn me not in mine extreme of misery.
"Siege of Valencia."

"O CHRIST, is there no remedy? Must my husband's name be thus wronged and my honour be thrown in the dust by the vile insinuations of some plotting monster? I cannot bear it. No; never! Let me die, O God, and be delivered from this heinous outrage."

Edith Woodhouse was raving, and she drew about her a number of sympathetic hearts as she poured forth the above words in her delirium. Dr. Fane, the medical officer of the district, had been summoned to her. His care was unremitting, and his professional skill was taxed to the utmost to preserve life in the unfortunate patient, whose nerves were strained to the utmost tension. He had administered sedative mixtures and a draught, which had given her a couple of hours' sleep, but now, like a lion at bay, Mrs. Woodhouse rose with dishevelled locks and bloodshot eyes. The doctor tried to compose her, but with little effect. He grew alarmed at the probability of dementia, and tears began to flow from his eyes. Mrs. Woodhouse, however, soon convinced him that she was not mad.

Miss Fairley and her father, the Rev. Mr. Fairley, entered the apartment and their presence had a soothing effect upon her,—she became surprisingly calm and composed.

"So, my dear Maud, you have come to see the poor

outcast?" she said, looking into Maud's eyes, with tear-stained face. "I, the outcast, who have been branded with calumnies as black as hell itself, still possess the friendship of a pure soul like you."

"Oh, my dear Edith, how can you fancy yourself an outcast? Your life has been too exemplary to be affected by any base accusations made against you. Compose yourself and believe that whoever has placed this bitter cup to your lips will receive his deserts at the hands of Heaven. None who know you would believe that you were unfaithful to your husband."

"Do you really think so, Maud?" asked the unfortunate woman, who clutched at this flimsy straw of hope to establish some peace within her bosom. And she buried her head in her hands and wept aloud.

Maud's heart was ready to burst with mingled pity and love. Mr. Fairley and the Doctor were deeply moved at the scene, but said nothing.

McIntyre entered the room, and after interchanging civilities with those present, took a seat near Mrs. Woodhouse.

"Do not be so distressed, poor dear creature," he pleaded. "It is the Lord's will that this sore trial should come upon you. Acquit yourself like a woman, and be strong. 'Cast your burden upon the Lord for He careth for thee.' I am certain that Burleigh did not destroy himself in his sound mind. He must have sustained some injury, which temporarily deranged him, and impelled him to commit the awful deed. Take hope, my dear Edith, that you will be sure to meet him again in that beautiful land where partings are no more and 'Where the wicked cease from troubling and the weary are at rest.'"

"Thank you for your comforting words, George; but

tell me nothing about my husband's committing suicide,—that is out of the question. I shall never believe such a thing; he was murdered,—yes, murdered by some foul being, who for his own ends has also bruited it abroad that I have been unfaithful."

"Unfaithful? Why, that could never be! No intimation of that has as yet reached my ears."

"Strange! Have you not observed that this morning's paper had no hesitation in libelling my character in unmistakable words. I am sure you read the papers."

"I have not yet had time to glance in the columns of a newspaper, so much have I been engaged with your affairs."

"I thank you, George, for your kindness. If I have spoken harshly, I am sure you will attribute this to the unhappy state of my mind."

"Poor dear cousin, my heart yearns for you. I fully realize that in your excited condition you are not accountable for any impolite expressions that may fall from your lips. May you have the support of Him who is the Father of the fatherless and the Judge of the widow, in this your terrible trial!"

McIntyre turned to leave the room, when he saw old Zac approaching him with the words:

"A servant wants to see you, sir."

"Where is he?" enquired McIntyre.

"Not my business, sir; so I didn't take the liberty to enquire."

McIntyre did not stop to reply but ran downstairs as fast as his legs could carry him, muttering as he went: "Damn it; all this fuss could have been avoided with a little more discretion! But I have some splendid cards to play yet."

THE SWORD OF NEMESIS

At the door a cab was drawn up, on the box of which sat a burly-looking coachman just in the act of drawing out his pipe to enjoy a pleasant whiff; a good-looking face, which bore the marks of tender youth and a high degree of intelligence, peeped out anxiously from between the curtains.

"Oh, is it you?" asked McIntyre, as his eyes fell upon the gentleman. "Why, I thought you were abroad," he continued in an undertone, advancing meanwhile toward the vehicle.

"No; not yet abroad. I am, however, going straight off with my impedimenta. I have a full quarter of an hour to spare. It is now a quarter past eight. The steamer leaves at half-past, and as our arrangements have been so hurried, I came this way to learn if there are any further instructions, and also to wish you good-bye, and to thank you once more for your kindness to me."

"Nothing more than we have spoken of. You will be looked out for at Melbourne, and when you land, you must enquire for the house of Webster & Cheeseman. I have already replied to their private telegram, and have said that you will positively sail this morning."

"Then, according to arrangements, I shall expect to enter upon my duties immediately."

"As a matter of course, my boy; and according to my recommendation, I predict a speedy promotion for you. In addition to the five hundred dollars already presented to you, I shall add twenty more,—and here is the money. Whatever your necessities may be, they will be well attended to by my brother on your arrival."

"How can I thank you sufficiently, Mr. McIntyre?

I hope to repay you some day for the extraordinary interest you have taken in me."

"Don't say a word, dear Heineman. I'm much older than you,—in fact, you are but a mere boy to me,— but I have a special fondness for you. The fact that a youth like you is so far away from home causes me to entertain for you a kind of paternal sympathy."

Heineman then parted from his benefactor, and the cab, laden with the baggage, pursued its course to the pier.

"My lack of foresight has cost me very dear," mused McIntyre, as he retraced his steps toward the house. "Nevertheless, I must continue to be Jesuitical,—the end justifies the means. One cannot launch on any great enterprise without making sacrifice."

One or two words of the conversation that had been carried on between Heineman and McIntyre had been heard by Lindsay and Hugh, who had seated themselves at a window overlooking the street, after their recent arrival. A venetian blind had hidden them from outside view, but gave them the advantage of what was taking place in the street.

"That youth has been duped," said Highfield; "I'm positive of that."

"Why do you think so?" enquired Lindsay, who, despite his eminence as a lawyer, was not as farseeing as his companion.

"McIntyre's benevolence could never reach that standard if he were not playing some extraordinary game. My experience of his character, as obtained in a very recent conversation, proves conclusively that he is not what he seems. I tell you, Lindsay, I have an unconquerable repugnance for that man."

THE SWORD OF NEMESIS

It was not long afterward that McIntyre came in contact with Lindsay and Hugh.

"So you have heard of the awful tragedy, gentlemen?"

"Yes, Mr. McIntyre," was the laconic reply.

"And what do you think of it?"

"I firmly believe, sir," ejaculated Hugh with great emphasis, "that a barefaced murder has been perpetrated, and that by no stranger, either. Probably some trusted person did the foul deed. I am further convinced that the revolver found near the dead man is as innocent of the crime as are these fingers."

"You are quite singular in your belief, Mr. Highfield," replied McIntyre.

"Yes, sir; as sure as that I am alive and that there is an avenging God above, the red-handed villain will one day pay the penalty of his monstrous crime."

"It is my sincere desire that that may be so ere long," said McIntyre.

Mrs. Woodhouse was much better when Lindsay and Hugh entered her apartments. She was relating to the Rev. Mr. Fairley the premonitory signs by which she had been warned of the approach of some very grave event; she told how for several days a bird had been perched on a beam in the house, and after having engaged the attention of all the inmates of Elmsdale, had mysteriously disappeared, no one having seen when it took its flight. She also recounted the frightful dreams that had for some time been disturbing her rest.

At this the countenance of the clergyman grew serious, and his thoughts went back to the dreams of Joseph and the mysterious visions of Daniel. He realized at once that humanity, under the Theocracy, with its mysterious phenomena was identical with humanity under the Christian dispensation, and he began to think that what he had been denouncing from the pulpit as ignorant superstition and the natural outcome of fallacies of the brain, as John Stuart Mill would say, had an impregnable foundation in Holy Writ.

"This is really an interesting study," said he, "and your sad circumstance, Mrs. Woodhouse, has given rise to new ideas in my mind. I am convinced that God still continues to make dreams a medium of communication to his people, but there are no Daniels to give the interpretations and prepare us to receive our good,—or bad,—fortune."

At this the eyes of all present were simultaneously turned on Zac, who was standing like a statue in the middle of the room, with his mouth wide open, listening attentively to the clergyman and drinking in every word that fell from his lips.

"But there is a Daniel, or rather a Samuel, in our midst," interrupted Hugh. "I mean the venerable Zac whom I heard with my own ears foretelling the calamities of Elmsdale."

"Yes, indeed; there is something inexplicable in connection with this old man," remarked Mrs. Woodhouse feebly, "and he really possesses some prophetic gifts."

"He has a remarkable appearance," said the man of the cloth; "but so far as I am led to understand from certain members of my church, his light is associated with the black art, or something diabolical, and I have had occasion to speak to him on the subject more than once."

At this juncture some one intimated that the Coroner had arrived. Mrs. Woodhouse was sitting in a melancholy mood, and her thoughts appeared to be far away; but at this important announcement she sprang up wildly, rushed upon Maud's neck, and then dropped down unconscious.

All hands present found something to do toward helping to retore her. She was carefully and tenderly laid on a couch, and the doctor placed Maud to watch over her. The rest of the party, except Zac, returned to the study.

The faithful servant would not leave the room under any consideration. He watched with anxious eyes the throbbing breast of his mistress, and as she lay in her tranquil beauty, with eyelids closely shut and the stamp of inexpressible sorrow imprinted upon her face, he thought of the terrors of death, and sent a prayer up to the Throne of Grace that his beloved mistress might be spared a little longer.

CHAPTER VI

> All, all look up with reverential awe
> At crimes that 'scape or triumph o'er the law,
> While truth, worth, wisdom they decry.
> Nothing is sacred now but villainy.
>
> Forgiveness to the injured does belong,
> But they ne'er pardon who have done the wrong.
>
> *Pope.*

NINE of the principal men of the town were selected for the jury at the inquest, and the Hon. Patrick Chalmers presided as Coroner. Dr. Fane gave evidence as follows:

"I was summoned from my house by Sergeant Hollingsworth, to view the body of the deceased, at about a quarter to four this morning. I found the body steeped in blood, with a revolver,—the probable instrument of destruction,—in close proximity. A bullet had pierced the frontal lobe of the skull, pentrating the right cerebral hemisphere of the brain, and making its exit near the occiput. Death, I believe, must have occurred instantly. I believe the deceased committed suicide while in a state of temporary insanity."

Several witnesses were examined, from whose statements was elicted the fact that Woodhouse had been apparently buoyant and gay throughout the evening preceding his death, and that there was nothing to create the impression that anything of a serious nature rested on his mind. The jurors seemed puzzled. Ref-

THE SWORD OF NEMESIS

erence was made to the paragraph that appeared in the *Chronicle* of that morning, relative to the tragedy, and the Coroner felt desirous to know from what source the paper had gathered certain important details, which could not have been in possession of the general public. Acting upon this suggestion, the jury searched the corpse and, among other things, Woodhouse's will was found in an inner pocket, also the letter that Zac had testified to having seen McIntyre reading. The Coroner looked grave as he ran his eyes over this letter and handed it to the foreman of the jury, with a request that he should read it to his confrères. It was addressed to the wife of the deceased, and ran as follows:

DEPRAVED WRETCH! My life is a blank; and though I have often drowned the thoughts of my cursed lot in the Lethean springs of poisonous distillers, yet can I no longer bear life's stings and arrows since your infidelity has now reached an irrepressible and horrible stage. Edith,—my once loved Edith!—whom I adored with a transcendent love, now that you are converted into a veritable Messalina, I hate and despise you.

BURLEIGH.

When the letter was read, the assembly seemed stricken as if with catalepsy. Mrs. Woodhouse was leaning on McIntyre's arm, while Maud applied to her nostrils a vinaigrette. She had recovered somewhat and Dr. Fane had advised her to attend the inquest so that, if necessary, her evidence might be taken. All eyes were now turned upon her, and even hisses were levelled at her. She treated them with dignified scorn, which only intensified the contempt that was fomenting against her.

A sad expression came over the face of Mr. Fairley. There were tears streaming from his daughter's eyes, but she continued in her work of love. McIntyre seemed stung by some venomous reptile, and with an air of offended pride, withdrew his arm; but his place was immediately taken by Hugh, who cast a stern and severe look at the man whom he disliked so much, and called him to his teeth "an inhuman dog."

"The letter! the letter! Let me have a glance at it," cried Lindsay in a tone of deep excitement.

It was ordered to be handed to him, and as he looked at the writing his visage changed immediately. He became ashen pale and from his trembling hands the paper slipped upon the ground. Maud took it up, and, before she could look at it, Mrs. Woodhouse suddenly seized it.

"Yes, it is my husband's writing," she exclaimed vehemently. "Is this a vision? Am I in dreamland? Yes, it is my husband's own writing. O merciful God!"

And she fell to the ground senseless. The Doctor was immediately in attendance.

A voice burst from the crowd:

"Hypocrite! she is only shamming."

How complex indeed are the elements that constitute our nature, and how our impulses are marvelously stirred to action often in diametrically opposite directions within the space of a few minutes, according to the circumstances by which they are around. A few moments before there was a wave of indignation against the woman who had dared thus to offend society, and now, as she lay cold and senseless upon the ground undergoing the penalty of her suspected unfaithfulness, there was deep pity for her and curses and execration for the inhuman wretch who dared to strike such a foul blow at such a moment. It was afterward ascertained that McIntyre was the offender, and the Coroner sternly rebuked him.

THE SWORD OF NEMESIS

This was the third time that Mrs. Woodhouse had swooned within the space of a few hours. Dr. Fane expressed the opinion that her illness had become quite serious, and he ordered that she should be immediately removed to her apartments.

The inquest continued. Zac gave his evidence in much the same strain that he had done before. Lindsay then moved forward and said:

"It is obvious from the evidence we have heard that the *Chronicle* had some authority whereon to found the comments produced this morning in its columns. In the absence of further evidence, we must necessarily arrive at the same conclusion. But the question narrows itself to this: Whence did the *Chronicle* get the knowledge of certain private matters, which are not the property of the public, and which they could never have known; and how was this distinguished journal in a position to solve this knotty problem of murder or suicide? There is a great mystery connected with the matter, which, in my opinion, gentlemen, ought certainly to be cleared up."

"Very good, Mr. Lindsay," said the Coroner and jury with one acocrd.

The Coroner put the following questions to McIntyre:

"Did you, Mr. McIntyre, examine the body of the deceased and therefrom extract certain documents?"

"I did overhaul the body, sir, but extracted no documents."

Professor Zac advanced with rapid strides, saying: "Do not hide it."

But before he could go further he was instructed by the Coroner to sit down until he was required.

"You said then, Mr. McIntyre, you did not interfere with anything on the dead body."

"Well, er—er, sir, I—I—I did see some papers that dropped from the coat pocket, but I immediately put them back, knowing that I would not be justified in removing anything until the body was handed over to the Crown."

"You did not read any of them, did you?"

"Of course not, and even if I was disposed to do so, I had no time at my disposal."

"Can you give me any idea of how the reporter came into possession of certain very confidential details in connection with the domestic affairs of Elmsdale?"

"I am strictly of opinion that they must have leaked out through some servant, as is generally the case. The letter read awhile ago was discovered unsealed. I regret much that I went beyond my province in touching the papers, but I must again impress upon you, gentlemen, that I did not probe into the contents of this remarkable letter."

Old Zac now came forward at the Coroner's request. He began:

"Mr. McIntyre said he never read the letter, but he did open it and read it in the presence of myself and Tommy Blackburn. I'll swear to it, sir." Then waxing warm, he thundered forth, clenching his fist with violence: "You're a liar, George McIntyre, and may the curse of Ananias fall upon you! May the leprosy of Naaman cleave to your tongue, and before you meet with the death of Judas, may you be half-eaten by worms like Herod; only let me have a chance to do you the goodness of twisting the rope for your neck. You prince of Hell,—you child of Beelzebub! The curse of God is upon you and your seed forever."

While the old Negro poured forth his anathemas, the Coroner endeavored to stop him, but found it impossible to do so.

McIntyre,—in fact the whole assembly,—was struck by the vituperations which were hurled at him, but he gathered courage to speak.

"It is unnecessary," said he, "to convince you that I am ignorant of the malicious charge made against me by this old man. I am positive that none of you gentlemen who know my reputation and who have listened to the vile ravings of a man who has long borne the reputation of being stark mad and a creature of questionable morality, would for a moment regard his evidence as more valuable than mine. He has wilfully lied against me, and endeavoured to permanently injure my character."

At the conclusion of his evidence, McIntyre came out the victor. None could look at those large, mild, grey eyes of his, which adapted themselves to all circumstances, and not see in them honest indignation, mingled with the apparent straight-forwardness that innocence always imparts.

One of the jurors suggested that the evidence of Blackburn should be taken. This individual had not been summoned in time and had gone to his work in a distant part of the country whence he would not return for a fortnight. After a brief deliberation it was decided unnecessary to adjourn the enquiry to obtain the evidence of a person who, in all probability, could not be relied upon for his veracity. The jurors were ultimately satisfied that no information concerning the private matters of the deceased and his wife had reached the public through McIntyre.

The enquiry was adjourned for a couple of hours,

and on its resumption the editor of the *Chronicle* was called upon to give evidence. He was a tiny old man, whose head was covered with a wealth of silver locks falling profusely on his neck; his features were wrinkled, and under a pair of pebble glasses twinkled two brilliant orbs, which told that their owner was blessed with a high degree of intellectual power.

"Mr. Perkins," began the Coroner, "you're responsible for the report that appeared in your paper this morning concerning the death of Burleigh Woodhouse of Elmsdale, and as the reporter who obtained the news might be able to throw some light on the mystery that now engages our attention, it is your duty to let us know who he is."

The editor took off his glasses, wiped them, and replaced them on his nose; then, looking the Coroner straight in the face, he said:

"The article in question was unfortunately not sub-edited by me before its publication. I did not happen to see it until a copy of the *Chronicle* was handed to me at my house this morning. When I arrived at my office I naturally enquired who was the author, as I was much concerned about the sad passing of my lamented friend. None of the reporters could account for its authorship. I, therefore, examined the original manuscript and found it was in the handwriting of Robert Heineman, a lad of estimable worth, who hails from England and recently identified himself with the *Chronicle*. He is an adventurous and harebrained youth, of eccentric habits and quick impulses, and bent on making his fortune by leaps and bounds. I was therefore not surprised when he announced to me at my home this morning that he had a few minutes before received an unexpected appointment somewhere in Australia and that he would

THE SWORD OF NEMESIS 51

leave by the steamer that sails to-day. I advised the boy against the step, but he refused to hear me. I have since discovered that he has carried out his intention, and left by the *Muriel*, a P. and O. liner."

"At what time daily does the *Chronicle* usually appear, Mr. Perkins?"

"Usually at 5 a. m.; but this morning, a little earlier."

"Now, are you of opinion that Heineman is directly or indirectly connected with the tragedy?"

"Certainly not, sir; he is a gentleman in every sense of the word, and would spurn to be an accessory to anything that bears the nature of crime. I agree with Mr. McIntyre that it is a probability that the news reached him through some one intimately connected with Elmsdale."

After some other questions had been asked and a few other witnesses examined, including two female servants and a groom, from whom nothing of an important nature was elicited,—the jurors unanimously returned a verdict of "Death by Suicide!"

The Coroner, in the course of his summing up, said:

"This enquiry is one in which some very curious elements are involved. There is not the slightest doubt that Woodhouse's death is of a mysterious nature, from the Doctor's evidence, and from the disclosures made by the papers found on the dead body. I think the idea of foul play is out of the question. With regard to the newspaper report,—that has been cleared up by Mr. Perkins, who leaves us to conclude that young Heineman, late of the *Chronicle* staff, was the author of it, and that his information was supplied by some unknown meddlesome person who had access to the documents discovered on the body. It is therefore evident that Woodhouse, goaded by domestic troubles, became insane, and in this condition committed suicide. I deem it necessary to hand these documents,—the will of the deceased and this letter,—to his attorney, Mr. Lindsay, who will, no doubt, care safely for them."

Hugh and Lindsay, when the inquest was ended, became engaged in a deep and earnest conversation.

"I am not at all satisfied with the turn the enquiry has taken," remarked Lindsay. "There is a great deal yet to be unravelled. I will not believe that Burleigh committed suicide, nor am I of opinion that his wife has been unfaithful to him, and yet that letter,—that startling letter, undoubtedly written by himself,—terrifies me. I am greatly perplexed and know not what to say."

"Take my word for it, Oscar, George McIntyre is closely connected with this tragedy. I do not like that man's actions, and I can almost read 'guilt' written on his brow."

"Nonsense, Hugh! He may be a villain, but he surely would not take his cousin's life to secure his wealth. That would be too dreadful to contemplate; and, moreover, up to the present I do not see anything that directly fastens suspicion on him."

"Ah, my dear friend, you are much older than I am, but my experience of mankind is somewhat extensive, and my impressions are not easily shaken. The schemes of a villain are beyond conception, and the foul tactics he employs to perpetrate his dark deeds often affect probity and unsullied innocence."

"That is so," Lindsay agreed, toying with a manuscript of his dead friend which he had found in Woodhouse's library that morning; "and if this man has any connection with Burleigh's death, as you seem to think,

THE SWORD OF NEMESIS

he should be hanged a thousand times, were it possible."

Little did Lindsay imagine that in the roll of paper that he held in his hand he possessed an invaluable key to the Elmsdale mystery,—a fairy wand whose magic touch would change the whole obscurity surrounding the death of Burleigh Woodhouse.

CHAPTER VII

> Blow, blow, thou winter wind!
> Thou are not so unkind
>   As man's ingratitude.
> Thy tooth is not so keen,
> Because thou art not seen
>   Although thy breath be rude.
>
> *Shakespeare.*

A FEW months after the death of Woodhouse there was a general change at Elmsdale. The property passed into the hands of McIntyre, who, to the entire satisfaction of the authorities, was proven to be the sole beneficiary of the will. There was the proverbial nine days' talk, and then the matter quieted down. There were some who considered that Mr. Woodhouse was a thorough demon for having cruelly disinherited his unoffending son, even though he might have thought it right to make his wife suffer; but there were others who thought he was perfectly justified in leaving his fortune to his next of kin, and bequeathing nothing to the child who, inheriting the taint of vice, would ultimately use his legacy for evil ends.

By a few persons McIntyre was still regarded with distrust and suspicion and among these his success did not tend to promote the least familiarity, but outside of this circle he was received with open arms; for, since fortune had specially favoured him with her choicest smiles, why should not his friendship be considered a desirable thing? He played billiards with gentlemen of unimpeachable character into whose society at one time he never aspired to enter; and with the greatest *sang-froid* and air of chivalry offered his arm to ladies who before had contemned him. No longer did the characteristic tranquility and soberness of Elmsdale impress the passer-by, for it was now converted into an Epicurean haunt, where drinking and vice ran riot.

Nevertheless, although McIntyre was a true child of Epicurus, he was not a fool but a man of some method, and laboured earnestly to keep his estates in prime order. He never ran into more debts than he was able to pay, and this was considered a marvel and departure from the regular course of such debauchees.

Night after night the revels of Elmsdale sounded far and wide. It was a peculiar and noticeable fact that McIntyre was never seen to enter a certain room within Elmsdale House. This particular room was kept locked. Some people thought it was a sort of Ali Baba cave where he kept his treasures, but the servants held a belief that it was the haunt of some demon with whom McIntyre was closely connected, and thus, holding it in superstitious awe, they never ventured to approach it if they could possibly avoid it.

It was Christmas Eve. The shades of night were rapidly falling, and loud peals of thunder, accompanied by fearful flashes of lightning, were heard from the west. It was evident that a storm was approaching. A slight rain began to fall, and gradually increased until it poured down in torrents. As night advanced the blackness became intense. The wind howled dreadfully among the branches of the tropical trees, bending to the earth the tall, slender cocoanut palms. Yet above the terrible and confused music of the storm rose the stentorian voices of young men who were gathered at Elmsdale to drink to the health of their convivial host, who was celebrating his fortieth birthday.

While these Bacchanalian orgies were transpiring within, outside, under the friendly branches of a towering ceiba tree, stood a frail female figure draped in black, holding by the hand her only child. They were evidently listening to the hubbub of voices that came from within the mansion. Neither the blackness of the night nor the violence of the storm impressed them; the rain beat their forms, and the lightning flashed into their faces, yet no thought of the danger of their position occurred to them.

"I, the unfortunate castaway!" said the woman, and she sent forth an hysterical laugh that thrilled the soul. Reader! pray that never may such a sound fall upon your ears. It was so full of untold sadness and ringing with scorn.

Cold and shivering, this weeping Niobe pressed in her arms the child, who now seemed anxious for the storm to cease; and when she had whispered to him a few words pregnant with maternal tenderness, she continued to give vent to her emotions.

Her friends had almost all forsaken her, and the thought of this filled her cup of sorrow to the brim. Where were the friends who once shared the joys of this poor woman? Like migratory birds, they had flown!

"Oh! if there were only some one to whom I could look to defend my cause!" she sobbed bitterly.

"I will fight to the end for you, Mother," said the child with emotion.

"You are yet so young, my child; and I shall be under the cold earth before you are big enough to fight my battle."

"I shall be a big man soon, Mother. God will let me live. I know he is good and hears the prayers of little children, and I will wait patiently until the time comes for me to fight your battle. It is I who must do it."

Little did the child imagine that these words were prophetic.

"Your fate and mine are in the hands of a good Providence, and whether you or another be the instrument selected by God," returned the woman, "I have strong hope that I shall live to see my desire upon mine enemy."

"I shall pray, Mother, that I may have the privilege of finding out the man who killed my father and brought you to this condition. O God, look down upon thy child, and help him to make his mother happy."

The distressed mother found a ray of pleasure steal into her heart as she thought of the earnestness with which the boy sent up his petition to Heaven in her behalf, and in her heart of hearts she prayed, too, that the Almighty would look down in His mercy and spare her darling.

The storm abated. Streams of light began to pour from the windows of neighboring houses, which had been temporarily closed on account of the rain, and Edith Woodhouse, the disinherited widow, stole from her shelter with her boy, whose hands she firmly grasped, and without a moment's further delay they wended their way toward a miserable little dwelling in which they had found refuge since being driven from the luxuries and comforts of their beautiful home.

As Mrs. Woodhouse and her child entered the house, a kindly voice greeted them; it was that of an old woman on whose brow were traced the wrinkles of three-score-and-ten summers. She had had the honor to have been Burleigh Woodhouse's nurse, and her hospitable roof was voluntarily placed at the disposal of his deposed widow.

"Ah, you unruly runaways! where has you bin all this time?" asked the old dame with a smile on her lips. "I sure you been exposed to the wind and rain, you are shivering so much. Don't waste a moment; tek off those wet clothes immediately, my dear, and get into something dry. Why, poor little Mass Carl, you seem to have a hard time. Look how the chile's teeth chattering."

While Mrs. Woodhouse and Carl have retired to change their wet clothing, and kind-hearted old Candace is busying herself about lighting a fire to prepare as quickly as possible two cups of invigorating ginger tea, we will give the reader a description of the modest home of this hospitable old creature.

It consisted of two small rooms, used respectively as hall and bedroom, and an adjoining gallery served the purpose of kitchen and pantry. The floor of the hall was scrupulously clean, and the entire furniture consisted chiefly of two straw-seated chairs, a rocker, and an old couch, while a rickety mahogany table, situated in a corner of the room, testified also to the cleanly habits of the inmate.

The building, however, showed the ravages of time, in spite of the frequent attempts of industrious hands to repair it by nailing pieces of tin over the gaping apertures, or stuffing rags into the crevices. Branches of bay leaves and pretty flowers smiled from every corner of the cot and formed a beautiful arch over the doorway. There stood in the gallery a table covered with a white cloth, and laden with tempting and appetizing viands. The stuffed, roasted pig grinned menacingly in an ocean of rich gravy. Boiled and roasted chicken, a square-cut piece of cheese, and a pan loaf, a dish of soused pork, and several kinds of vegetables made up the menu.

The reader would naturally imagine that these preparations were intended for the entertainment of some expected guests for whom every provision had been made to tempt their dainty palates. Certainly this, in a sense, would be correct, the only difference being that the expected guests were certain disembodied beings who by her class are designated "jumbies," and who, in accordance with traditional customs, assemble on Christmas Eve to make merry at the feasts that are usually prepared for them. Marvelous powers are ascribed to these mysterious spirits, who are in a position to affect for good or evil the condition of mankind, according to the believers in this curious myth. So Candace had done her part to entertain her visitors in right good order, even though she could ill afford the expense.

Mrs. Woodhouse and little Carl appeared much revived by the change of clothing and the warm ginger tea.

"Now tell me, my dear," said old Candace to Mrs. Woodhouse when they were both seated, "how you spend de afternoon, w'ah you bin, and who you see?"

"We have been to the churchyard," replied Mrs. Woodhouse, "and we whiled away the hours in the labor of love that pleases us so much,—that is to say, clearing away the wild weeds which overrun the resting-place of our dear departed one, and, oh,—what a beautiful lesson did we learn this afternoon! The lilies, which we despaired of, have now bloomed sweetly, so will our darling bloom on the resurrection morning when the angel shall wake him from his slumber."

"I tart you had gone to ta'k with the dead. You must not go dere to grieve so, my child; you must leave off your sorrow and de Lord will lighten your burden, and after de night de morning will soon come, dat shall give gladness to your po' heart."

"Gladness! Ah! my poor Candace, when shall that be?" And Edith drew from her bosom a miniature photograph of her dead husband and kissed it with much tenderness.

"Dear Mistress, remember what is the message tomarrah marning is bringing us all. Fancy you is hearing the angel singing the glad song of joy and telling you to cast your cares away."

Mrs. Woodhouse was about to reply when she was interrupted by the intrusion of Old Zac who had come to spend a half-hour with his beloved mistress, and to administer some words of consolation before retiring to sleep.

"Well, Candace," he commenced when he had respectfully saluted his Mistress and had taken a comfortable seat, "what's all the news to-day? I hope you are taking care of the Missis."

"O, go away, you old devil! Does you fancy you only one loves Missis and can take care of her. You always come annoy me bout you nonsense."

"Never mind, old gal, don't insult me like that," said the Professor, kindly; "you just give me a grog. I'm sure there is something good in the house to-night. Afterward we will knock old story. There is something I want to talk to you about."

The old dame, happy at the thought of joining in some interesting gossip, quickly rose from her seat and entered the gallery. Zac followed, and in a few minutes he was sitting at the table with Candace and testing the virtues of some very old rum. A smile lighted up the face of Mrs. Woodhouse as she mused on the oddities of the old people and their attachment and devotion to her.

"Now, Candace," said Zac, adjusting his pipe and preparing to have a good smoke, "I think we shall have to seek out some Egypt to send the young saviour of Elmsdale to before he gets into the hands of Herod."

"I don't understand you, man. Speak plain; a little larning is a bad ting foo niggars like you; good old Massa couldn't ha do a wusser ting dan foo get you eddication."

"Well, I'll tell you plainly what I mean," Old Zac explained, pleased at the reference to his superior knowledge. "I have had a hint that that vagabond George McIntyre is up to some of his tricks, and he is trying to get rid of that poor little boy who is so dear to his mother's heart. It would be very sad for the little fellow to part from his mother; but he must for the good of them both."

"Do you mean dat dat beast want to kill de chile, too? He not satisfy wid de blood he already shed? But tell me, Zac, how you know de intention of dis devil?"

"You know I do not go through the world with my eyes shut, old lady. But to the point. I'll tell you how I see through the villain's plot. Last night about half-past eleven o'clock I was passing by Elmsdale, and when I arrived at the gate I saw a person coming from the yard. I stopped back awhile and hid myself, when I heard George McIntyre close the gate, whispering at the same time to the person: 'Do your best, man. Remember it is five hundred bright canaries.' I said, 'Something is up.' You know I don't trust that rascal, because I will never lose sight of the fact that it was no other but him who murdered Mahs Burleigh, no matter what judge, jury, or any earthly man may say to the contrary. Well, to go on, I followed at a distance, and what was my surprise when, after half an hour's walk, I saw the form before me go into Fish alley,—the nastiest place in the town. I marked the house in which he went, and in the morning when I went back I found it was Dick Ray's house."

"Dicky Ray?" interrupted Candace, much alarmed. "My God! the worst wretch that God make upon the face of dis earth, but go on, Zac; dis story is very serious."

"I put my brains to work, and to-day I went to feel Dick's pulse. I sent for some of Allan's Old Tom, and when Dick had swallowed a plenty he spoke unadvisedly with his lips."

Upon these last words Zac laid a great stress, and Candace once more reproved him for using big words, at which he laughed haughtily and remarked:

"But I'm talking scripture, you big dunce; why not read the sacred volume? Well, then,—to talk so that you can understand,—Dick Ray vomited many more words than I expected. He told me that he had not seen McIntyre for some time; he joined with me that he was nasty fellow, and said that he was of opinion that Mahs Burleigh was murdered by him to get his wealth, and that the right heir of Elmsdale would, if he lives, come in for his property. Well, you can't see through the thing as I can, but I'm sure you have enough brains to see what's what."

When Zac had finished he looked intently at Candace, to observe the impression that his words had produced.

The old woman nodded her head and sighed, then ended by dropping a tear, and exclaiming:

"De Lord be praised. We will save de chile."

She had not the privilege that Zac had had of obtaining a smattering of education, but she was naturally endowed with a vast amount of common sense, strengthened by the wide experience that her many years brought her; and so Zac's narrative seriously perplexed her, and caused her to think deeply. After having carefully weighed the subject, she could not but arrive at the conclusion that McIntyre had contemplated the destruction of the harmless child, and in perpetrating his wicked designs had employed the services of the most renowned brigand available.

These circumstances were related to Mrs. Woodhouse the same night. She actually broke down, although the wary Zac had brought into operation all the philosophy that a buoyant optimism could devise, in order to console her. At last the broken-hearted mother yielded to a suggestion made by Zac to put Carl under the care of Mr. Highfield, who, it was agreed, would give him every possible attention.

From the first day that he formed the acquaintance of the Woodhouse family, Hugh had been esteemed as a friend, and in his intercourse with them exhibited every mark of sincere friendship, which did not terminate with the sad change of circumstances. This resolution was, however, subject to the sanction of Lindsay, in whom all had the greatest confidence.

Hugh would be off to Trinidad in a month, and there should be no time lost in fixing matters up. So it was arranged that, as soon as practicable, there should be a general conference on the subject.

CHAPTER VIII

> Come, ye disconsolate, where'er ye languish,
>   Come, at God's altar fervently kneel;
> Here bring your wounded hearts, here tell your anguish—
>   Earth has no sorrow that Heav'n cannot heal.
>
> *Moore.*

> See, see thou dog what thou hast done,
> And hide thy shame in hell!
>
> *Macaulay.*

CHRISTMAS day dawned. It was one of those lovely mornings when all nature in the tropics smiles sweetly and lends the most charming aspect to things both animate and inanimate. The air was cool and balmy, and the tints of light glorious. In the eastern sky a beautiful picture presented itself. There one could observe banks of clouds of exquisite loveliness, ever changing in form and color. Every bush and flower was bedecked with rare beauty, which seemed to be specially imparted to them on that December morning; and as the radiant sun rose majestically above these clouds, they appeared to extend gracefully their fronds and petals to receive Sol's gentle kiss.

Bright and happy faces came and went along the streets, and blithe hearts poured out merry greetings. The night before had been spent in jovial nonsense and merriment. Well-to-do citizens indulged in whiskey and soda, and argued vociferously as the liquor inflamed their brains. Middle-class folk enjoyed themselves as best they could. Some went to hear Mass at St. Patrick's, while the more mischievous played fantastic tricks, to the great discomfort of their friends and neighbors. Several families found themselves barred up in their houses, and it was only after much trouble and expense that they were set at liberty. Fruit trees of all kinds were stripped of their fruit. Even the tallness of the cocoanut tree did not deter the rash poachers from indulging in their little joke and carrying off several bunches of cocoanuts.

When the morning dawned merchants and shopkeepers felt a little irritated when they discovered their signboards removed from their proper places; old maids complained that they were unable to find the whereabouts of their step-ladders, and many proprietors, with a suppressed laugh and a cry of "Mischievous rascals!" replaced their gates which they were fortunate enough to find only some yards away from where they should have been.

Divine service was held at all the churches at eleven o'clock in the morning, and a large congregation assembled to thank the Almighty for His mercies in sparing them to join in the pleasures of another Christmastide, to swell the strains of "Hark the Herald Angels Sing," and hear the minister's eloquent presentation of the lessons that the day brought with it.

Peace on earth, good will to men; man's redemption a reality; Eden is restored to the fallen sons of Adam!

On this day of days there was, however, among the vast congregation gathered in St. Mary's Church a heart overwhelmed with a sorrow that knew no bounds. It was that of Edith Woodhouse. There in that sacred edifice, at whose altar she had often knelt and obtained strength to bear her troubles when everything else proved ineffective, she now found herself growing more and more miserable. The tremulous peals of the organ as they swelled to the rich volumes of a soul-stirring fortissimo, or faded away in the sweet cadence of a pathetic pianissimo, had no charm for her. These were lost,—entirely engulfed in the sad memories that the associations of the day had revived. There was no more a loving husband to take his seat by her side and join in the chorus of joy that was ascending to heaven. The affectionate glance that greeted her when the moment arrived for approaching the Lord's Table had gone forever. A stranger took possession of their seat in the church; and in the world, alone with a helpless orphan under the ban of a terrible ostracism, she had not even the wherewithal to supply any part of the customary good cheer which the poorest at this time provided for feasting and merrymaking.

The poor woman in her widow's weeds bent her head upon her breast and wept. The Rev. Mr. Fairley appeared touched to the heart as his eyes stole upon her now and then during his discourse. Edith remained in the church with her child until all others had gone out, and as she rose and directed her steps toward the door, a voice greeted her:

"The Rev. Mr. Fairley wishes to see you, ma'am," said the sacristan, quickening his steps and advancing toward the mother and child.

"He is yet in the vestry, I suppose?"

"No, ma'am, he has gone on to the rectory and desires you to follow."

"I will do so. Come on, my heart."

And she took Carl by the hand and followed.

Gathered in the minister's drawing-room were Lindsay, Hugh, Mrs. Fairley, and her daugher Maud. They were, of course, no strangers to Mrs. Woodhouse. They were the only friends she had left in that circle, and she felt at home among them. But when her eyes alighted on the form of McIntyre coming in with the Rev. Mr. Fairley, all the bitterness that was pent up within her breast revealed itself in the frown that knit her brows.

McIntyre approached with an air of gallantry and extreme politeness. He shook hands with Mrs. Fairley and Maud, and made a very polite bow to the others. Mr. Fairley and he then retired for some time, and engaged in an earnest conversation. Not long afterward Mrs. Woodhouse was invited to the clergyman's study to talk over some private and confidential matters. The audience seemed astonished and anticipated something unusual.

"You certainly do not desire me to face Mr. McIntyre in any affair whatever, my dear Mr. Fairley?" protested Mrs. Woodhouse. "If this be so, I shall be placed in the awkward position of having to refuse your request."

The minister smiled sweetly.

"Why is this, Edith? Is your hate made of such implacable stuff that you cannot be amenable to reason of any sort?"

"Then you contemplate a reasoning of some sort. If it be with my arch-enemy, I must again strenuously decline to take any part whatever in it."

"Do you forget that it is Christmas day, and the heart takes holiday from cherishing personal dislikes, and shuts out all thoughts of wrongs?"

"Not such as I have suffered, sir!"

"Oh, be not so obdurate, my child," persuaded the minister. "I promise that you need have little to say to Mr. McIntyre, and you will do me an immense favour if you will attend."

Mrs. Woodhouse cast a glance at Lindsay and Hugh, and in their faces she read assent to the proposal; while "what harm can reach you when we are here to protect?" seemed to speak from their eyes. Then, rising from her seat, she accompanied her pastor into his study. Carl followed, unobserved by her.

McIntyre was sitting with his legs crossed and a newspaper in his hand. As Mrs. Woodhouse appeared he assumed the dignity of a Turkish Pasha. Mr. Fairley beckoned the lady to a chair, and as he glanced around him, his eyes fell upon Carl.

"You are not wanted here, my little man," said he to the child. "Will you retire until your mother is through?"

"Excuse me, sir," sharply responded Carl, "wherever my mother is there will I be. Do you forget that I am her protector and the only one she has in the world?"

Mr. Fairley looked his admiration of the spirit the child displayed.

"There can be no harm in his remaining, since he will learn nothing to his detriment nor get any harm."

And so he did not longer resist Carl's desire.

After directing his attention to Mrs. Woodhouse, he said:

"Mr. McIntyre is desirous of showing some sympathy toward your child, and has suggested making arrangements for his education with Mr. Kuhner, the principal of the High School here, if you will only give your consent. He assures me that he has been much concerned about Carl's progress, and although the boy has been shut out of his father's will, he considers it his duty as a Christian to help him on and bury all previous feuds. Mr. McIntyre desires to approach you on this all-important subject, feeling sure that the chord which Christendom strikes to-day is vibrating as powerfully in your heart as in that of any other earnest disciple of Christ, and will lead you to forgive and forget hatred, malice, and all uncharitableness. Meanwhile you will be securing the proper training of your boy. Now what do you say to this?"

Mrs. Woodhouse curled her lips, and her eyes sparkled with indignation.

"Do you deem me such a sycophant, Mr. Fairley, that you did not anticipate my emphatic refusal in this matter? By influencing me to face this man, with the view of accepting his proffered baits, or to bring about any reconciliation between us, I cannot hesitate in saying candidly that, although you have hitherto extended your sympathy to me, you tacitly conclude that I am guilty of the black charges of which I have been accused by this scoundrel and his set; for who but a vile and degraded wretch,—lost to every sense of honour,—would consent to receive any favours from the man who has ruined her life, dragged her reputation in the dust, and, not content with this, seeks further to satiate his thirst for blood?"

"Do not be angry. I had no intention of offending; and if I have acted in any way unwisely, I did so in the interest of your child's education. In my capacity as an apostle of peace, I certainly would not shirk my responsibility as a mediator."

"I am surprised to hear Mrs. Woodhouse speak in such vengeful terms against me. I bear her no malice, and shall only attribute her remarks, which are so pregnant with rancour, to the rashness incident to woman's nature. I have done you nothing but good, Madame. It was no fault of mine that I became your husband's heir, and my sense of manhood, coupled with an innate and uncontrollable desire to be generous, has prompted me to make the offer that I have, through our beloved pastor, as a first step toward bettering your own condition and that of your fatherless child, and adding to your general comfort. Believe me, it will relieve the burden with which I am afflicted by my too sensitive and kindly nature if you will permit me to feel that I have done something toward ameliorating your present condition."

"George McIntyre, the honey of your words can never conceal the adder's poison that stains your lips. Do you think to charm me now? No; you need some rarer music. Leave me and my child to live in that peace which our unsullied consciences afford us. As for your part, your doom is sealed according to the words of Him who said 'vengeance is mine,' and who clothes the lily of the valley and protects the fatherless and widow. Mr. Fairley, will you take your Bible and read for Mr. McIntyre's instruction from the seventeenth Chapter of Jeremiah, eleventh verse?"

The clergyman took the Bible and read:

"As the partridge sitteth on eggs and hatcheth them not, so he that getteth riches and not by right shall leave them in the midst of his days, and at his end shall be a fool."

"That constitutes an unpleasant insinuation, but as far as I am concerned it is quite irrelevant, for I have not got riches unlawfully. You labour under a wrong impression, and your words do not affect me. But a truce to all this, I beg your forgiveness for my harsh dealings with you. My conduct was justifiable accord-

THE SWORD OF NEMESIS

ing to my sense of right; and if I once spurned you, it was because my prejudice prompted me so to do. I, too, have my shortcomings; and as I look more closely into my own heart, I find, with intense regret, that I have been often uncharitable toward you. Madam, I ask once more your forgiveness."

The strong, stern man seemed metamorphosed into a lamb, and knelt before the frail woman and implored her pardon.

"Are you so barefaced as to come to the cast-out adulteress, the pretending hypocrite, to sue for pardon? Has your morality grown so feeble that it now bends to recognise a polluted wretch like me? Strange, sir, —strange indeed!"

"Yes; for the tempted needs more sympathy than the tempter."

And as these words escaped McIntyre's lips he fixed his eyes upon the pastor.

Then a moment's quiet ensued during which time a fierce fire shone in the dark eyes of Mrs. Woodhouse before she burst forth with vehemence:

"What do you mean by those words, Mr. McIntyre?"

"Your clergyman may explain, if he chooses," was the laconic reply.

"So you dare to insult my mother?" interrupted Carl, who clearly perceived the approaching storm.

"Confound you, boy; do not vex me!" retorted McIntyre in exasperation. "I shall not fail to give you your deserts if you assume the man with me."

He turned to go, after bidding Mr. Fairley good-bye; but before he reached the door, Carl impetuously threw a ruler at his head, which sent McIntyre reeling on the floor, with streams of blood flowing from a gaping wound. Mr. Fairley had never before found himself in such a quandary while exercising his sacred function as an advocate of peace. With nervous lips he ordered his buggy, in which McIntyre was placed and driven hurriedly home to Elmsdale.

CHAPTER IX

Whether of open war or covert guile
We now debate. Who can advise may speak.

Milton.

It was a dark and misty night when two muffled forms were seen advancing towards Elmsdale. The clock had just struck twelve, and a policeman had taken up his beat in the vicinity of this palatial residence; but despite the apparent vigilance of this custodian of the peace, the two forms quietly effected an entrance within the precincts of Elmsdale. They were conducted by McIntyre,—who had evidently been awaiting them,—into a cosy apartment, where a small lamp placed upon a table burned dimly. Upon a shelf stood a tiny clock whose weird ticking fell monotonously upon the ear, and three chairs, placed together in a corner and overrun with cobwebs, gave one the idea that this apartment was certainly not frequented except at rare intervals.

"Sit down, by boys," said McIntyre, when he had lighted a cigar and was himself duly seated. "I have signally failed in my attempt. My cock won't crow, and I will have to try some other stratagem to get the little scamp and his mother within my grasp. Now, Dick, what do you say?"

"Fifty guineas more, and I will suggest a better plan," whispered Dick Ray, his face ablaze with enthusiasm.

"What is it?" enquired McIntyre.

"Only promise that you will add the sum asked and we are your humble servants."

"Very well, Dick, I'll promise to give you fifty guineas more, in addition to the handsome sum already agreed upon. Let me have your plan without delay. I know you can be trusted,—and you have already given ample evidence of your originality."

"Excuse me, sir; I am not disclosing the plot that Dick and I have arranged, as you might be somewhat nervous and over-anxious," put in the individual who had hitherto kept his peace. "We will pledge you our word, upon the honour of gentlemen, that we will perform our duties to your entire satisfaction. What say you?"

"Your plans might involve me and get me in a serious mess, hence, I should like to know what you are about before you begin to work."

"You might hamper our movements," put in Hawkie.

"Oh, balderdash!" said McIntyre with impatience. "My aim is to put that little monkey where he ought to be! and it does not matter what means are adopted,—rifle-shot, cyanide of potassium, or whatever you choose. Do you see this, Hawkie?" And he took off his hat and exposed a wound at the back of his head. "The little urchin has given me this mark, and do you think I could imagine any death too hard for him to die? But you must be quick with your plans, as I have been made to understand that mother and son sail shortly for Trinidad."

"Oh, we are aware of that. Don't fear, Mr. McIntyre; your prize is worth fighting for, and we shan't disappoint you."

"But I implore you once more to let me into your secret?"

"*Never!*" thundered Hawkie, almost annoyed; and Dick Ray joined in the refusal by looking his accomplice in the face and giving him a negative shake of the head.

"Very well, my jolly boys, I leave the matter entirely in your hands," agreed McIntyre, handing over the sum demanded. "When shall I get news again from you?" he asked.

"When the thing is done, and you get the evidence."

Matters having been thus arranged, McIntyre accompanied his companions to the gate, and they, congratulating themselves that they had happily escaped the vigilance of the police,—who was still monotonously pacing up and down the street,—retired to their respective homes.

Hawkie was a monster of Herculean form, with perfectly developed muscles; his face was broad and of a low type, and his retreating forehead, high cheek-bones, large dilating nostrils, and thick lips presented a most repulsive appearance. His eyes flamed in their sockets and seemed ready to fall out, and yet it is an incredible fact that there were times when they wore a mild appearance, especially when not distorted by the effects of alcohol. His voice was deep and powerful, and often brought into requisition to awe ill-behaved children into swallowing nauseous potions, or to run off to the village school. He was a terror in the community in which he lived, and nobody dared disobey his order or incur his displeasure, for fear that, irrespective of any consideration whatever, his brawny arm might send his victim to measure his length on the ground. His crimes were numerous, and the prison had often been his home. Yet this man, with the seeming characteristics of the brute of the lower creation, had been known to weep profusely over his mother's grave, to give his last penny to a famishing beggar, and to almost sacrifice his life to save a man who had once been his inveterate foe.

Curious medley of the *genus homo* indeed was Richard Fullerton, alias Jack the Butcher, alias Hercules, alias Hawkie. And this brings us to the conclusion that, no matter how low a being may sink in moral degradation, there is yet something Divine within him, though it be warped and suppressed by the contamination of evil environment and choked by the vicious passions and impulses of his lower nature.

Dick Ray, Hawkie's companion in crime, was a tall, sinewy fellow, who possessed fairly well-chiseled features. He had received his education in the three R's at a public school and had progressed favorably in them. When a boy, he had been designed to fill a decent vocation in life, but being of a degenerate turn of mind, he was led away by evil companions, and subsequently broke his mother's heart. He thereupon stifled the voice of conscience and commenced a life of unmentionable infamy. The rector of the parish could not influence him by his forcible arguments grounded on the Scriptures. Dick read Tom Paine and the translations of Voltaire and similar infidel authors, and he agreed with them that the things of this life are sufficient in themselves to employ our undivided attention, without groping in the dark for what does not concern us. He wanted to be happy here and leave the hereafter until he got into it before fixing his plans for eternity. So he fell into the life of a noted brigand. He had shut his ears to the cry of the defenseless traveller, had set his heart against the widow and the orphan, and wore on his brow the eternal stamp of Cain.

In South America, where he began his nefarious profession, the blood of many innocent victims cried out from the ground against him. It was recorded of him, on the most unmistakable authority, that he poisoned a benevolent uncle of his to secure four hundred and eighty dollars, and sold his own daughter to be another acquisition to the harem of a well-known debauchee.

Unlike his accomplice, he was not susceptible to the emotions that pain or suffering induce. His heart was like a piece of granite within him, and no deed could be too infamous for him to undertake, so long as it carried with it the anticipation of pecuniary gain.

CHAPTER X

> His life was gentle, and the elements
> So mix'd in him that Nature might stand up
> And say to all the world: "This is a man!"
> *Shakespeare.*

"MAMMA," said Carl to his mother one afternoon when they were sitting together in the churchyard near the last resting-place of their beloved dead, "do you know that I love you more than I can tell."

"But all nice children love their parents, especially when they are kind and loving. Why, therefore, do you say this to me, my sweet?"

"My love is not like that of other boys and girls. It is more than theirs. I am happy that I am the son of such a noble mother as you are, and since you spurned that villain who wanted to give me schooling at his expense, I feel that I could die for you. Mamma, when you were talking to that man, I remembered the sad story of poor Virginia and her father, which papa often told me, and I now confess that if you had consented to take anything from George McIntyre for me this knife I now show you should have been pressed against my heart, and my father's spirit would have driven it in deep."

Mrs. Woodhouse read in the child's face a fixed determination, and whether from joy or sorrow at this startling demonstration, she trembled with emotion, buried her head in her hands, and wept.

THE SWORD OF NEMESIS

Carl was an impulsive child, full of vivacity, with eyes that sparkled with precocious intelligence. He was extremely adventurous and wild, and could hardly be kept indoors for a single moment,—"Always up to some mischief," as his father used to say. But he was kind and generous, with a heart always ready to deny itself for others. Often did he divide his lunch among his poorer school-fellows and go without himself. He could not bear to see an advantage taken of another, and on one occasion he nearly got the life knocked out of him by a much bigger boy whom he had attacked on behalf of a smaller schoolmate. At home he was trained at his mother's knees in all the sublimer teachings of the Bible,—teachings that he arduously labored to put into practice. His deep reverence for Christ was admirable. He loved to read the story of the crucifixion, at which he would weep bitterly; and there was not a single day that he omitted to read the Sermon on the Mount, which so influenced him that whenever he was about to do anything of the rectitude of which he was uncertain he would ask himself, "Would my Lord have done this?" and act according to the answer that conscience supplied. Carl had never taken much interest in arithmetic, but delighted in history and classical knowledge, and his father, encouraging his hobbies, had taken pains to fill his youthful brain with the rich legends of ancient Rome, the story of the valor of classic Greece, and the departed chivalry of France and Spain, and the boy, with open mouth and rapt attention, would hear Burleigh Woodhouse tell of Romulus and Remus, and of Horatius at the bridge, while the extraordinary deeds of Sparta kept his spellbound, and his very soul would become aflame with interest as he listened to the tale of surly Diogenes and Alexander, or to the ludicrous exploits of Don Quixote and his valet Sancho Panza.

Woodhouse, who was somewhat of a psychologist, had done all within his power to educate his son's character, and naturally employed such materials as would tend to produce the best results. He taught him to ride with the ease and grace of a knight-errant, and no boy, for miles around, of Carl's age and size could surpass him in the art of swimming.

Although Woodhouse was born "with a silver spoon in his mouth," as the expression goes, he had not been without some trials in his early youth; but by dint of courage, resolution, and a proper sense of rectitude, he laboured to overcome them, though in many cases they loomed dark and high. From his own experience he taught his boy some valuable lessons, had thoroughly inculcated in him the spirit of courage and perseverance, and had caused to be engraved on the child's heart the bright motto, *"Nil Desperandum."* Buddhist philosophy, in a measure, teaches this and Sakya Muni enjoins his followers to believe that to attain Nirvana,— the state of sublime forgetfulness,—it is necessary to scale the mountain of difficulties constantly menacing them and arresting their onward progress.

As little Carl's mind developed under such healthy and loving influences his character gradually shone forth in the brightest colors. At the public school not far from where his mother lived, which he attended, he had won a place of favour among the other boys. One day he was induced by a harebrained impulse to take a cricket ball on which the master had placed his veto, from a table drawer in the schoolroom in order to revive the excellent game of cricket, which had been summarily stopped through the ill conduct of some naughty boys. Mr. Parker, the schoolmaster, was a strict diciplinarian and was extremely annoyed when he returned from luncheon to find that his orders had been disobeyed.

"Who removed this ball from where I placed it?" was the stern query. The boys all trembled in their shoes and a chorus of voices pointed out Jeremiah Jacob as being the offender. This unfortunate boy was perfectly innocent, but his name and nature were repulsive to his schoolmates. He was the *bête noir* of the school, and was selected as the scapegoat to bear the others' punishments. He now remonstrated and protested his innocence, but to no avail. The master's authority must be maintained. A thick cane, customarily used in cases of graver offence, was soon in evidence, and two of the biggest boys were called upon to hold the offender.

Just as Jeremiah Jacob was seized by the two burly boys, who were exulting over their prey, Carl entered, and having been informed why Jeremiah was about to undergo such stern punishment, he gave a look of evident displeasure at his school-fellows and bursting into passionate tears he sobbed:

"I took the ball from your drawer, Mr. Parker, and I cannot see Jacob whipped for what I did."

Mr. Parker brought down the uplifted rod. A momentary smile beamed on his face, but it was quickly followed by a dark cloud of indignation. He ordered the unfortunate Jeremiah to be released, commended Carl for his honesty, and sense of justice, which recommended him to pardon, and administered a severe thrashing to the wicked boys who had stooped to involve themselves in such an unmanly plot.

CHAPTER XI

Through grief and through danger,
Through sin and through shame.

Moore.

POOR weak woman! who will pity thee when thine unwary feet are caught in the meshes of thine own frail humanity? Even though remorse haunts thy better self and thou strugglest to reform, thou art only too harshly dealt with by the pharisaical prejudices of silly conventionalism. Thy crime becomes unpardonable in the eyes of thine accusers, who would banish thee without the gates and level at thee impious execrations, unmindful of the voice of conscience that sternly rebukes them for the dark stains which desecrate their own lives, but which lie hidden beneath the thick veil of hypocrisy; unheedful of the master Master's echoing word: "He that is without sin among you let him cast the first stone." And so, relegated under the ban of a hideous conventionalism to an atmosphere where the sunshine of human sympathy penetrates not, thy moral sensibility becomes warped, thy self-respect decays, thy love becomes hate, thy once refined tastes resolve themslves into brutal abandonmnt, thou at last fallest headlong into the pit of complete destruction. Alas! heartless men, that ye would so cruelly deal with the lost sheep whom the Saviour loves and so ardently seeks to bring home to his fold.

Mrs. Woodhouse felt her position acutely when she

realized that those whom she once considered her faithful friends, and in whom she had placed the greatest confidence, had entirely forsaken her. Of course, there were a few exceptions among them. Lindsay and his clerical companion clung tenaciously to the deposed creature; their experience and human philosophy had ripened to the conclusion that she was entirely innocent of the charges brought against her. The whole affair seemed dark, but they were determined to clear away the mysterious clouds and convince the world that she had been the victim of trickery and duplicity unparalleled.

Mr. Fairley, the pastor, seemed to have caught the general contagion; for, although he had been most gracious at first, he now began to assume a somewhat unpleasant attitude toward Mrs. Woodhouse. His wife also became distant, and it was only the affectionate and kindly-disposed Maud who could not under any circumstances be led to entertain an ill thought against her friend or believe for a moment that she was guilty. She openly expressed her opinion that nothing but a startling revelation from Heaven would convince her to the contrary.

Hugh gladly undertook to take Carl under his care, and promised that he would leave no stone unturned to secure his education. Of this Mrs. Woodhouse felt perfectly certain, and, moreover, had every confidence that when once her son's lot was cast in with such an amiable character as Hugh there need be no doubt as to his general welfare in the future.

After due deliberation she determined also to leave the uncongenial atmosphere where her life was gradually decaying and try to recuperate her health and strength in some fresh field, where the sunshine of a genuine smile would light the dark corners of her heart, or the kindly words of unprejudiced souls reanimate the dying embers of hope within her. She would accompany Carl to Trinidad, where he was to stay with his kind guardian, and still continue to drink in the only happiness earth afforded; namely, to watch carefully her child's moral and intellectual progress.

One evening, as she and Maud were sitting at the rickety table, under Candace's roof, the latter remarked sadly and with much feeling:

"I cannot tell you how much I regret your approaching departure, my dear Edith. I cannot, however, but hope it will be for your benefit in every way; we have been such good friends for such a long time that I do loathe to part with you."

"Ah, my darling, my misfortunes are great! I have drunk of the waters of Meribah; my people have cruelly despised me, and I am counted as a thing of nought amongst them. Maud, you love me, I know. Such love can never perish; it is not inspired by Mammon; it is Divine and cannot die; it is born of Heaven, and comes down on earth to illumine the souls of men; it will still link us together although the clay may be separated when we are divested of the frail tabernacle which hampers us now so much and, then, as pure and ethereal spirits we shall live and love in the presence of our Father which is in Heaven."

Maud sighed deeply.

"Do not be sorrowful, my dear," continued Mrs. Woodhouse. "I have a prophetic feeling which convinces me that we shall meet again in the flesh, though miles of water may divide us for many years."

"God grant it!" whispered Maud with overwhelming emotion.

At this moment the Professor's voice was heard, and as he approached, Mrs. Woodhouse got up from her seat and went toward the door.

"What news?" she enquired as soon as the old man had respectfully greeted her.

"Very good news, Mistress,—never had such good news in all my life. I had to take a good grog on the strength of it."

And Zac laughed with all his might.

"What is it, Zac? Do not keep me in suspense any longer."

"Well, Mistress, I only feel a little disappointed that I did not get all I expected, but I got enough to last me for some time and——"

"Oh, to the point, Zac!" interrupted Maud, who had been led to believe that the Professor had come in for some good fortune.

"Ah! Miss Maud, you're there? Well, I'm glad. I am going to give you the nice little news that Mr. George McIntyre, Esquire, of Elmsdale, was horse-whipped and almost kicked to death!"

"By whom?" "When?" "Praise be to the Lord!" were the expressions in one chorus from Maud, Mrs. Woodhouse, and old Candace.

"By the young parson!" ejeculated Zac in a ringing tone.

Mrs. Woodhouse looked surprised, but Maud's colour changed and she trembled like a leaf. This did not escape Mrs. Woodhouse's quick perception. Candace enjoyed the news and looked forward with delight to further details.

"So me little parson hab blood den? Well, dis man is de real debil when de angel of de Lord hab to come and administer judgment upon he."

"Go on, Zac," commanded Mrs. Woodhouse.

The old man continued:

"I did never believe Mr. Highfield had so much pluck. This afternoon McIntyre and he met on the Sims road. Mr. Hugh asked him for some explanation about something which I could not hear, for I was a little distance away from them. McIntyre was very rude and answered the gentleman as if he was a nobody, but Mr. Highfield showed him that he was somebody when he gave his six fine lashes with the head of his horsewhip. The brute twisted like the serpent he is; and when he tried to defend himself, Mr. Hugh gave him a few cuffs, threw him down, and then kicked him all about. I was waiting to see him give him a last one to roll him down the precipice of the narrow road and finish with him, but the bloomin' parson in the man must have remembered that 'the quality of mercy is not strained,' and,—by all that is good and great!—I didn't get all I wanted. However, I am satisfied that Mr. George McIntyre went away swearing vengeance against the wicked parson."

"And where were you when this happened, Zac?"

"Hidden away in some bushes, and neither of them knew that they were watched by mortal eyes."

"I wonder what can be the reason of this unfortunate conflict," said Mrs. Woodhouse. "I am certain that something serious underlies this, which perhaps we shall soon hear about. O Zac, how you exult over your enemy! That is not a Christian spirit. I assure you that I dislike the man, but I own your narrative makes me feel for him."

"Do you, Mistress? Then earth is no place for you; you are too much of an angel to live among people who can't get the old Adam out of them. But I have to be

THE SWORD OF NEMESIS 87

away to see Mr. Fairley before it gets later. I shall
soon return to assist you in your packing and to give
you a hand in whatever else you have to do. You know
the schooner will sail to-morrow morning positively?
Captain Dalmetty told me so."

"Very well, my dear old Zac," fondly replied Mrs.
Woodhouse.

Then she turned, moving toward the bedroom with
Maud, when Zac softly touched her hand. She halted;
the old man, assuming a sacrastic air, whispered something in her ear, and soon afterwards she went on to
join her companion.

Then Zac made his exit.

The two friends,—Mrs. Woodhouse and Maud Fairley,—were bending over various pieces of clothing scattered here and there upon the floor, and out of the
chaotic jumble endeavouring to put things in order,
when Carl entered. He had been about the garden all
the afternoon, chasing the little gay butterflies on gilded wings, and flitting about with the busy bees, trying
to imprison them as they buried themselves in the calices of wild flowers. As twilight approached he had
secured a dozen or so of the fireflies. Perfectly satisfied with his rambles, he now came in to nestle in his
mother's arms, and to learn the lessons of love that he
delighted to hear fall from her lips.

"Good evening, Miss Maud," said he, approaching
the lady and extending his little hand.

Maud took the proffered delicate hand in hers and
pressed it gently while she bent and kissed the child.

Mrs. Woodhouse then drew her boy to her arms and
in her turn smothered him tenderly with kisses.

"Now, dear Maud," she said; "you will please hand
me that silk dress, while I shall place at the bottom

of my trunk, also that cream satin. They shall never again cover my back, but must become a feast for moths."

The dresses of which she spoke were extremely costly, and had been made by the most renowned dressmaker of the town. In them, at the zenith of her prosperity, she had shone like a queen, and now that her sun had been clouded, she resolved to condemn these possessions to eternal disuse.

"And where are you going to put this likeness?" queried Carl, taking up a picture of his mother and father taken together. "I will keep it and wear it next to my heart so that I can always look at the face of my dear Father."

"No, my boy, you shall have this instead."

And his mother took up a small medallion, containing a miniature portrait of her late husband, and attaching it to a bit of ribbon, hung it around the child's neck and carefully adjusted it under his shirt.

Carl smiled approvingly, and gracefully thanked his mother.

"Shall I put this in now?" enquired Maud, laying her hand upon a ball dress of white satin, trimmed with fine chiffon and lace.

"Certainly, my dear. It must take its place with the rest at the bottom of my trunk. It was the last gift I received from Burleigh, and I well remember now the beaming smile that lingered on his face the day when he brought it to me and told me I was expected to eclipse everybody else in the ball-room as he had spared no pains to secure good materials and had ordered Madame Doré to exhibit her finest artistic taste in the work, which she evidently had done. Ah, me! This dress will ever remind me of that fatal ball and of the darkest days of my life. Fold it neatly, Maud, and put it here. Ah, but wait!—you had better place this coat in first; it is that in which he approached the altar with me; and I deem it a most precious relic."

An hour and a half elapsed, and the packing was done.

Maud was tired after all the tedious work of readjustment and of consigning to the flames such things as were thought to be of no further use and which time had swollen into prodigious heaps. She now sat down upon the bed, and Mrs. Woodhouse, bending over the small table that stood in the room, with her head resting on her elbow, seemed wrapped in deep meditation. The shrill voice of Candace, however, aroused her.

"The good gentleman is outside, Mistress," announced the old dame.

Mrs. Woodhouse knew at once who were her visitors, and rising quickly, went out to receive them. Maud followed and in a few seconds found herself face to face with the only man she loved, who greeted her with a warmth that lent colour to the rumours current about the town.

Mrs. Woodhouse was very pleased to see her friends, and soon a general conversation began, touching the occurrence of the afternoon of which Zac had brought the information. The causes which led up to the incident could not be ascertained from either Lindsay or Hugh. The laconic explanation that Hugh gave was simple:

"I have been vilified by that infamous rogue McIntyre, and have given him his deserts."

Whatever else there might have been lay buried in his breast.

CHAPTER XII

Slave to no sect, who takes no private road,
But looks through Nature up to Nature's God.

Pope.

"Good night, parson," said the Professor as the minister extended his hand toward him, a genial smile resting on his face. Mr. Fairley was evidently in the best of moods and seemed for once to curb his prejudice against the noted parson whom he considered an emissary of the devil, and who was in his opinion engaged in sowing tares among the wheat in his field of toil.

This unexpected change in the clergyman's demeanor impressed seriously the wily and experienced Ethiopian, and he immediately resolved to adopt a certain line of tactics to cope with the requirements of the situation.

"You know your Latin and Greek, Mr. Parson," thought he, "and can tell me what street Theon most frequented, and what was the colour of his favorite tunic; how Julius Cæsar escaped drowning when he swam the Tiber; how many stars are in God's firmament, and what kind of people live in them, and such like learned stuff, but I have my senses, and I use them well. I study the great book of Nature; all men and things are leaves; I turn them over carefully and with greater observation than you take with the thing you call 'learning'; I pile experience upon experience till I get a solid mountain of knowledge, which is more substantial than your air-bubbles. The labour of men like me cut out the road on which you walk easily. Ah, Mr. Parson, you may fry me for a fool, but you will lose all your fat."

"I am happy to see you looking so well, Zac," said Mr. Fairley, "but may I ask if your soul is as healthy as your body seems to be?"

"Thank you, sir, thank you, sir, for the interest you take in me. I am sorry that it is not, for times are bad and leather is scarce." And Zac, with a grave and solemn countenance, held up one of his boots to the minister's gaze.

"I mean your inward soul, your spirit, the energy which inspires your actions."

"Spirit, sir! I am not inspired by any at all, for I will swear that I have not tasted anything strong to-day."

"Don't be a jackass; you will make me lose my temper, sir."

"I never intended to be one, sir, nor have I any wish to enter your society. I accept your valuable advice as the fruit of your experience, and will not be a jackass."

"A truce to your insolence, old man. Now, come, be a rational being and answer the question I shall put to you. Do not spoil your wit by making it obnoxious. Were you not baptised?"

"I do not know, sir, for certain."

"Why, did not your parents have you christened in your infancy? Zac, you astonish me."

"I have heard that they did."

"Did you not say that you did not know?"

"I did."

"And why did you lie?"

"I did not lie,—I told the truth. My people told

me I was christened; this is a matter of faith; I can believe them as well as not; but I only know what I am myself conscious of and cannot rely on what I have heard."

"Where were you born?"

"On a silk cotton bed."

"I mean what country gave you birth?"

"My mother gave me birth."

"Where did you live when you came into the world?"

"I believe it was in a house."

"Well, if ever there was a madman, you are one. Tell me, my man, in what country your mother gave birth to you?"

"In Jamaica, sir."

"In what year were you born?"

"Leap year, sir."

"I don't mean the kind of year,—I mean the time."

"I cannot say. Remember nothing about that. You're asking me questions which I cannot answer."

"How do all sane persons know their ages?"

"They can do as they please; that is nothing to me. I speak that alone which I know."

"Do you know that you are not respecting your minister by your rudeness? David says 'touch not mine anointed and do my prophets no harm.'"

"Yes, sir; but David spoke of the man whom God sent and not those who heard the wrong call. David meant the men who sacrificed their happiness to make men better, and walked with publicans and sinners. I'm sure the wise old man didn't mean those who borrow the parson's robe to make themselves rich and live in luxury. No; he was inspired; and do you not think he knew what sort of being it was who should reign in the new kingdom,—a man so poor that he had to catch a fish to find in its mouth the money wherewith to pay the tax of Cæsar's government?"

"Oh, Zac, you are becoming intolerable and blasphemous. It seems to me that you have some animus against me; if so, I must decline having any further conversation with you, and postpone the inquiry I intended to make."

"I am not against you, sir, but I must say what I think. I am from the brave Zulu race, with no mixture. I fear no man; if I did, how could I worship the Great Being to whom alone all homage is due and of whom you white men have taught me such beautiful things. Though you think I look like a monkey in this black skin, I don't care a jot. Look here, sir; I think it much better to have a black skin than black tricks. My appearance will some day change into the brightness of the stars of the morning, according to the Blessed Book, but where will those ugly tricks which your race have been practising for so many hundred years bring you? Ah, my God,—Into utter darkness! I know the traditions of our great Zulu people, and I know their nature. They are mild, constant, full of noble courage and affection, but stormy as hell when they rise,—excuse me, parson,—so the old man gets hot sometimes. I didn't mean to blaspheme, though. Time is going. Let me hear what you have to say."

As the last words fell from Zac's lips his countenance, which had hitherto been as strong and fierce as if set in marble, now completely changed, and a pleasant smile played about his mouth. This was induced by a certain consciousness that he had disappointed the minister, who had underrated his abilities, and whose chagrin was now evident by his frowning lips and wrinkled brow.

It was but too true that Mr. Fairley had eagerly desired to have a friendly tête-à-tête with Zac on a matter in which he was interested, and Zac by intuition realized this. The wily clergyman, into whose vocabulary the word "beaten" did not seem to have entered, now made a bold attempt by putting the question.

"There is a rumor that Mr. McIntyre has been waylaid and beaten by Mr. Highfield. My informant said that you knew all about the matter. Is the affair reported correctly or not?"

"Glory be to God! Correct, sir; as correct as Moriah."

"Then I am disappointed in Mr. Highfield. It is certainly not in accordance with the spirit of his profession as a minister of the gospel to resort to such scandalous methods of adjusting matters. He might have waited. Well—ah,—since he has not found it beneath his dignity to blackguard himself in that way, I may as well believe. Mrs. Woodhouse accompanies Mr. Highfield, you say? Remarkable!"

Rev. Mr. Fairley had necessarily to stop short his conversation with Zac as George McIntyre knocked at the study door.

"Very well. Come in, Mr. McIntyre," was his greeting. Then, turning to the Professor, he continued: "I am quite finished with you, Zac. You may go now."

"Thank you, sir. Good evening."

As Zac came towards the door his gaze fell upon McIntyre, who would have preferred to have been a mile away rather than meet once more the withering gaze of those condemning eyes, which seemed to shoot fire at him.

As Zac retraced his steps homeward, he mused:

"Well, well, there is something at the bottom of all

this. You never see smoke without fire. He 'may as well believe' what? 'Remarkable!' that Mistress should 'leave with Mr. Highfield!' Why, the wise parson betrays himself to simple foolish Zac, and more's the pity he doesn't know it. Pooh! pooh! By Moses and the Lamb—more treachery heaped on! O Heaven, pour down the thunders on that son of Belial, that Prince of Hell, that accursed and uncircumcised dog!"

CHAPTER XIII

"One gaze again,—one long last gaze, adieu, fair France, to thee."
The breeze comes forth; she is alone on the unconscious sea!
"Mary, Queen of Scots."

PARTING! What a sad reality is this! What anguish of soul and sorrow inexpressible overwhelms us at the thought of being severed perhaps forever from those loving hearts with which we have always associated and with whom our very lives seem to be linked by the conditions surrounding our early youth, and cemented by the sweet affection which the hand of Time has rendered well-nigh indissoluble. It is then that the floodgates of human sympathy burst asunder with the might of a current of emotion, indescribable, wild, terrific, venting itself in a torrent of tears that pour down blanched and saddened cheeks, and as we raise our pinions to fly toward the distant haven, where may be found conditions more congenial to our temporal advancement, we look back sadly and reverently upon the spot we once called 'home.' Then everything seems to grow more attractive and lovely, and as these things stand out in pathetic silence, seeming to bid eternal farewell, we turn away the lingering glance, utter a silent prayer, muse philosophically upon the unstability of human existence, then cast our burdens upon the kind Providence that directs the course of our destiny.

Edith Woodhouse felt all of these emotions as she stood upon the pier with her little son by her side ready to embark on board the schooner *Alice* while Lindsay, Maud, Zac, and Candace were prominent among the small circle of friends who had gathered to say good-bye. They were anxiously awaiting Hugh, who did not, however, keep them long in suspense; for he soon appeared, walking at a rapid pace toward the party, with a smile upon his face. He saluted them, and then turning toward his friend Lindsay, he said, with a contemptuous laugh,

"You know what I have left behind me, Oscar. It's all over now. *Honi soit qui mal y pense.* You will, of course, apprise me of developments, and of how my friend's bruises get on."

"Indeed I will, nor shall I cease to think of you in the connection by which you have avenged your honor."

Mrs. Woodhouse, who was in a deep and earnest conversation with Candace and Zac, looked up with astonishment as Lindsay's last words fell upon her ears. Zac seemed also much concerned, but surpressed his emotions.

There was little time left for many words. The boatman had unfastened his boat from the pier and in a hoarse stentorian voice was announcing his eagerness to be away. Condace fell upon Carl's neck and kissed him eagerly.

"I will neber see you again, my own chile; but may de blessing of de Lard res' upon you and bring you back to you country safe again. Only, how me heart bleed! My! my! dis is what Mars Burleigh wife and chile come to! It's better I didn't live to see dis."

The affectionate old creature was frantic with grief, and she wrung her hands in wild despair. Zac's emotion was not less, and as Mrs. Woodhouse pressed his hands and sobbed: "Good-bye, Zac. May God bless you till we meet again,—if not on earth, in heaven!" the old man's tears trickled down profusely and fell on his luxuriant grey beard. When his grief permitted him to speak he said:

"Should you at any time want your old servant, only send for him, Mistress."

Maud and Oscar, although touched to the core, still endeavored to restrain their emotions, and the sadness that marked their farewell to their friends was so deeply engraven on Mrs. Woodhouse's memory that neither time nor circumstance ever effaced the sorrow of that parting.

Soon the gallant *Alice* was hoisting her anchor and lifting her sails aloft, as the merry voices of the sailors rang out in some of their favorite ditties and blended with the creaking of the ship's tacklings and the whirr of the heavy anchor, as it gradually rose from the sea.

Captain Dalrymple was a jolly fellow, a trustworthy seaman, and a navigator of exceptional ability. He enjoyed the confidence of all who travelled with him, and his kindly disposition had rendered him extremely popular. One of the first things he did when the *Alice* was under weigh was to pay special attention to Mrs. Woodhouse and Carl. He offered them his own stateroom, but Mrs. Woodhouse preferred to remain on deck, so the good captain handed over to her his doghouse, while Carl and Highfield were provided with excellent berths.

As the vessel distanced the shore, Mrs. Woodhouse strained her eyes looking at the various familiar objects that were fast disappearing from view. Carl retired to rest after having been a trifle seasick, and Hugh was lying meditating in his birth. Alone, therefore, silent and sad, the melancholy widow sat brooding over her past and speculating on the future, which loomed ominous and dark.

Things went on tolerably well for the first day and a half; but on coming under the lee of the French island of Guadaloupe, a dead calm stopped the progress of the ship. It was monotonous to linger there. The captain and crew became impatient as the ship rolled to and fro like an imprisoned monster in the throes of unutterable agony. The expansive, limitless, unfathomable ocean seemed majestic in its tranquil and mysterious stillness, as—contrasted with its severer moods, when with appalling fury the breakers rise mountain high and bear upon their foaming crests the helpless trembling bark that staggers to and fro at the mercy of their wild caprice.

Carl did not, however, seem much troubled about the monotony; he was preoccupied watching Mother Cary's chicks swarm around the vessel and as the gay little birds picked up the crumbs which he continually threw to them, he became more and more delighted. Mrs. Woodhouse sat upon the deck with her Bible on her lap listening to the flapping of the sails and the noise of the booms, while the *Alice* tacked here and there, anxious to catch a breeze. Hugh was whiling away the hours conversing on nautical matters with the genial, experienced captain. Twilight came and went, and the moon began to look down solemnly upon the restless bark on the bosom of the vast deep. A melancholy shade passed over the face of Mrs. Woodhouse, and she seemed enrapt in grave thought. Captain Dalrymple spoke kindly to her, and did his best to dispel any unpleasant sensation that she might be experiencing.

"What ails you, Mrs. Woodhouse?" asked Hugh,

coming toward her. "You seem rather sad this evening."

"I cannot help being sad, Mr. Highfield. I have very gloomy forebodings of impending evil. I do not know why such a feeling has crept over me and entirely dampened my spirit, but I am almost positive that something is going to happen to us before long. Do you remember how I explained to you my feeling a little previous to my husband's death? There is now a recurrence of this feeling. It seems to me as if I have a natural, unaccountable instinct within me, which always warns me of misfortune."

"God forbid that any further calamities should happen to you than those which have already embittered your life! You must not give way to these sad apprehensions that make you so unhappy. We are under the merciful care of a kind Providence, who will not fail to protect us. Have you not firmly clung to Him who by his mystic voice charmed the roaring billows into gentle sleep? Then do not despair; though the waters rage, His voice will yet whisper to the troubled element, 'Peace, be still.' Cast your burden upon the Most High, and He will bring you out of the night of sorrow to look upon the morn of radiant joy."

Raising her mournful eyes, the widow answered:

"You are very kind and good, Mr. Highfield, and I shall always feel myself indebted to you for the consolation that you have given me from the treasure-house of God's Holy Word."

"It is my duty as a man to extend to you my protection, which I will certainly not fail to do; and it is my mission to dispense to you the comfort which our holy religion offers. Be of good cheer. You will soon learn to forget your misfortune, and as your boy advances in life he will restore your smiles and labor to supply your every want."

"Thank you, thank you, Mr. Highfield. Heaven will repay your goodness."

A slight breeze struck the water and caused a sudden stir, while the *Alice*, relieved awhile from the charm which had kept her spellbound, moved steadily on. A dark cloud crept over the face of the moon, and the mate sang out to Captain Dalrymple.

"See signs of a fierce battle to-night, sir."

"Yes, Tom, I agree,—we are going to have some weather. Keep your eyes out. What's that, a sail?"

The mate took the telescope, and looking through it, descried on the horizon a sail coming toward them.

"Yes, sir," he replied; "appears to be a sailing boat. Must be bound for Montserrat."

"It'll have a hard time, I guess. Squall ahead, boys! Mrs. Woodhouse, you had better retire at once. Don't get sprinkled."

Edith at once turned into her quarters, drawing Carl with her. Highfield was too adventurous to be alarmed at an approaching squall, so he remained on deck, eager to tender his assistance to the crew in case they needed it. A few minutes and the ship was riding majestically on a fast-flowing sea, and quickening her onward pace.

"Stand fast to those halliards!" shouted the Captain. "Lower your flying jib off there! Heave to."

These orders were echoed by the mate and borne to the farthest limit. The squall did not last so long as was expected; however, it contrived to give the *Alice* a march on of a few knots. Then everything became once more as calm and serene as possible.

It was now about eleven o'clock, and all had long since retired to sleep, except the captain and a sailor who stood at the helm. The sail, which they had espied, bore down upon them until they could see that it was an ordinary sailing boat. In a shorter time than they imagined, the boat was within speaking distance of the ship, and Captain Dalrymple shouted out in a friendly voice:

"Where are you bound to?"

"Just a minute, Cap'n, and you'll understand," returned a rough voice.

And before the Captain had time to collect his thoughts two ruffians, wearing long beards, threw themselves from the boat and rushed on the deck of the vessel. The more bulky of the two seized the Captain and had him thoroughly gagged while the other did the same to the unfortunate mate at the helm. Both of the ruffians held revolvers over their victims, who were almost dead with fright.

"Now, Cap'n," said the big fellow, "you needn't be afraid,—if you will only do what we want. First of all, do not resist. Keep your d—nd self quiet, and only let us know where that queen of Sheba is,—I mean that woman you call Woodhouse, Stonehouse or the devil knows what kind of house. If you do so, you are free; if not, you're a dead man."

The Captain attempted to resist but it was of no use; he was too firmly manacled. He gasped for breath and tried to bawl out; but this he found impossible. He delayed betraying the whereabouts of the unfortunate woman whom the villains were determined to kidnap, thinking that some one might turn up to his assistance. But no! Every soul on the ship was indulging in quiet sleep. Even the next hand who was to take the rudder at the stroke of "eight bells" was also wooing Morpheus as ardently as any other. It was a tall slim fellow who

THE SWORD OF NEMESIS

secured the mate and bound him to the wheel of the rudder. The poor fellow struggled with all the strength of his being, but in vain.

The Captain with a heavy sigh directed the attention of the ruffians toward the dog-house, where slept soundly Carl and his mother (for the child did not leave her that night). After having been threatened with a loaded revolver, the Captain was bound to the mainmast as a punishment for his reluctance and the trouble he had given.

The unfortunate woman and her son were dragged from their resting-place by these cruel men, who lowered the ship's boat, placed their victims in it, then got in themselves and rowed toward their boat, which had drifted some distance away. All this had been done in an exceedingly short time.

When, shortly after, the morning soon broke, the boat with the pirates was nowhere to be seen.

CHAPTER XIV

> Through ocean's mirror dark and clear,
> Reflected clouds and skies appear
>   In morning's rich array;
> The land is lost, the waters glow,
> 'Tis heaven above, around, below.
>
> *Montgomery.*

"You will not throw me overboard, will you? Have you no pity for a frail woman's tears? Ah, heavens! What have I done that thy harsh judgment should thus pursue me? I do not know you, good men,—I have never seen your faces before, but I know that you have hearts throbbing within you which will not permit you to wantonly destroy the life of a woman who has never done you harm. Think for a moment of your mothers. Do you not remember their love to you? If you do, you will, I am sure, think a thousand times before you drown me. Has no woman's gentle hands lingered caressingly on your brow when you had a fever or when your hard day's work made you tired and you went to her suffering from a headache? If you were ill, my womanly instincts would impel me to watch over you and tend you,—if you had no one else to do it for you. Oh, think of this and spare me!"

"No use talking, my lady, The thing must be done; and if the old Nick stands at the door you must spend your night down there," said the thin sinewy rogue, pointing to the fearful, expansive ocean, over which the boat was swiftly gliding.

"Will you be so hard? Only spare me, and I will be your slave."

"Mamma," said Carl. "What do you say? I would rather see you die than be this wicked man's slave. Don't be afraid. I am not afraid to die. Does not Christ remain with us in death as well as in life!"

These spirited words of Carl imbued Mrs. Woodhouse with a sense of fearlessness. As far as she herself was concerned, death was no terror to her, but she wanted to save her child from the terrible and untimely end that threatened him. Now that she had ample evidence that, with heroic courage worthy of any son of Demetrius and with stern Christian fortitude, he was perfectly prepared to face death, she felt satisfied, and awaited the inevitable.

"You won't stay long to give much more of your impertinence," was the brutal comment, "so you may amuse yourself as much as you like for the short space of time you have left."

The burly pirate, who had all this time kept silent, now spoke.

"Look here, Dick; we will not throw the woman overboard, but we will send her adrift in the boat we took from the schooner. I tell you, man, her words have pierced my heart, and I couldn't bear to see her die under my eyes after all that pleading."

"Oh, man, don't make a baby of yourself."

"Never mind, Dick, what I say must be done."

The heartless Dick had to submit to the desire of his companion, who was none other than our acquaintance Hawkie, and agreed that Mrs. Woodhouse should be placed in the schooner's boat and turned adrift. She wept bitterly, and imprinted a long, loving kiss on her child's lips.

"Oh, Carl,—my darling Carl,—what ill-starred mortals are we! Since it is thus that we must part, may God be merciful to us, and may the Saviour guide our souls into His Eternal Presence. My child, my child,—adieu until we meet in a lovelier world!"

She again clasped the boy in her arms and kissed him tenderly. Dick Ray brusquely parted them and deprived Mrs. Woodhouse of a massive gold ring, on which her initials were beautifully engraved. Then, placing his hand upon the frail woman, he bade her prepare for her fate. The small boat was put out, and in it she was placed, with six loaves of bread and a bottle of water. This merciful provision was made at the suggestion of Hawkie.

Under the soft, glowing light of the moon, the little craft, unmanned, sat upon the crest of the waters with its solitary passenger, who awaited patiently her awful doom. As the boat glided on toward its unknown destination the woman strained her eyes to catch a last glimpse of her child. But, ah! the crisis of her grief was reached when she saw poor Carl's tender body cast out into the sea by the hands of the foul villain, Dick Ray.

Nature could endure no more; and Edith Woodhouse sank senseless to the bottom of the boat.

CHAPTER XV

> Be still, thou seabird, with thy clanging cry,
> My spirit sickens as thy wings sweep by.
> *Mrs. Hemans.*

A GOOD breeze sprang up and the *Alice* drifted considerably out of her course. When watch came to relieve the mate at the helm, he was staggered at the scene that met his eyes,—the mysterious situation of the Captain and his mate. The first thing the sailor did was to release them, after which he was soon put in possession of the terrible incidents of the past night. The description of the pirates was given, but there was no clue that might lead to identification.

The whole ship was startled at the ill news of the kidnapping of Mrs. Woodhouse and her son. Highfield was at first frantic with rage, then suddenly became calm and began to weep like a child. He could do nothing to remedy the evil.

"They are good enough to die, poor creatures!" said Captain Dalrymple. "Better they than I, because I am weighed down with iniquity. I tell you, sir, I myself narrowly escaped being choked to death, or having a bullet sent through my brain by one or other of the villains."

No other unusual incidents happened during the continued voyage of the *Alice*. The Captain, according to his accustomed habit, kept under the lee of the lovely chain of islands that rose one after the other out of the Caribbean waters. A voyage of five days and a half brought the seafarers to their destination.

It was with intense relief that the passengers and crew of the *Alice* hailed the first glimpses of spires and the beaming grey hills that appeared to their view as the schooner neared the harbor of Port of Spain.

"Our voyage has been a most adventurous one," said Hugh to the Captain, as he stood before the mirror in his stateroom adjusting his neckcloth.

"Yes, certainly sir; and such a one as I should not like to see again. I am an old salt and have fought many battles with fiercer seas than you experienced during this voyage, but I have never had my spirit cowed or my blood thrilled as they were by the voice of that poor woman whom those beasts of hell kidnapped for reasons I cannot guess. Poor creatures,—think of their carcasses having been eaten by fishes! I don't know, sir; but I have a mind there is something very nasty at the bottom of this thing, and I fancy we are going to make some discovery sooner or later. You see, sir, the scamps wanted nothing else but the woman and her son. They never looked for any valuables aboard the ship. I would rather they had broken into my chest and taken all I had than to have taken away those poor people. I believe, sir, the rogues had a special object in view."

The Captain laid great stress upon the last words, making a wistful movement of the head and pointing gravely with the index finger of his right hand.

Hugh did not reply but earnestly looked into the Captain's stern countenance on which were printed the indelible marks of deep experience and worldly knowledge. He was wrapt in deep thought, as a result of which he unceremoniously turned away from the Captain with Newtonian absentmindedness, knitted his brow, and snapped his fingers. Captain Dalrymple was astonished, and he left off buttoning his waistcoat to watch the peculiar movements that Hugh was exhibiting. As he noticed drops of perspiration profusely pouring down the young man's face he could not but fancy that he had discovered some important link in the curious concatenation of the kidnapping affair.

The harbour-master soon arrived, so that there was no time to enter into further conversation. The whole ship was astir from stem to stern; those who were engaged in getting up their baggage were now rushing forward to answer the formal questions put to them by the revenue officer.

It did not take Captain Dalrymple much time to settle his business with the officer, who returned to the shore in his little skiff.

Hugh was among the first of the passengers to place his feet once more on his dear native isle, and he breathed a sigh of relief as he found himself seated in the train puffing a cigar and once more holding in his hand a copy of the *Port of Spain Gazette*. He was on his way home to St. Joseph; and as each scene once more familiarised itself to his ardent gaze, he could not help giving utterance to spasmodic ejaculations nor could he refrain from quoting Scott's lines:

> "Breathes there a man with soul so dead
> Who never to himself hath said:
> 'This is my own, my native land'?"

That night as he sat down to tea with his only brother and a few intimate friends who had come to welcome him, he appeared absorbed in deep meditation despite his repeated efforts to make himself jovial to his friends. His usual buoyancy of spirit was lacking, and he failed to produce the brilliant flashes of wit and humor which his companions delighted to listen to. He naturally put the best forward and did all in his power to create the impression that nothing extraordinary occupied his thoughts. He flattered himself that he had scored a victory in the art of dissembling, and took comfort therefrom. But he was mistaken. His genius in endeavoring to present the spurious for the genuine utterly failed, and all present felt satisfied that the pleasant and witty Hugh had some secret absorbing his mind. His ordination as deacon took place shortly after his arrival and he was sent as Curate under Rev. Mr. Drayton of St. Patrick Parish. There he proved a valuable and energetic assistant displaying in his contact with his parishioners noble Christian virtues and manly straightforwardness which endeared him to all in no small degree.

CHAPTER XVI

> His ready smile a parent's warmth expressed,
> Their welfare pleased him and their cares distressed;
> To them his heart, his love, his griefs were given,
> But all his serious thoughts had rest in heaven.
> *Goldsmith.*

SEVERAL years after his elevation to the priesthood Canon Highfield was sent to a remote district in the country to take up the cure of the Parish of St. Michael's. The place was neglected and both energy and physical activity were necessary to bring it up to a proper standard.

The Canon was one of those who believed that the salvation of men's souls is certainly of greater moment than meaningless controversies over forms of creeds or ceremonies. He sought out the people of all denominations and carried the sunshine of the gospel into their hearts and homes. Catholic or Protestant, it mattered little to him. His mission was to reveal to his brethren Christ and the scheme of salvation. Much of the nimbus that surrounded Christianity he considered was born of conceit and selfishness, which tended more to foster disunity than to promote the bonds of holy brotherhood. This fundamental principle he never lost sight of and ever carried into his daily ministrations. He kept a school for the purpose of imparting sound knowledge to the youths around, and the fruit his efforts bore from year to year was incalculable.

It was a lovely afternoon,—when the western sky

was radiant with a splendor indescribable, reflecting its brilliant rainbow hues upon the verdant hills and temporarily gilding the window-panes of clustered houses in gold,—that Rev. Canon Highfield "more bent to raise the wretched than to rise," bestrode his favorite pony, an iron grey of imposing beauty, and proceeded toward the remote district of X. The ride was a pleasant one. Now uphill, now downdale, through forests of *theobroma cacao*, relieved here and there by open savannahs, where horses, mules, and donkeys grazed lazily on luxuriant plots of grass; or by silvery rills echoing their monotonous murmurs as they flowed steadily along on their everlasting course.

A distant noise fell upon the clergyman's ear; he stopped to listen, and Charlie the pony also felt interested as he pricked his ears and awaited his master's directions.

"This way, Charlie," said the parson, turning the horse's head in the direction from which the sound appeared to come.

Canon Highfield was soon gazing at a scene of which he had often heard but never before witnessed: It was a celebration in memory of the death of a prominent individual, usually called, "the eighth-day wake."

A throng of people was assembled about a dingy hovel, which one would hardly have believed to have been the residence of a Spaniard who owned over nine hundred and twenty acres of cocoa plantation, which broke him a splendid annual revenue. Around this queer apology for a house there were in evidence the vendors of cakes, fruits, and sweetmeats. The indiscriminate distribution of the coarsest rum, which was quaffed in large quantities, caused the brain of many to burn with frenzy, and elicited from them gestures and antics that seemed to argue in favor of Darwin's theory of the simian origin of mankind. An old woman sat upon a stone a few yards from the hut, smoking a dirty clay pipe, while a few gay damsels danced around with all the characteristic hilarity of unhampered youth.

The noise and hubbub were almost unbearable and the clergyman felt a sickening sensation creep over him as the air, which was charged with the unpleasant odour of rum and tobacco, saluted his olfactory organs. He passed into the house, where he observed a well-lighted room wherein burned innumerable tapers. The principal object of attraction was an improvised altar, on which were several images and floral decorations. Upon a bed that stood near, and which presented a very clean and tidy appearance, was laid a crucifix, with lighted tapers surrounding it, while by the bedside knelt a beautiful girl of about fourteen summers reading prayers from a missal she held in her hand.

The intruding clergyman could not help admiring the girl, whom he thought worthy in every way of her noble ancestry, the "Sisters of the Sun," who existed in the era of the Peruvian Incas.

Rita, for such was the name of the maiden, did not appear in any way disturbed by the appearance of the "English Parson," for she soon rose from her kneeling posture and struck up in a melodious voice a hymn in Spanish. Those who were present took up the strain, and soon the jarring and confusing notes that fell upon the ear made one think of Bedlam.

It was indeed a pleasant relief when this Babel ceased and the calm, impassioned sweet voice of Rita alone rang out enchantingly on the air. Her superb tones commanded the attention of all present. The hymn she sang was as follows:

> O mi Dios, que a los apostoles
> Das la paz siempre dichosa,
> Tu resurrection gloriosa
>   Anunciandoles asi:
> Haz que me alma resucite
> Contigo a la eterna vida;
> Y dame esa paz querida,
>   Que solo se encuentra en ti!
> El mundo no la conoce.
> El mundo mas bien encierra
> Turbacion, discordia, guerra,
>   Odios, envidiar, y rencor.
> A ti pues vengo a pedirla
> Que la diste a tantos otros,
> Haz que siempre con *nosotros*
>   *Se la paz del Señor.*"

She ceased her song, and a solemn silence ensued. Her hymn had inspired a thoroughly religious sentiment among the audience, which was augmented as the girl recited in a clear and sympathetic tone the *Paternoster* in her own tongue. The devotion ended for the time being, the people began to withdraw from the room. Rita turned apologetically to the Canon, a smile beaming on her countenance.

"Buenas noches, Padre," said she.

"Buenas noches, Hijita," replied the Canon.

"You have come to pay us a visit, sir," continued Rita. "We love you, good padre, as much as we do our own, and we bid you welcome. Bien venito, Padre! Bien venito."

"Thank you, señorita, for your kind welcome. I feared that I had intruded; but I now feel that I was fortunately mistaken."

"No, no! how can you intrude upon us? Though

you do not pray to the good Virgin as we do, and to all the blessed saints in heaven, you teach us of the great Father who made all men,—of His Holy Son who died to redeem all. I once heard you preach when I was staying in your parish at the house of a good old friend, and I came home and cried because Father Barrett told us that all who were not Catholics were damned. I felt so miserable to think that a man who spoke such nice things should go to hell. But Carlito read to me from his Bible, and made me change my opinion according to God's word."

"I am glad you have changed your opinion, Hijita. Who is this person that has been so good as to enlighten you on such important matters?"

"Carlito, Señor Padre,—Carlito, whom my father used to call *hijo de la mar*, and whom I love more than any one else on earth."

"And what is his real name?"

"Carlito de la Mar only."

"Where is he now? I should like to find him you prize so much."

"He will be soon here; he went out a few moments ago. I am sure you will love him, dear Padre,—he is kind and brave and good and as handsome as can be."

As she finished, the subject of the conversation between the loquacious maiden and the Canon entered the apartment. He gave a smile and a gentle bow to the stranger, then, advancing toward Rita, he stood by her side and whispered in her ear. Rita retired a moment, and when she returned she found Carlito and the Canon engaged in an interesting conversation.

"So you said your father died lately and you are left an orphan in the world."

These were the enquiring words addressed to Carlito, which fell upon Rita's ears as she reappeared.

"Si, *Señor*," chimed in Rita. "He has no mother,—she died many years ago,—and my father took him. So we grew up together as children and found all the happiness this earth can give in each other's company. My father used to tell me that Carlito has a strange history,"—she smiled gaily,—"but he never told me what it was, and I never insisted upon knowing. I am quite happy with what I know about my Carlito, and I fear that I may become unhappy by any further knowledge. They say that all women are curious, but I stamp down my curiosity that I may not run any dangerous risk of loving Carlito less. That would be like losing my life. I'm sure if I found any serious flaw in him I would die. There is an old man in the village who knows as much of him as my father did. He is an old sailor named Francisco Verde; but I have never asked him anything about the dear boy, because I know my father would have been angry."

Carlito blushed deeply as his fair companion spoke so freely and flatteringly about him to the genial minister. There was no doubt that he had a history,—and a very romantic one, too,—but time had effaced many memories and there had only lingered some dim impression of early trouble which had gradually lost its importance through the association of happier circumstances.

This Carlito was a lad of fifteen,—stately, handsome, and refined,—who spoke little but thought much; and, in keeping with his natural taciturnity, he often chid Rita for her continual prattling, although he loved her ardently.

The Canon was delighted with his new friends. He

was in the best of moods and spoke to them lovingly, so that he at once made inroads on their hearts, inviting a respectful familiarity and dispensing with the obsequiousness so often demanded by those who wear the cloth. There was a wonderful, inexplicable and mysterious affection that spontaneously seemed to spring up between Carlito and himself,—a feeling for which neither could account, and which each felt would be productive of good fruit.

Filled, therefore, with joy and satisfaction, the good Canon took his leave, promising to return as soon as opportunity offered.

CHAPTER XVII

*Still doomed in sad suspense to bear
The hope that keeps alive despair.*
   Montgomery.

CANON Highfield had many things to think of when he reached his home; the array of thoughts that had occupied him as he rode slowly by moonlight toward the rectory was somewhat interrupted by the good news that the mail had arrived a day before it was expected, and that a heap of letters and newspapers on the study table were awaiting his perusal. His correspondence from the Island of X soon engaged his attention. It was a land where he had made sterling friends, a land which he entertained a mixed recollection of joy and sorrow; a land where the sympathies of his kindly nature had been for the first time ardently aroused in support of the cause of the widow and orphan.

Ever since his holiday trip to that lovely isle Hugh Highfield had been kept *au courant* with the general condition of affairs there, and each mail that brought him news caused his face to lighten with joy or darken with sorrow, according to the kind of information that he received. He took up from the table a letter, which he saw to be in the handwriting of his friend and quondam host, Oscar Lindsay. It read as follows:

                        THE GROVE,
                 ISLAND OF X—, 24TH MARCH, 18—.
MY DEAR HIGHFIELD:
    Your last brought with it its accustomed pleasure, and the news
you gave about yourself is highly gratifying. Maud and I are
looking towards the day when you may seek repose from your
arduous labors at our home and hearth in this dear little island
where nature unfolds her loveliness to enchant the soul, where the
rich skies in their azure beauty still await your genius to transfer
them to canvas, where the moonbeams seem to kiss more lovingly
the things of earth, and where the air is laden with the fragrance
of jasmine and lilies which used so much to delight you and
stirred your poetic soul with ardour.
    Things in general continue in much the same way, except that
I am the father of another bouncing baby boy which brings up
the sum total to four.
    I know it will give you pain to hear of the death of old Candace.
It is a wonder she lived so long after her unexpected shock. I
think I mentioned in a previous letter that she had a paralytic
stroke after hearing of the fate of Mrs. Woodhouse and her son.
From that moment she never rose from her sick bed until the hand
of death kindly removed her from the stage. The poor soul lived
lovingly and died happily. My wife,—who, by the way, is a real
sister of mercy,—was unremitting in her attention to the invalid.
The deceased always spoke of Carl and his mother, and hoped they
were safely at rest. Kind dear soul!
    Professor Zac still continues in his mysterious vocation, and
though everything points to the conclusion that his mistress and
her child have long ago been embosomed in the sea, he never
thinks of losing hope, but continually repeats the sad expression
which so startled you in your first intercourse with him: "When
the white dove no longer sits upon the wall, the dark lantern will
shine to draw the fox from his hole, the bones from the earth, and
give back virtue and order to Elmsdale!" Curious old chap; isn't
he? Instead of diminishing, his wit seems to grow daily. He has
access to my law books, and is "studying for the Bar," he says.
I have never met with a negro of such an extraordinary and varied
personality,—buffoon, wit, philosopher, all in one. His craving for
knowledge has not ceased one whit.
    McIntyre is in the zenith of prosperity. His health occasionally
is disturbed by insomnia. He wields the scepter of his power
furiously.
    There is hardly anything left to interest you, so I must bid you
adieu.
    Warmest regards from better half and little ones.
                         Yours sincerely,   OSCAR.

As Canon Highfield finished the missive and replaced it on the table he propped his head with both hands and appeared to think deeply. He sighed for some moments, tears stole down his cheeks. Soon afterward he turned to the rest of his correspondence; but there was nothing to interest him as had Oscar Lindsay's letter. The clock had just announced that it was past midnight and high time for all honest folks to be in bed, so he left off toying with the newspapers before him and retired to rest.

Hugh Highfield tossed wearily upon his bed and could not sleep, for his mind was filled with anxious thoughts about his former friends. The news which Lindsay's letter brought was of very great interest and carried him back to the good old days when he enjoyed old Zac's flow of wit, listened to Candace's funny expressions, and admired her kind and sympathetic acts, for although he was so far removed from them, he had always felt the keenest interest in them.

"So the old crank still believes his prophecy will come true!" he mused. "Well, I never! But there is a curious coincidence between the news of Zac's persistent belief in the restitution of young Woodhouse and his mother and what has been weighing upon my mind since my return from that fetish scene. It is possible that the boy may have been rescued from a watery grave; but how can it be? Captain Marryat may create a Schriften in his romance, but such things do not happen in real life. It is almost incredible. Nevertheless, I shall interest myself and make further enquiries. Did not the girl say his name is Carlito? Well, this is but the graceful diminutive that the Castilian language would give to the English name Carl. She said he has a strange history, and that her father used to affix the words *de la Mar* to the name. I know *Mar* is Spanish means 'sea,' and *de la* are the preposition and the article equivalent to 'of the.' The interpretation of the whole name would therefore be 'Carl of the Sea.' There is naturally some connection between the boy and the sea. His complexion seems to be darker than that of the child I know, and that scar across the face puzzles me; but it is possible that the effects of a warmer climate might produce a slight change in the cuticle; and the mark may have been the result of an accident. Fool I was not to have discovered this key before. I shall seek out the mystery at once. I'll call upon the man Verde as soon as I get an opportunity and see what information he can give me."

Having thus thought out his plans, the worthy cleric fell asleep.

CHAPTER XVIII

> Leave me! thou comest between my heart and heaven!
> I would be still in voiceless prayer to die!
> Why must our souls thus love and then be riven?
> Return! the parting wakes mine agony!
> Oh, yet awhile delay!
>
> *Mrs. Hemans.*

SILENT, sad, pensively musing over some sorrow which lay deep in her heart, sat Rita under the branches of an immortelle tree a few yards from her home. As the soft light of evening fell upon her dark brown face she appeared like some charming princess of the "Arabian Nights" mourning over the cruel fate of her enchanted lover. Then, as if she could no longer control the current of thought that was passing through her mind, she spoke audibly:

"Oh, I shall die if he leaves me; he is all that I have upon earth, now that my poor father is dead, and what shall I do if he holds to what he has said. Oh, will not my love keep him from what his high mind urges him to do? We can live and love together and spend our young days happily, because I have enough wealth for us both. But he says he must go out in the wide world to become wise. It is Francisco Verde who has filled his mind with his foolish tales. I wish I had never known him, and that he had never taught us to read about Don Quixote and his valet Sancho Panza; for it is only since Carlito has got so intimate with him that he has wanted to leave me. He has been so noble and loving, and now with one sudden blow he breaks my heart. Oh, I see, I see, too late!—he never truly loved me or he could not be so unkind!"

"Yes, darling, I love you dearly. How can it be otherwise, my own sister?" whispered a voice behind her.

Rita looked back, half ashamed and annoyed with herself for having betrayed her feelings, and her bright eyes, filled with passion, fell upon Carlito.

"O Carlito, I have been very weak; but forgive me!" she cried. "I cannot help thinking that you do not love me, since you have made up your mind to leave me alone in the world."

Carlito felt a torrent of emotion swelling within him, and he knelt down and imprinted a kiss upon the soft velvety lips of the maiden.

"Take this, and believe that I love you still as dearly as ever, although I must leave you, darling, for your own good. You are rich and will get some one to marry you. I am too poor and must go out to seek my fortune and gain wisdom. I am tired listening to the history of old Spain, and have no more pleasure in hearing of Don Quixote and Dulcinea del Tobosa or of Boabdil y los Moros. I want to be a wise and good man, and I cannot be if I remain here always."

"O cruel, cruel, cruel Carlito! I never thought you were so cruel," and Rita sobbed bitterly.

"Nay, not cruel. You will soon forget your sorrow at our parting, and when you become yourself again, you will regret you were so unwise as to cling so much to a poor orphan like me who has not a penny in the world."

"Do not speak so to me. If it is my riches from

which you run, then I shall part with all and become poor like you so that you may never leave me."

"Do you really mean this, my Rita?"

"As God reigns above." She spoke reverently, slowly, deliberately, and called upon Heaven to register the oath. "At this moment" continued she "I would destroy my father's will. It is in my power to do so, since I have it in my possession."

"But you are his nearest of kin, and his fortune would still be yours."

"Then I would give up all claims for your sake."

As these words Carlito looked tenderly into her eyes and read there the sincerity of the words that thrilled his soul. The feelings that overpowered him were such as he had never experienced before. He had been accustomed to look on Rita as a sister, a playmate, a friend, but now those tear dimmed eyes whose electric influence suddenly transfixed him to the spot where he stood; those last words spoken by the tender girl with so much earnestness and sincerity; that brow now darkened by unmistakable marks of bitter sorrow, all inspired him with an ardent, devouring, flaming passion. The fond sister was to him changed into a peerless queen of extraordinary beauty demanding his homage, and Romeo could not have felt deeper emotion when he entered the presence of his beloved Juliet than did he at that moment.

"My loving Rita," he said passionately, "how could I have been so cruel as to taunut you so much?" And he pressed her to his breast and kissed her fevered brow tenderly and passionately. "Rita, I shall never love any one else as I love you, and though we cannot marry now, as we are both too young, I shall give you this token to show you that I mean what I say. It has never left my neck since it was placed there; and now I shall put it on yours."

He took the medallion containing a miniature portrait from his neck and placed it around Rita's.

"And now, my sweet," he went on, "since I have promised you myself, you know that I will keep my word. But I must leave you for some time, in order to secure a broader education, which will make me—nay, both of us—happier than we are. I shall always come to see you, as I shall not be far away, and when we are both old enough to marry we can do so. This will, I am sure, satisfy you. Won't it, darling?"

"If I know I shall always see you," she innocently replied, "I shall not be so unhappy."

"Then let me tell you what will make you feel better. Do you remember the night of the wake, when the English parson came to see us and spoke so kindly to us?"

"Yes," was the eager reply.

"Well, when you left us alone he offered to take me home with him and teach me all that I should like to know, and I thought that was the happiest moment of my life. Of course I said I should be glad to go, and he promised to come and see me again. You must not be angry with me for not telling you this before. I met the good man to-day at Señor Verde's and I have told him that *la vieja* Matilda has given me permission to go to him."

"And when will you leave here, Carlito?"

"As soon as I can. I know you will see after my things and get them ready for me. I will depend upon you."

"I will begin to do so at once. Your grey suit is looking very soiled and needs washing, so I must ask *la vieja* to do this. I myself will starch and iron your shirts, so that you will look clean and nice when you go to the big people. You have no money; but I will get some for you, so that you can buy whatever you like."

"I thank you very much, Rita, for your kindness in offering me money; but I shall not want any just now. I have a few shillings saved to buy some books, and this is all I need. I will trust Mr. Highfield to give me all that I require. I don't care about spending money on myself."

Whether it was the independence of Carlito's character, or his fear that he might put Rita to some trouble to secure money for him, this deponent sayeth not, but he strenuously refused to accept a single farthing, and was prepared to enter his new home with the small earnings he had accumulated by the labor of his own hands.

La vieja Matilda, to whom reference was made in the course of conversation between Carlito and Rita, was some distance off while the young people were conversing, engaged in picking brushwood to keep a brisk fire under the pot of sancoche,[1] which was simmering on the fire. She was an old dame of over sixty who hailed from the Spanish Main, and had not lost the characteristics of the Indian race to which she belonged. Her complexion was of a deep tan color; her face was broad, and her forehead extremely flat; there was scarcely a streak of gray in the coarse black hair, and to the casual observer she would have appeared twenty years younger than she really was. It was she who had the charge of Rita; for it was the special desire of old José

[1] Sancoche is a soup composed of various kinds of meats and vegetables, cooked together and seasoned with pepper and herbs.

Cedeño that this should bo so. She was very much attached to her charge, and would indulge her in every whim and caprice.

Carlito came in for a good share of her affection, and she would never do anything to render unhappy the handsome, pleasant-faced *negrito* to whom her compadre was so much attached. The good-hearted creature was reluctant to part with the boy, but she could never allay the ambition for learning which was devouring him and before which all other considerations were as nought. She therefore, with much regret, permitted him to pursue his plans unmolested.

Poor Rita had some difficulty in dispersing the unhappy thoughts that crowded upon her as she realized too truly that she would soon be severed from the darling of her heart, and that she would be compelled to drag out the time drearily and wearily until he should return.

During the few remaining days that Carlito spent in the company of Rita he had a greater insight into the depths of a woman's love than he had ever thought of. All of the latent strength of a love that was in every respect genuine and flawless was now called forth by the stern exigencies that every moment seemed to make upon Rita's heart. It came with all its eloquence of pleading, its infinite solicitude, its sacrifices and complete self-immolation in the interest of the being in whom that love was centred.

Carlito felt this keenly, and in his heart he called Heaven to witness his oath that as long as Rita Cedeño lived he would marry no other, whether he became a Crœsus or remained in his poverty.

CHAPTER XIX

But how should Prospero be living and be here?
Shakespeare.

CANON HIGHFIELD did not hesitate to seek out that important individual known as Francisco Verde. It was not a difficult task, however, because the old salt was known to everybody for miles around.

The Canon introduced to a lean man with a face revealing strong masculinity, and a frame lithe and sinewy, showing the marks of great physical activity, and indexing the spirit of adventurous daring. A large, bushy mustache partly concealed his thinly compressed lips, and a closely-cropped beard covered a broad, square chin. His eyes were mild and of a bluish cast, and his mouth well formed. His hair was of silvery grey, and judging from his appearance he might have been from seventy to eighty years old. He spoke the Spanish language fluently, and could also express himself very freely in English. He seemed to possess an ordinary amount of education, which, with the infinite store of experience he had gathered from his travels, placed him far above his neighbors in intelligence.

Francisco Verde was indeed no fool, but a man of excellent sense, who could be relied upon for advice. He was a native of Peru,—a half-caste, the child of an Indian mother and a Portuguese father,—and was quite familiar with the history and traditions of the mysterious aborigines of that romantic country. He had been twice around the world, through perils and dangers innumerable, and could relate wonderful narratives of his experience, with which he never hesitated to amuse the inquisitive listener, as his bright eyes lighted up his shaggy wrinkled face tanned by the fierce suns of many lands.

Canon Highfield rather liked his host, and was much entertained with his brilliant conversation.

"Can you give me any information about the boy, Carlito de la Mar, whom I met recently at the house of his late guardian, José Cedeño?" enquired the Canon. "There are very few youths reared under like conditions who exhibit such intelligence as I found in him."

"I, too, am of that opinion," replied Don Francisco. "The boy has some excellent parts and genius which will make him of note in the world some day. I take a great deal of interest in him, since it was I who picked him up, half-dead from exhaustion, one night about eight years ago when we were on a return voyage from Martinique, where we had just discharged a cargo of cattle."

Here the Canon could not withstand the wave of emotion that swept over him. He might have fainted,— so great was the nervous shock which Don Francisco's narrative produced on him at this stage,—had he not resorted to the use of his vinagrette, which he customarily carried with him. After a moment the clergyman regained his equilibrium, and Francisco continued his story.

"If we had not come upon this poor struggling form so soon he would surely have perished. We found him clinging to a piece of board, which must have formed at one time the seat of a boat. I presume he must have fallen overboard from a boat we espied crossing us. As

Captain of the vessel I ordered the boat to be lowered and the boy taken aboard. He could not have been very long in the water; the sea was as calm as a pond when we saw him. Were it otherwise, I am sure he would not have been alive to-day. Don José Cedeño was on board at the time. The poor child became completely unconscious a few moments after he was taken on deck, and with a heart filled with goodness and pity my poor friend Cedeño endeavoured with us to restore him to consciousness, but to no purpose. We, however, after hard work, managed to place him on the way to recovery. José Cedeño, with my consent, adopted him as his foster son. He had much trouble with him, as he remained in a state of semi-idiocy for a long period, until the aid of a clever French specialist in nervous diseases was requisitioned, when the invalid began to improve, and has made rapid progress ever since. Nobody ever mentioned this incident to him. The fact is, you are the only living soul here in possession of this strange story,—except myself."

"Was it you who gave him the name 'Carlito?' That seems Spanish, doesn't it?" enquired the Canon, after Francisco had stopped in his narrative.

"Don José called him so. The word Carl was the only name he could make out on his clothes, the surname having almost disappeared; and so this Christian name was converted into the Spanish 'Carlito.'"

"I see, I see," muttered the Canon, shaking his head. "Are you able to account for the scar which I observe across his forehead?"

"Yes; this was caused by the knife of the clever French surgeon, Dr. Raoul Angeron, whom I saw trepanning the child's skull with my own eyes. It was a horrifying sight; yet from the cold, self-reliant manner in which the doctor went to work, I took hope, and my spirit was buoyed up. I can hardly tell you how I pitied the poor unfortunate child in his suffering."

"I am sure, Don Francisco, that Dr. Angeron deserves credit for his brilliant operation in overcoming a disease in the treatment of which science has yet made such little progress. We have some hope that when our medical men shall be able to locate definitely and manipulate freely the tissues of the brain and nervous system, our lunatic asylums will have to be converted into some other institutions. You see, it takes time to do everything; science progresses slowly; and so we must be content to develop gradually until we reach the goal of perfection by sheer force of our experience. In the physical world we are all schoolboys,—be the branch what it may,—and are all struggling toward the everlasting, *but*, like the mirage, it seems still to evade us as we approach. The great medical profession contains many intricate problems which must be solved by man for the alleviation of the suffering of his brother man and increase his happiness."

"That has always been my opinion, sir, although I cannot put it in such words as you have done."

At this moment footsteps were heard on the pavement outside, and Francisco rose to welcome his visitor. It was Carlito, who had come to pay his usual visit to his friend. He was surprised to find the clergyman present, and expressed great pleasure at the unexpected meeting.

Canon Highfield showed no hesitation in expressing his desire to take Carlito home to his own home and educate him with the other scholars of his grammar school. Old Francisco willingly acquiesced, seeing that it would be a step of which the lad would no doubt gladly avail himself to secure his much-desired ambition. The sanction of Doña Matilda Luces having been obtained, it was agreed that Carlito should be lodged under the care of the Canon.

As the Canon bade good-bye to his amiable host and left his presence, many were the thoughts that crowded on Don Francisco's mind. He wondered over the divine elements in man's nature, which give birth to love and sympathy and goodness; and he concluded the world would be a thousand times better if those who have been favored with the special smile of Fortune would yield to the eloquent voice of Charity and stretch the helping hand to rescue from ignorance, vice, and irreligion their poor brother struggling in the black darkness of despair.

Similar thoughts connected themselves with other strange ones that were passing through the Canon's mind. His heart was overflowing with joy as he retraced his path homeward. It was indeed a reality that he had made a startling discovery,—namely, that Carl Woodhouse, whom he thought long ago to be dead, was certainly alive and well and, above all, soon to be under his own care.

Reader, can you imagine the good man's joy? It was indescribable; no words can portray its depth; it was for him another Lazarus—resuscitated. When he reached the rectory the words which fell from his lips were a portion of old Zac's prophecy:

"The dark lantern shall shine, and give back honor and virtue to Elmsdale."

When Carlito arrived home that night he imparted to Rita the news of the conference of the afternoon, and resolutely reiterated his intention to leave his old home.

THE SWORD OF NEMESIS

Naturally the Canon did not neglect to communicate the good news to his friend Lindsay, with the special request that it should be kept secret, at least for the time being.

CHAPTER XX

> Onward, onward may we press
> Through the path of duty,
> Virtue is true happiness,
> Excellence true beauty.
> Minds are of Celestial birth
> Make we then a Heaven of Earth.
>
> *Burns.*
>
> The rank is but the guinea's stamp,
> The man's the gowd for a' that.
>
> *Burns.*

CARLITO DE LA MAR, installed into his new home, began to experience the exquisite pleasures created by the surroundings of a healthier atmosphere. An utterly new life dawned upon him, and he appreciated in no small degree the opportunities of progress that were now afforded him. He certainly had not thrown away his time when in the wooded heights of his late home, amidst a variegated display of floral magnificence, he read "Les Fleurs de Dieu," seeing in each bud that burst forth the hand of a loving tender Faith; in each fruit that gradually developed from the parent plant, a creative and sublime power above the comprehension of poor mortals, and he acquired the wisdom and knowledge inseparable from the careful contemplation of mystic nature.

Now that he had for a time ceased to give his undivided attention to flora and fauna and to concentrate his intellectual faculties upon the study of classical literature, he could look back with pleasant recollections upon the happy days spent under silvan shades when in absolute innocence he had collected much of philosophy that would prove useful to him in after life. The rapid strides that he made in his studies were remarkable, and Canon Highfield considered him a prodigy. Each morning saw him rise with the crowing of the cock with book in hand on his way to some sequestered spot where he diligently poured over his lessons. And the last thing he did at night was to place his books containing the lessons for the next day under his pillow, in accordance with a superstitious custom in which most schoolboys have faith.

Carlito's intellectual advancement did not fail to impress his schoolmates, and, with one exception, they admired him and respected his marked abilities. The Canon's attachment grew stronger each day. The good clergyman, however, never mentioned the extraordinary circumstances connected with the history of his charge. He had even steadfastly withheld them from his brother, who was in other matters his chosen confidante, and this latter gentleman had learned to look upon Carlito as one of those earnest students whose peculiar abilities had recommended them to Hugh's benevolence. For this he commended the Canon, and always showed some attention to Carlito, although in so doing he felt that he was making some sacrifice in stepping down from his social rung.

Two years and six months had elapsed, and Carlito found himself fully competent to translate perfectly Cicero's "De Senectute" and Virgil's "Eclogues," and though he had some hard work over passages in Bacon's "Novum Organum" he always came out victorious in the end. He took great delight in translating "Télémaque,"—Archbishop Fénélon's remarkable production, which most schoolboys know,—and his passionate love for the French language led him to dive deep into "Tribolet," and to gather some of the delicacies from "Les Misérables" and "Quatre-Vingt-Treize."

One night, after he and his guardian had returned from a long and tedious ride, during which they had experienced much discomfort, the Canon persuaded him to retire without reading, as he needed immediate rest. Carlito, of course, consented to do this and meant to keep his word, but after having reached his apartment and undressed, he recollected that there was a problem that he had to work out for the next day, and he thought there would be no harm if he spent just a short time in solving it. But he was unable to concentrate his mind. He drew from a coat pocket a letter which he began to read pensively. It was written in Spanish and ran thus:

My dear Carlito:

I know you never loved me, or you could not treat me so. You have been so long away, and only twice I have heard from you, and have never seen you once though you promised when you were leaving that I would often see you. I shall surely die if you continue to treat me so heartlessly, and would prefer to do so, because no sad thoughts will make me miserable in the grave.

I remain your own true,

Rita.

This simple yet soul-touching letter from his first love quite upset Carlito, and one by one a series of ideas piled themselves up in his mind. When first he came to the parsonage the image of Rita lingered on his memory for some time, during which he had dreamt beautiful dreams, and even anticipated a happy future when she and he would be as one, never to part till death. In fact he had given place in his breast to all those ecstacies which are born of deep affection, but alas, time and mental occupation tended to produce a lukewarm feeling, and he had gradually ceased to think of the Spanish maiden with the same thoughts as he had been wont to in the first flush of his attachment. He had often to chide himself for his neglect in not writing to her, but consoled himself with the thought that Rita would attribute this to the great lack of postal facilities. This, indeed, was in a certain sense true; but if he had exerted himself he would have found the means of communication. As he leaned over the table where a shaded lamp burned dimly with his left hand supporting his forehead, he mused silently.

"After all, I could not really have loved poor Rita, who above all mortals deserves my warmest and deepest affection. It was but the momentary vibration of a chord in my sensitive nature when she so ardently appealed to my affection that caused me to cast myself unreservedly at her feet; if not, why then do not those sensations which I experienced at that never-to-be-forgotten moment still abide? They say that youthful love is strong and irresistible.

> Much enforced it shows a hasty spark,
> And straight is cold again.

"But time and circumstance have quenched the ardent flame which has been short-lived because the material from which it was kindled was not genuine. I own I possess yet a sort of love for the fair creature, but it is in no way different from that which I felt when we were innocent children together. The tidal wave had swept vehemently over my heart, but the waters now have receded to find their level and things remain in their normal and undisturbed condition. But how unkind am I, how unkind towards the girl who would have sacrificed so much for my sake. I cannot be less than a man of honor and integrity, and though the heavens fall, I will respect my vow,—I will not forsake her."

Once again he turned to his studies, but his thoughts continued to wander and he pushed the books from him.

Two days afterward, as he was strolling amongst the flowers in the garden surrounding the rectory, intensely enjoying the cool and invigorating morning air, he suddenly and unexpectedly came upon a young lady whom he had often met and conversed with. He was surprised, for he was certainly not aware of her presence at the rectory. Nevertheless his slight perturbation did not prevent his lifting his hat with the usual display of easy grace and chivalry that was characteristic of him. The stranger was a girl of about his own age; she was tall and handsome, with captivating blue eyes, a commanding forehead, a Roman nose, and full, curved lips. Though an octaroon, and the great-granddaughter of a slave, she might have passed for white. Her hair fell in golden clusters upon her swanlike neck, still further enhancing her beauty. Her voice had in it a musical ring which impressed those who heard it. Carlito could not help being struck by her charms from the moment of his first intercourse with her.

"I am indeed pleased to see Sappho paying her respects to Flora," was Carlito's greeting.

"I am rather flattered by your remark, Señor de la Mar, though I delight in paying homage to Flora, I can certainly lay no claims to the mantle of Sappho."

"Your good sense and womanly modesty certainly guard you from sounding your own trumpet, but your poetic genius, with which I have the good fortune to be acquainted and which has been most prominent in your latest production has, my dear Miss Highfield, somewhat of Sappho's melting pathos."

The young girl smiled bewitchingly, then said:

"Ah me! Were I conscious that my poetic abilities could soar to such lofty heights as those of the tenth Muse, in view of the generally acknowledged axiom that history repeats itself, I should soon begin to grow anxious for fear lest I be unattended with the calamities which befell my fair prototype."

"But who would dare to be the Phaon that would thwart thy love and cause thee to take the fatal leap? Rest assured, there can be no Phaon who could possibly resist your charms."

"You are certainly very complimentary this morning, Señor de la Mar, but I shall not be intoxicated by your chivalrous remarks. I shall attribute them to a praiseworthy element of your nature,—the desire to please. But, aside from this, I shall be spending some months here with Uncle Hugh, and shall have a literary companion in you, and one in whom I may rely for valuable assistance in learning the language of the immortal Dante. I have not made as much progress as I should like, but, with you to help me, I shall soon be able to satisfy my ardent desire to study the literature of romantic Italy, the centre of Latin civilization. I want to follow minutely the history of her famous painters, sculptors and poets, and to gather from her own treasure-house the rich harvest that I earnestly seek. Furthermore, I have an uncontrollable desire to read Leo Africanus."

"Does the Moor interest you, Miss Highfield?" interrupted Carlito.

"Certainly, his is a most entertaining history."

A gleam of pleasure fell over Carlito's countenance, and he remarked:

"I am glad to know that you can look away from self and lend your thoughts awhile to your darker brothers and sisters. I always had an idea that you were free from the prejudice of the mulatto, and this has been greatly confirmed since you have, with all the energy of your poetic soul, so sweetly sung of the loves of Andromeda and Perseus. But stay, Miss Highfield; do you really mean to remain so long with us? I'm sure your presence will be the means of making things look much livelier at the parsonage. What pleases me most, however, is that you will add fresh impetus to my desire to study."

"Oh, I shall be pleased, my dear Mr. de la Mar, if my stay here in any way enhances your pleasure."

CHAPTER XXI

'Twas gold instructed cruel hearts
In treachery's more pernicious arts.

Anon.

"Say, hello, Melville,—look at that stupid bookworm! He isn's fit to be alive. If he should isolate himself from the rest of mankind, I fancy he would feel quite happy in that condition."

"Yes, Cyril; that's a fact, and I confess I hate him, and were I to follow the dictates of my own mind at this moment, I'd punch him through."

The last words of the speaker were uttered with much emphasis, and his eyes sparkled with indignation as he advanced toward the spot where Carlito de la Mar lay reclining on the ground engaged in translating one of the "Carmina" of Horace.

"You dog!" he thundered. "I will make you answer for your impertinent allusion to me, which came to my ears much sooner than you expected."

"Bertie Melville, look before you leap," coolly replied Carlito, laying down his text book on the sod, "or you will have reason to regret your bitter words. How are you metamorphosed from smiling, pleasant Bertie to a lion's whelp. Impertinent to you! I cannot understand the mystery. I did not think my nature rendered me capable of offending the humblest of God's creatures, much less one whom I have always recognised as among the most intimate of my schoolmates."

"I want none of your hypocritical palavering. Come to the scratch at once. Did you not say that I was a low-born scullion and unworthy the love of Mary Highfield?"

"Oh,—how could you believe such a thing! Even though my brain were converted into a temporary whirlpool, my tongue could never have taken such liberties."

"You are a liar,—and you know that you are lying."

"Don't indulge in such harsh epithets, Bertie; only let me know who is the author of this falsehood."

"I have no right to say; and further, I am bound to secrecy. I suppose this will save you the trouble of further protestations."

And he handed to Carlito a dirty piece of paper on which the words "Low-born Scullion unworthy of" could be made out,—the other portion not being legible.

"Isn't this your own handwriting?" vociferated Bertie.

"It is," replied Carlito in a moderate yet impressive tone, "but——"

He had not finished his reply when Cyril, who was listening to the altercation a few paces apart, drawing near, said something to Bertie *sotto voce*, and patted him on the shoulder. But the latter, in a paroxysm of rage, tore himself away, and like an infuriated tiger made for Carlito, inflicting a severe blow upon his head with a stick he held in his hand. Carlito made no resistance, not even raising his hand against his foe. Bertie took advantage of his passivity and inflicted another blow, which sent poor Carlito reeling on the ground, bathed in blood.

But the blow had only stunned Carlito, and when he again opened his eyes it was to see his assailant standing over him and gazing at him with that triumphant air with which a cat looks upon its trembling prey before destroying it. But there was in Bertie a certain change of feeling which seemed brought about by the effect of Carlito's pitiful eyes as they rested upon him. It might have been either fear or shame, for he turned to fly. When, however, he had got a few paces from the scene where he had wrought such havoc he found himself suddenly grasped by Cyril.

"What does this mean! Let me go, Cyril. Must I exclaim like Satan 'which way I fly is hell?'"

"No, you fool! Have you allowed fear to take all the starch out of your collar? Let's out of this mope's sight, and I will explain why I held you."

Carlito picked up the piece of paper, which had fallen upon the ground, while the two retired out of his sight and hearing. Then Cyril began:

"You did it in a masterly manner, Bertie, and deserve all possible credit."

"Did I?" replied Bertie trustingly, "but then, why did you lay hold of me when I was leaving the scene. I am beginning to feel a kind of remorse, you know. It may seem unmanly to you; nevertheless 'tis true."

"I never thought you had so much of the woman in you. My reason for stopping you in your flight was to hand you this, which I saw fall from your pocket."

So saying, he handed Bertie an official communication, which the latter had taken from the post office that morning for his father, Dr. Sidney Melville, the medical officer of the district. Bertie fully knew the consequences which the loss of this very important document would have entailed, and he therefore thanked Cyril exceedingly. In another moment he unceremoniously withdrew from Cyril and started homeward as fast as his legs could carry him.

Meanwhile the unfortunate Carlito had gained sufficient strength to stand on his feet, whereupon he was soon rejoined by Cyril, who had only reappeared when he was certain that Bertie was out of sight.

"What an awful and lamentable thing has happened, my dear Carlito!" he croaked, assuming an air of the sincerest sympathy. "That vagabond, Bertie Melville, should be made to suffer for his outrage on a poor unoffending youth like you. I did my best to capture him after he had wounded you, but I suppose he escaped by reason of his superior strength. Nevertheless, be sure that Nemesis is at hand and will overtake the villain."

Carlito looked up at Cyril with that calmness and suavity of expression on his features which can only characterize a lofty, elevated, and dispassionate soul.

"Never mind, Cyril," said he; "I cannot allow you to call my friend a villain in your anxiety to espouse my cause. I must protest against such a word being used in connection with Bertie Melville. There is a vital screw loose somewhere, and when it is adjusted we shall meet again as better friends than before."

"Maybe,—or rather, I hope so. I shall be very sorry indeed if your misadventure prevents you from attending the examination. We feel certain that you will win the prize for that essay on the French Revolution. The examiner, Mr. Bridgewater, has promised as a gift to the winner a splendid silver watch, besides the prize of fifty dollars. This was told to Bertie by Miss Highfield, so it is no longer a secret. Bertie and I intend to wrangle for the second prize, which is, as you know, a mere begatelle as compared with the first."

"Why, do you think I will be the successful competitor? The chances are not equal. You and Bertie are mulattoes, and closer to that intellectual race which has evolved most of the arts and sciences of which civilization boasts to-day. You would, therefore, be quite illogical, with the evidences of hereditary superiority before you, to suppose that a poor embryo like me could rival you."

"But we have measured your abilities with ours and we have found ourselves considerably wanting."

"Then perhaps the defect is in the proper application to your studies and the want of due concentration of your powers."

"I follow the wise and patent theory of evolution and the results of natural selection which have obtained among white people for so long; and it does seem phenomenal to me that there are so many full-blooded negroes who, granted the same privileges, are able to surpass in intellect so many of the whites."

"Well," said Carlito with a smile, "I suppose these may be the exceptional 'reversions' to some far off progenitors, as travellers tell us that in some portions of the dark continent there are evidences of a high order of civilization having existed at one time."

"The cause may lie somewhere else, because it is a recognized fact that the average unmixed negro, given the same chance, can successfully compete with the average white man. Even James Anthony Froude admits this."

"But the white race has been struggling through mists of doubt and fear, of hope and dismay, of failure and trial, until they have been repaid with the bright smiles of a radiant day. But we have the difference of a sudden transition from darkness to resplendent light; and while we must admit the advantages of this, we are without the impregnable foundations reared in the progress of gradual development."

"It would nevertheless argue well in your favor that, even though this be taken into consideration, yet the craniological difference between the pure blacks and the pure whites is not greater. It shows you are equal as a man and a brother, though you be more distant from the Caucasian than I happen to be; and your ability to make the proper use of your privileges is manifest."

Cyril had for good reasons adduced these arguments though he felt inwardly the insincerity of them. At heart he was prejudiced against his darker brethren and would rather have seen Carlito dead a thousand times than to have considered him his equal. But he had some important cards to play, and it would be to his benefit, he thought, to impress Carlito with his magnanimous and philanthropic sentiment.

Cyril was Carlito's senior by a couple of years, and though he evinced a most crafty and subtle disposition, he was far below young de la Mar in intellectual capacity. Born of fairly wealthy parents, he had been placed under the careful tuition of Canon Highfield when he was twelve. He had always pretended to be on excellent terms with Carlito, and was often to be seen in his company. This attachment, however, seemed somewhat spurious to Carlito, when on one occasion he recognized with deep regret the utter selfishness that Cyril exhibited in a matter that considerably affected him. The kind and forgiving heart of Carlito soon learned to forget the circumstance, and the accustomed friendship was, unhappily, resumed. It was, therefore, without the slightest doubt on his mind of the sincerity of Cyril's sympathy for him that Carlito rebuked him for another unkind remark which he made concerning Bertie.

"Cyril," said Carlito, "I seek no revenge for the wrongs I have innocently suffered. I do not court Adrastia's patronage in this lamentable affray. I would not be a Timon who, brooding over the unkindness of his race, can only find amidst the haunts of savage brutes an unction for his misfortunes. Nay, not so, Cyril. We must not be too pessimistic and choleric. There is something good, after all, in humanity. Life is not all thorns; there are roses, too. The thorns sometimes cause dreadful harm, but if the roses be cared for and nurtured they will always fill the atmosphere with their delicious perfume. Though I must exclaim 'Et tu, Brute!' I again repeat that I shall see Bertie Melville repent of his outrage upon me yet. He will be sorry for it one day, I tell you. Though he has not asked it, I shall forgive him. This day, before God, I do."

Having said this, Carlito bade Cyril good-bye, and each took his respective road homeward.

CHAPTER XXII

> Fleecy locks and black complexion
> Do not forfeit nature's claim;
> Skins may differ, but affection
> Dwells in white and black the same.
>
> *Cowper.*

WHEN Carlito had reached a distance of about fifteen yards from the rectory he observed to his great dismay that blood was still oozing from the wound a trifle above the temple, and his efforts to staunch the flow were without effect. What could he do? He did not wish to alarm the inmates of the rectory, nor did he desire that there should be any discovery of the accident, as this would necessarily lead to further complications, which would ultimately result in Bertie's getting a rough handling from his austere father. He endeavoured to obtain a remedy to stop the flow of blood. It was half past six o'clock, and he considered, could he succeed in this, he would reach home in the twilight and avoid detection.

He noticed a bird's nest almost hidden among the branches of a tree above him. It did not appear to be tenanted, and he thought of obtaining some of the soft down that enters into the building-material of birds' nests and apply to the wound.

"It never rains but it pours," said he delightfully, and starting on his way to set his thoughts in operation, he put his hand in his pocket, where he discovered a very small phial containing laudanum.

THE SWORD OF NEMESIS

There was some difficulty in climbing the tree, but Carlito ultimately succeeded in reaching the nest. A possibility that at first did not enter his mind now dawned upon him, and he felt disappointed as he saw in the tiny receptacle three small tropical birds, wrapped in balmy slumber.

"I will not disturb you," said he. "Poor little things, you will not suffer inconvenience at my hands."

He heard a rustling and it appeared as if some one had spoken. But having listened carefully, and finding no further evidence of the presence of any other person, he concluded that it was the rustling of the wing among the branches. When he reached the ground he took out of his pocket a silk pocket handkerchief, and with the words *"necessitas non legem habet,"* tore off a bit, which he saturated with the laudanum and placed on the wound. With the other portion he bound his head.

He had succeeded in almost reaching his quarters when he was suddenly met by Miss Highfield. He came well-nigh fainting when he saw her eyes resting steadily upon him. Though his hat had been carefully placed over the bandage, it occurred to him that the prying gaze of the young girl had observed something unusual, when in a tone faltering with emotion, she said:

"I see you have sustained some injury, Mr. de la Mar."

"I have met with an accident, Miss Highfield; but it is of no great importance, and I hope to be soon all right."

He wished to evade his fair enquirer and was proceeding onward, when she suddenly electrified him with the words:

"I know a part already, and you would do well if

you were to make a clean breast of it and give me the history of your adventures, which have resulted so disastrously to yourself. I saw you when you climbed the apple tree, and from my hiding place watched all your movements. I heard your tender, manly expression when you refused to disturb the little birds in their cosy nest, and my heart became filled with emotion at your tenderness,—this evidence of your humanity. I felt for you, I must confess, Mr. de la Mar, and I preceded you home and prepared to do my best to alleviate your suffering. Only let me know how you came by your wound."

Carlito was struck at the peculiar candour of the young girl, and though he would much rather have kept the affray of the afternoon to himself, he could not help satisfying her curiosity,—on the condition that she should not reveal the secret. He told her of the unexpected attack which Bertie had made upon him, how her name had been associated with the matter, how he had refused to deviate from the principles that underlie sincere friendship, although Bertie's conduct was so reprehensible, how he refused to give blow for blow.

Miss Highfield had always entertained a high opinion of Carlito's moral character, but the incident of the afternoon had raised him to the standard of a hero in her estimation. She promised to keep the secret of the story that she had heard and, though she thought deeply, she made no comments whatever.

Mary Highfield had now been six weeks at the rectory, and in her frequent intercourse with Carlito she had often deviated from the narrow and convential code that society prescribes for the upper classes; she had recognized his extraordinary talents, and a great friendship had sprung up between them. But Miss

Highfield, being of a naturally proud and haughty disposition, had always about her a certain something,—call it "dignity" or what you will,—which regulated wisely the admiration which genius so strongly called forth; and so an unwholesome relationship was thereby prevented.

Carlito for his part had always before his mind's eye the status in society where providence had placed him. Ofttimes he was compelled to condemn himself for unfaithfulness to his first love, Rita,—to whom he had so faithfully pledged his word,—when he permitted his thoughts to linger lovingly upon Mary Highfield, who, with all the fascinating graces of excellent womanhood, at times captivated him. He strove nevertheless to cure himself of this madness. Whenever Miss Highfield would honor him with her presence (and the occasions were frequent) or exhibit her unusual attachment, to him he would demolish the magnificent air-castles that presented themselves to him one by one by musing thus:

"I could never be so absurd as to imagine that Miss Highfield could love me. She could never lavish that sweet passion upon me,—the poor charity boy whose only claim to her slightest notice lies in his being favored by her generous and noble uncle, who has introduced him into a circle which he had not even hoped to enter. My color is another insurmountable barrier. No! no! the casket cannot please, and the priceless gem which it may contain must therefore be deemed worthless. I cannot be the Dark Othello who wins this fair Desdemona."

Miss Highfield did all in her power to administer to Carlito's sufferings, and her dainty hands seemed to have produced marvellous effects whenever they rested upon his brow. Luckily the Canon had been absent for the last two days and was not expected to return for four more. It was a young clergyman who had lately left Codrington College that had relieved him of his duties,—both in the church and school,—during his absence. It was, therefore, expected that Carlito would be all right before the return of the Canon. The staid housemaid was bought over and was, on her peril, charged to say nothing about Carlito's indisposition. Though she had grumbled much at the extra amount of labor it entailed upon her to convey his meals up to his room, she consented to carry out Miss Highfield's request, as that would secure for her a good many more tips. Besides, she had a care for her little granddaughters who could not afford to lose the presents of worn skirts and pretty petticoats, which Miss Highfield had been in the habit of giving them.

Carlito's wounds soon began to heal, and in the space of a couple of days caused him but little pain. A slight fever, however, lingered which was combated with febrifuges and other remedies. Three days after the attack upon him he was able to sleep to his entire satisfaction,—a luxury which he had not enjoyed since the encounter.

It would have done one's heart good to see the noble lad resting peacefully. Though he was almost black, his features were not at all those of the characteristic Ethiopian. He partook of the beautiful ebony complexion of his mother and the commanding and captivating features of his father. His brow was lofty, but upon it still lingered some signs of the suffering which he had experienced in earlier days. The marks of the surgeon's knife could not be mistaken. His finely-shaped head argued a well-developed brain. Well arched brows shaded glowing and penetrating eyes. His nose was not aquiline, but was large and refined and thoroughly in proportion with the rest of his face. The lips were not thin, yet it could not be said that they were of the Ethiopian type. In them there was perhaps a harmonious blending of the forms peculiar to his progenitors, while a slight curve in the under lip enhanced its beauty of expression. Love, affection, and nobleness were unmistakably indicated there. As he lay dreaming, his face illumined with a gentle smile, he would have furnished an excellent model for a sculpture in jet, and even Michaelangelo might have been happy to add to his laurels by a true representation of such a picture. In the regions of dreamland he saw his friend Miss Highfield weeping over him, her tears were dropping fast, while she tenderly wiped his brow with a lace handkerchief. She had altogether lost that haughtiness that had characterized her and was transformed into the most ardent of lovers. She knelt over and pressed her rosy lips on his as she whispered:

"How I do love thee, my Carlito! Never, never shall I cease to love thee, noble boy!"

To the dreamer's fancy it seemed that the emotions of her heart were excited by some powerful passion that flamed high within her and seemed to consume her, while upon her face was revealed what she felt within. He knew that this was love; and he felt translated into a region of happiness where all was poetry and love; where roses smiled and blossomed under their feet.

In his ecstacy he laughed triumphantly, and subsequently awoke to find, with all the horror of disappointment, that he had but been dreaming. It was like a sudden transition from the grotto of Calypso to Dante's Inferno. His face had been all this while turned to the wall, and as he looked in the opposite direction, he saw Miss Highfield calmly standing over him much the same as he had seen her in his dream. As his eyes rested upon her she turned with a graceful air and left the apartment. Strange thoughts now took possession of his mind.

"There are more things in heaven and earth than are dreamt of in our philosophy," he murmured. "Those abstruse questions which have been exercising some of the ablest minds for several generations may some day be exposed to the light, when an advanced philosophy shall open the invaluable treasure-house, explore its hidden secrets, and classify its vast treasures, thereby increasing the power and happiness of men, and mitigating their sufferings. Can it be possible that Mary Highfield loves me! O Heavens! can it be possible? Then, alas! we shall both be martyrs."

CHAPTER XXIII

Come to these arms and meet in this embrace!
The vows you never will return receive;
And take at least the love you will not give.
                Pope's "Translations."

CYRIL, having once begun his nefarious mischiefmaking, could not easily desist. He very ingeniously led poor Bertie to believe that Mary Highfield had been carrying on frequent flirtations with Carlito de la Mar, and indeed these tales were so plausibly told that the least credulous person would have taken them as plain, unvarnished truths. He nevertheless sought Miss Highfield's company whenever it was possible, and even had the audacity to speak to her of his love. She, however, rejected his overtures with a hauteur as stern as it was scornful. This did not deter him from the main object which he kept continually before him,—to persevere until she should favor him with her heart and hand. It was not that he really cared for her, but, as in the case of Midas, it was gold,—the all-ruling powerful motive,—that had caused him to fix his thoughts in that direction.

Mary Highfield was wealthy, and this was enough to make the target worth hitting at any cost. She was the only daughter of John Babcock Highfield, proprietor, who had been one of the sugar lords of the West Indies and who was considered to be the possessor of about seventy-five thousand pounds in cash and landed property. There were those who said that her father's estates were heavily mortgaged, but nobody knew for certain. Mrs. Grundy was always busy, and none need bother with her tattlings. His younger and only brother, Hugh, was much attached to him, and had for the most part obtained his education at his own expense. Mary was at an early age placed under the most careful tutors, and at the end of her sixteenth year could boast of a first-class education, in which poetry and art were not the least of her attainments. She was peculiarly fond of literature, and it was to satisfy her desire for a companion in the study of languages and the fine arts that she consented to remain the guest of her uncle; for although she often went to the parsonage, she had never remained there more than a few days. Bertie and she were first cousins,—Mrs. Melville and Mrs. John Highfield being two sisters who had always lived on the closest terms of friendship. Their children had always been together, and the happy hours of childhood were spent in each other's company. Bertie evinced a passionate fondness for Mary, but, though she loved him as a relative, she could not consent to his frequent pleadings that she would one day become his wife. Whenever Bertie introduced the subject Mary evaded it, or turned to something quite different. Nevertheless, the lad did not despair, and sought by every means available to make some cleft in that obdurate, granite heart of hers. But woeful ballads, piteous sighs, and promises fraught with the sweetest affection were found utterly useless.

The reader can therefore imagine what was Bertie Melville's chagrin when he understood that there was a dangerous rival in the field in the person of young de la Mar, whom he had always believed to be the sincerest of friends. Since Cyril had pitted him against him he actually hated Carlito as much as he had loved him.

"'All's fair in love and war' is an old saying," he thought, "and if Carlito can believe in it and be treacherous enough to allow such sentiments to influence him to my detriment, I see no reason why I should ever think him worthy of my,—or any other honorable gentleman's—regard."

Dr. Melville, whose practice was somewhat limited, certainly was not rich, and he looked forward with much anticipation toward a closer relationship between Mary Highfield and his son, which would place his own exchequer upon a surer foundation, as well as enhancing Bertie's prospects.

It was the day after Canon Highfield's return that Mary for the first time during many days took an evening stroll and found herself in the churchyard, a few steps from the rectory. She had not been long there when she saw her cousin Bertie coming toward her with an expression of much concern upon his face. She sat down upon a small bench under a cluster of palm trees and awaited him. After the usual greetings were passed and some remarks made about the weather and a few other trifling matters, Bertie, assuming an air of gravity, spoke in a faltering voice.

"Mary, you have often told me that you cannot give me your heart, but only during the last few days has the terrible reality dawned upon me that you are in earnest. You have been the bright star to which I have always looked with unfathomable hope. All my thoughts have been centered upon you; you have been the idol set up in my heart, which I adored with feelings of intense homage. All my aspirations, my ambition, my struggles, have sprung into restless action from the all-preponderating desire to have you as my own. I had ventured to hope that my frequent appeals would one day procure your consent, but, alas! it seems now more hopeless, since you have come down from your lofty pedestal to bestow your affections upon one who will disgrace your ancestry and humiliate you before all. Consider this mad step, my cousin,—for God's sake,—before it is too late to repent of your folly and indiscretion. You may deny it, but I am satisfied that if it had not been so, this surreptitious monster, Carlito de la Mar, would not have calumniated me as he has done. This has been the method which he has adopted to prejudice you against me. Once more, darling, I implore you, leave me not without a word of comfort, or I die of a broken heart."

Mary sympathized with her cousin; and she could not stay the tears that trickled down her cheeks. His words had pierced her heart, and she wished she had never heard them, as she mused over her inability to grant him his request.

"But, my dear cousin, I do not think that a heart like yours should buy a spurious love. You are worthy of something better than I can offer you; why should you have worthless brass for your brilliant diamond? If it were possible for me to make the sacrifice and consent to be your wife I would be deficient of those indispensable elements which genuine love produces to join hearts in one, and support marital relationship upon the sure foundation intended by God. Bertie! Bertie! we are not ordained to be one. Do not be angry with me. It is the decree of fate! 'Everything works together for good to them that love God,' and though you may deplore your disappointment, be sure you will

THE SWORD OF NEMESIS 159

in the future see enough to make it clear to you that 'all discord is harmony not understood.' You will soon learn to forget this trying moment when you will find some heart to reciprocate your affection as you deserve."

"Your words are not just, Cousin Mary. You might have tried to love me had it not been for Carlito, whom, I again repeat, you passionately love. The hardest steel relents, and flint cannot resist the effects of perpetual contact of other forces. Is the human heart more obdurate than other things in the realms of Nature?"

"You are raving, Bertie! Who could have told you that there has been anything like a mutual understanding between young de la Mar and myself? He has always comported himself with due respect toward me, and has never once even so much as spoken of love."

"Never spoken of love! Cousin Mary, you astonish me. Would that I had never lived to hear you utter such a falsehood."

"Falsehood! Do you say 'falsehood?'" Mary grew indignant with rage. "Am I not as much alive to the dishonor of a lie as you are, then?"

"Stay, you astonish me," said Bertie, meekly, seeing the storm which his imprudent remark had raised. "You need not be angry with me. I am rather buoyed up with hope to hear so stout a denial from lips that have never been tainted with a lie. If I mistrusted you for once, it was because I had been told certain things apparently supported by plausible evidence, which at least wore the aspect of truth."

"And who may your informant be that knows so much about my affairs?"

"Cyril Merton," was the straightforward reply.

"Cyril Merton!" reiterated Mary. "Has this barefaced Iago no other way of spending his time but in mischiefmaking! How can he befriend you when he speaks derogatorily about you and has laid damaging information against you in the unfortunate circumstance between yourself and Mr. de la Mar."

"This cannot be! Cyril Merton do this! How can I understand this inconsistency? Pray, then, does every one know of the conflict?"

"I cannot say that everybody knows, because I have heard nothing since I saw Cyril and asked him to keep this disgraceful matter under cover. Your victim is much distressed at your treatment and wonders how you could have been so blind as to act in the way you did. He has been most magnanimous, and even wished to hide the matter from me, though I made the discovery that he had been wounded, under peculiar circumstances. He believes, as I do, that you have been duped, and therefore cherishes no ill will against you."

"But I saw in his own handwriting the evil insinuations he made against me."

"I regret to say it, dear cousin, but I am positive that the wily Cyril has been playing a double part for his own benefit, and such a person is not a meet companion for either you or Mr. de la Mar. That piece of paper which has been the foundation of the whole trouble will on proper investigations be found to be a huge fraud, and if not a forgery,—take my word for it,—is something near it."

Bertie seemed to be almost stunned at this intelligence, and after endeavouring to say something in reply to the startling information he got from his cousin, he found himself utterly unable to speak coherently for some moments. During the momentary spell of silence he became wrapped in profound thoughts, which produced a painful expression on his face. When he had recovered from his aberration, he tenderly and pleadingly looked into Mary's eyes and said:

"You know our final examination comes off this week at the grammar school. My father awaits anxiously the result, which will decide whether I am to go into law or medicine. Soon, therefore, I hope to be on the broad Atlantic bound for England. Consider, therefore your decision, my life, and say whether you will send me heartlessly away a despairing, disappointed, and wretched mortal,—exiled from his native shores forever by a heart which felt no pity for the pangs of unrequited affection,—or say whether you will imbue me with vigor and ambition to go forth and study the profession that soon will place me in a position to gain eminence in life and procure the wherewithal for making you happy as my queen."

Trembling with emotion, Bertie took his cousin's hand in his and kissed it gently, kneeling upon the lawn. He anxiously awaited her reply, and the few moments which intervened seemed like weary years of waiting.

"Mary, cousin Mary," he pleaded passionately when the suspense had become unbearable; "you will not say no to my appeal. You cannot surely be so unkind. It is a question of life and death, and upon your answer hangs my fate."

Mary had never in her life experienced such a severe trial, such hard struggling with herself. At one moment her pity seemed to be gaining ascendency, and she was sorely tempted to yield; but a silent prayer sent up to the Throne of Grace imbued her with strength and impressed her more strongly than ever with the conviction that she did not really love Bertie. She remembered the words that he had just used: "It is a question of Life and Death," and verily it was. Had she in a weak moment, for pity's sake, yielded herself, it would have been the sowing of the first seeds of sorrow, for which repentance would have come too late. She at length summoned up courage, and with tears streaming from her sad eyes, she whispered,—nay stammered,—the words that fell upon Bertie's ears like a fatal cannon shot.

"It is of no use, my dear cousin. You can never be my husband. Do not think me unkind again, I implore you. This decision is for our mutual good. You are noble and generous and worthy any woman's love, but the connection which has hitherto caused us to live so familiarly has produced its own peculiar affection. If you had been absent from me and I had not known you before, I think perhaps I might have loved you as my husband; but that we have grown up together as children is certainly no fault of mine. I am sorry, my dear cousin, that once for all I must ask you to cease to think in this way of me."

Bertie rose from his knees, his eyes red with weeping. His mental suffering had produced deep marks of anguish upon his features, and he looked like a criminal being led to the scaffold.

"The storm has now burst with all its terrific fury," said he, "and I find myself a wretched being. The clouds have obscured my beacon light, no longer visible, and I must now be tossed upon the remorseless ocean of life,—helpless and forlorn. Straightway from your presence I go, a changed mortal, and these eyes of mine must cease to look upon you. Ambition beckons me on no longer. Good-bye, and 'If for ever, still for ever, fare thee well!' God bless you. I will not forget to pray for you, though you may forget that there is on this planet a being like myself."

Mary's heart was touched and she flung her arms around Bertie's neck and kissed him; but he straightway withdrew from her clasp and walked hastily away.

A few days afterward she received the following letter from him:

MARSDEN VILLA,
DEC. 5, 18—.

MY DEAR COUSIN:

My life is a blank. The main object on which my thoughts and energy have been concentrated cannot be attained. I have therefore resolved to enlist as soldier in the West Indian regiment which embarks from St. Lucia for St. Helena in a few days. A bullet shot may one day perform the kindly act of closing the career of an ill-starred being like me. Again I reiterate: God Bless you.
Farewell!
Your broken-hearted Cousin,
BERTIE.

CHAPTER XXIV

A soul as full of worth as void of pride
Which nothing seeks to know or needs to hide
Which nor to guilt nor fears its caution owes
And boasts a warmth that from no passion flows.

Pope.

THE examination of Canon Highfield's Grammar School came off. It was the last that many of the advanced students were to see at that excellent college, which had produced so many brilliant scholars and always paved the way smoothly for those destined for the liberal professions. There was a great deal of interest shown by those acquainted with the students, and the results were looked forward to with great anxiety. The Rev. Mr. George Bridgewater was the chief examiner, and looked through all the papers in Divinity, Classics, Mathematics, French, and Natural Sciences. The other subjects were covered by Canon Highfield.

As had been expected, the highest number of marks was taken by Carlito de la Mar, Bertie followed, and he who was expected to take the third place,—Cyril Merton,—fell extremely short and was outstripped by a lad many years his junior from whom such results had never been expected. It was indeed a gala day for the whole school and the lads, with the exception of Cyril, evinced much animation. The prizes were promptly presented on the same day, Carlito receiving the prize of ten pounds from a certain fund raised for that purpose, besides a silver watch,—the gift of Mr. Bridgewater.

A couple of days after this event Bertie sent a note to Carlito, couched in very friendly language, inviting him to meet him on the St. Cyr Cricket field after sunset that day. Naturally Carlito was eager to know what business Bertie could have with him, and impatiently awaited the appointed meeting.

It was a quarter to six when he arrived at the spot, but he had to wait many minutes more before Bertie appeared. When he did put in his appearance, Carlito was surprised to see the change that had come over his countenance. It was a serenely calm and sad expression that now marked the once bright and lively eyes, and the complexiou had grown much paler than it was wont to be. Carlito wondered what were the causes that had brought about such a penitential air.

"I am glad to meet you again as a friend, Carlito," said Bertie, extending his hand warmly.

"So am I," replied Carlito, with a smile. "I have no doubt by this time you have discovered your mistake."

"I have, beyond the shadow of a doubt, and I am come to make *l'amende honorable*. I never thought you had such a noble soul, Carlito, and that I have so basely wronged you will for many a day fill my soul with remorse."

"I knew that would one day come and I have waited anxiously for it. Is this not more in accordance with what the Master enjoins upon us than to have endeavoured to convince you of your error by more forceful methods?"

"It is Cyril Merton who is the villain, and not you.

It is his duplicity which had brought about this conflict between us. He laid before me false statements purporting to have been statements made by you impugning my character, and I took them for gospel truth. Then, again, he produced such plausible evidence in that piece of paper in which your handwriting undoubtedly appeared. But I do not question its origin since I am convinced that you really love me and could never have hoped to harm me in any way whatever. I am perfectly sure, Carlito, that you will forgive my unpardonable wrong, and upon my knees I implore it, since you have shown yourself a worthier being than I."

Bertie had fallen upon his knees and had clasped Carlito's hands with energy. The latter bade him rise, and as a token of his forgivenness, embraced him and kissed his cheeks. When this imposing little melodramatic scene had ended, Carlito said:

"Verily, Cyril Merton stands in the category of the basest of mortals. His wicked tricks, although having worked a temporary suspension of our friendship, have ultimately proved abortive, and he has now shown himself in all his true colors without succeeding in his plans that were to cause a separation between us and thus give him a better opportunity for carrying off the prize when we were incapacitated. I saw him snatch something from your pocket on the day you attacked me, but I did not dare accuse him of theft then. I do so now, however, since I find him capable of such duplicity."

He paused in his rush of words.

"My God!" ejaculated Bertie; "can human nature sink so low?"

"I shall satisfy you with tangible evidence that you

cherished a serpent in your bosom whose fangs have played complete havoc."

So saying Carlito drew from his pocketbook the following letter:

DEAR CARLITO:
I wish to see you personally, but at present such a thing is not possible. I am the victim of a somewhat troublesome cold. As the exam. comes off soon our efforts must be directed towards getting that pedant Bertie Melville somewhere in the corner. He makes a fool of himself by boasting that he intends to win the first prize and if you agree with me, let me know at once.
Yours sincerely,
CYRIL.

"This is my reply," showing to Bertie this copy:

DEAR CYRIL:
Yours received. My motto has always been *Palmam qui meruit ferat*. If Bertie boasts, that is his personal business. I would prefer to meet on fair grounds, so that we may compete by sheer force of intellect. Your suggestions are not charitable, and I cannot lend myself to any conspiracy against Bertie. A low-born scullion, unworthy of the name man, I should deem myself under such circumstances. I hope the day will come when we shall mutually coöperate in some laudable cause worthy of true gentlemen.
Yours truly,
CARLITO DE LA MAR.

Carlito had read this correspondence hurriedly. Since the letters were written, this was but the second occasion of his looking at them, and it did not appear to him that there was anything striking in them. But Bertie, who was always on the *qui vive* detected something at once which made him put the question to Carlito:

"Have you preserved the piece of paper that did the mischief," he enquired.

"I have," was the reply.

"Then," continued Bertie, "it will not be difficult to

discover how Cyril prepared his plans, since I have found the key."

The remarkable scrap of paper was produced; and, as Bertie anticipated, it was found to be a part of Carlito's letter to Cyril refusing to coöperate with him against Bertie. The ingenious Cyril has requisitioned the use of the ink-eraser for perpetrating his villianous act. On referring to Carlito's copy it was discovered that the full stop which was placed after the name Bertie was erased and the verb *is* took its place; the words "of the name man" were replaced by the name *Mary Highfield* and defied detection by the ordinary observer. On the whole, it was a cleverly executed fraud, and both the young men thought the author would make something in the world if he only turned his ingenuity in the direction of Virtue and Honor. They spent some time in giving their personal experience of Cyril's conduct, and by a comparison of their notes it was necessary to arrive at the conclusion that the delinquent should be sternly tabooed.

Just two days afterward Bertie and Carlito met again. It was to exchange words pregnant with sincerity and to shed tears at parting. On the same night Bertie bade good-bye to his beloved country and, with a heart bearing the burden of rejected love, was on his way to St. Lucia to join his West Indian regiment.

CHAPTER XXV

> Beside yon straggling fence that skirts the way
> With blossomed furze unprofitably gay
> There in his noisy mansion skilled to rule
> The village master taught his little school.
> *Oliver Goldsmith.*

CARLITO, having left college, selected the vocation of a schoolmaster. Canon Highfield was not financially in a position to send him to the continent to take up a profession, but gave him all encouragement for the future and buoyed him up in his ambitious projects.

At a quiet little village situated about a mile and a half from the parsonage young de la Mar spent his days in imparting to boys and girls the rudiments of education. His kindly disposition suggested to him the method of teaching by love and not by force. He soon won their hearts, and they all began to look upon him as a friend whose companionship became invaluable. There was a word of encouragement to the dull little fellow who could not for all the world take in what two from ten would leave, and the seven-year-old maiden who wearily and monotonously tried her efforts to spell "circumlocution" would be handed back the book with the words: "Take it, darling, and try again." The result was that she went away fully resolved to give the kind master no more trouble.

Though a student of moral philosophy, Carlito did not in every case conform to the theory of the Hinterschlag professor of Carlyle's "Sartor Resartus" who "acted upon the faculty called memory through the muscular integuments by means of birch rods." He did not believe that the powers of the brain could be developed by means of excessive castigation, and it was only in the case of inattention or downright carelessness that he resorted to the birch to accomplish his ends. With a patience worthy of Plato, he explained each subject that he took up, and no scowl sat on his face nor hasty expression escaped his lips when he found that at the end of his instructions the results were far from being satisfactory. Being strictly moral and religious, he never failed to inculcate the principles of virtue in the minds of his pupils by means of lectures and pertinent illustrations. Selfishness was an element that formed no part of his moral composition, and the same spirit of communism that he exhibited in his earlier days now showed itself in bold relief. Being of a gentle, quiet disposition, he was dubbed by his friends and admirers "Le petit prêtre."

An incident, however, occurred one day, which made it patent that he was an advocate of muscular Christianity and could use his strong arms and agile body with advantage to protect the weak and oppressed.

It was an afternoon when the rain was falling in torrents,—and the stream which he had to cross on his way home had swollen a great deal,—that he saw a poor black woman standing on the bank with an Indian basket on her head, hesitating as to whether or not she should risk fording the stream. She might not have been more than forty years old, yet she seemed worn with care. Her once sable ringlets had been almost entirely converted into silver threads, and an expression of unmistakable sorrow rested on her face. Her clothes

THE SWORD OF NEMESIS 171

were none of the best and were stained with mud and dust. It was evident that she had come some distance. There were a few persons standing by, some of whom viewed her with curiosity, while others cast insults at her. One man remarked that she was a witch who had come to dupe the place. When Carlito saw her his sympathy was awakened.

"Where do you come from, madam, and where do you wish to go?" he tenderly enquired.

This unexpected approach on the part of the young schoolmaster was received with amazement by the stranger, who was at first inclined to believe that he was one of the mocking crowd; but when on a nearer scrutiny she observed the kindly expression that glowed in his eyes and the books he carried under his arms, she was impressed with his sincerity and ventured to reply:

"I am a stranger, sir, in search of employment, and, for heaven's sake, I implore your aid and protection."

"You shall have them by all means, my poor woman; but you seem feeble, and can never cross this stream with that huge basket. I will take it over for you and assist you across."

"You are not going to help that she-devil, Mr. de la Mar," said a chorus of mocking voices. "You have forgotten you are a gentleman, sir."

"A gentleman! Aye, what's a gentleman?" asked the young man in a sarcastic tone, as the dignified passivity of the strange woman powerfully impressed him.

A stalwart youth who was laughing heartily at the idea of what he was pleased to call Carlito's craziness drew near and pushed the helpless woman so that she staggered and fell on her face to the ground.

Carlito gazed at the cruel perpetrator of this inhuman act with a rage that seemed unbounded. Never before had his temper so completely mastered him. He seized the ruffian by the collar and shook him. A fierce combat ensued. They seemed equally matched. Now Carlito's strong arm dealt a severe blow on his opponent's eye, now the latter returned another, which also took good effect. Ultimately, however, Mars decided in favor of Carlito, and with a well-aimed blow he sent the other reeling senseless to the ground. De la Mar immediately took off his books and rolled up his trousers, and having taken the basket from the helpless woman, he carried it across the stream.

"Hurrah! Nobly done, my boy!" shouted a voice that Carlito knew.

The voice was that of Canon Highfield, who, with his niece, had just come upon the scene and in a moment had taken in the entire situation.

The benevolent youth looked at them in amazement and smiled pleasantly. It was not the time, however, to listen to flattering compliments, and the next thing that he did was to escort the woman over. This done, he now entered into conversation with the Canon and explained the circumstances as they had happened. The woman also was conducted to the rectory and placed in the charge of old Annie, the housekeeper, who, despite her idiosyncrasies and fits of disagreeableness, manifested an extraordinary amount of fellow-feeling and was "wondrous kind" to the distressed tramp.

Weary, exhausted, and sad, the poor creature appreciated beyond expression the dainty supper and comfortable lodgings with which she was provided. She felt as if she were in an elysium, as her thoughts ceased to dwell upon the sad things that had hitherto occupied them, and she began to enjoy the comforts which were so kindly lavished upon her. Out of pity she was taken into the service of the Canon as assistant housekeeper.

Ellen, as she was called, exhibited astonishing intelligence considering the sphere to which she appeared to belong, and the evidences of her strict probity were numerous. This delighted the clergyman, and proved a great meed of satisfaction to her benefactor, Carlito.

One fine afternoon some time after Ellen's installation at the rectory, Carlito and Mary were sitting together upon a bench half hidden away in a grotto of flowers, conversing on some subject that considerably interested them, when Ellen happened to pass, and her gaze became fixed upon Carlito.

"Why do you stare at me in that manner, Ellen?" enquired Carlito.

"I really can not tell, Mr. de la Mar, but whether it is from the obligations under which you have placed me or some other unaccountable reason, I must confess (excuse my presumption, sir) that my maternal instincts have been aroused whenever I look upon your bright and intelligent features."

"You pay me a compliment really, my poor Ellen."

"So you are or have been a mother," put in Mary. "You are ambitious, Ellen, when you compare your offspring with one of Mr. de la Mar's type."

A gentle rippling laugh set the girl's face aflush. Her words were uttered thoughtlessly, and she would gladly have recalled them, but it was now too late, for they had already made deep impressions on de la Mar's mind. He, however, very adroitly endeavoured to rid her of her embarrassment by continuing his interrogation of Ellen.

"You say that you have been a mother, Ellen?" he questioned.

"Yes sir, I have been, but O Mr. de la Mar, for God's sake ask me nothing further, and do not probe the wounds which the kind hand of time has wellnigh healed."

"Another victim of man's perfidy, alas!"

"No, sir, no, sir,—but ask me no more, I beseech you." And she covered her face and sobbed aloud as she withdrew from their presence.

"That woman has a history surely," said Carlito, "and I feel great sympathy for her. There is a secret in her life which seems to haunt her. Perhaps she has been deceived by some demon who has completely darkened her life. The secret may come out one day. Time will tell."

"Ellen wears the insignia of marriage," said Mary, "and perhaps her husband has been unfaithful to her. Poor woman! I believe this is the cause of her suffering. Alas, how unthankful is the sterner sex now-a-days, and how often men steel their hearts against the tender graceful being that perfumes their lives with the incense of faithful love. If men could only realise the tenderness of a woman's affection I'm sure they would think a million times before they crushed it with their heartless words or deeds."

"You speak strongly and appear not to be a stranger to what true love is."

Carlito spoke the words mechanically. He scarcely knew the real force of his words, and in his emotion his hand fell on Mary's. She had not replied to his question nor did she withdraw her hand from his gentle pressure. He had read the answer in her eyes which were glowing with the strange light that love lent them. At one time he might have thought it more probable for a queen to bestow on him her affection than to cherish the remotest idea that the haughty, brilliant and erudite Mary Highfield should fall under this spell. But what he had lately begun to imagine in a half-hearted manner now appeared to be an incontrovertible fact. He lifted the delicate hand to his lips and kissed it with tenderness and emotion.

"Do you love me, Mary?" he asked, peering into the sweet liquid eyes.

"I do, Carlito," she replied, tremulously.

The curtain was lifted, and the drama commenced.

CHAPTER XXVI

> In action faithful and in honor clear,
> Who broke no promise, served no private end.
>
> *Pope.*

It was in the stillness of the night, when Queen Mab had set out on her tour drawing her cobwebs athwart men's eyes and playing fantastic tricks, that she alighted on Carlito and delivered him of the thoughts which had filled his breast to overflowing. The light of the silver moon which had just risen fell upon his face through an open window. A solitary star struggled to peep through a floating dark cloud and seemed to look down kindly upon the sleeping youth. The effulgence proved too much for him, and he suddenly released himself from the Fairy Queen and shut out the light which had disturbed him. He did not return to dream. A weight came over him that he could not throw off, and he labored without effect to court sleep.

To be in love is serious. It is a reality that perhaps is not duly considered, because men sometimes mistake ephemeral passion for the transcendental principle of true affection. Carlito had made this mistake. His pity for Rita and his sympathy for her devotion had roused in him a feeling that he had mistaken for genuine love,—a feeling that had caused him to pledge his word to her. Now that his heart had told him that that simple yet warm-hearted country girl could never gain the place in his affection of which she was indeed worthy, he became burdened with the most poignant grief, and his sufferings were doubly augmented when he recognised the fact that he had now found his real love and his true ideal; and yet he was forced by the voice of conscience, the arbiter that fixed the standard of his moral responsibility and to which he had always listened, to sacrifice the elysium he would, under other circumstances, have given his life to possess. He must be true to his word, true to himself, true to his God whom he had called to witness that, though the heavens fell, he would not forsake Rita. He wished that that moment had never come that had seen Mary confess her love, had seen him yield to the irresistible fires that had all along been inflaming his being, and as the reality of the situation stared him in the face he clenched his fists, bit his lips, and cried like a child.

Why was he so weak as to have betrayed himself and to have been guilty of the crime of fanning the love of that high-souled girl into intense flame by his imprudent conduct towards her? He made it evident that he had loved her, and she was convinced that there was nothing in the way of their love. A moment's resolution, a complete immolation of self, would have nipped the bud in its infancy and prevented an unprofitable growth. But no. He could as bravely and resolutely face death as any Spartan hero, but, alas! his philosophy could not render him proof against the magic charms of a woman's love.

Time wore on, and de la Mar threw himself more into his scholastic duties than he had ever done before. Several brilliant articles on educational subjects came from his pen,—articles that were valued by newspaper men as the productions of deep and earnest thought; and his moral essays which from time to time adorned the columns of a favorite periodical were highly commended, and raised their youthful author in the public's esteem.

Besides most of the classic tongues, Carlito studied Hebrew and Sanscrit with extraordinary application. In these labors he burned much midnight oil, and as he paced the room reciting selections from Homer or the Talmud, his eyes glaring with a brilliant light, one would have supposed that he had gone mad. But all this study could not serve, as he had hoped, to put Mary out of his thoughts. She had taken too firm a root there, and he found it impossile to dislodge her.

The intercourse between them had become less frequent, as he walked to school quite early and did not return until dinner time, which was 7 p. m. This he did with the object of avoiding Mary. But this apparent slight on his part seemed to cause her love to glow with greater ardour. From that first evening, when they had betrayed their mutual affection, the barriers had been trampled down and little or no ceremony marked their intercourse. Nevertheless, though Mary had often referred to their former conversation, Carlito steered clear of the subject, as by venturing upon such dangerous shoals he felt he would surely come to grief. This naturally led the young girl to fear that her affections may have been bestowed on one who did not really care for her. Mary had made rapid progress in Italian and had ceased to take lessons from Carlito, but as a means to an end she implored him to come home earlier from school in order that they might get through some pages of Tasso. Carlito, though he would have wished otherwise, could not refuse, and so he dismissed school earlier than usual that he might grant her request.

One evening as he with the Canon and Mary were seated at the dinner table the Canon remarked:

"My dear Carlito, you do not seem happy, and I have noticed for some time that you have grown paler and that your appetite is not what it was wont to be. I am afraid it is the effect of too much study, or else there is something which weighs heavily on your mind. You must not study too closely, my boy. There is plenty of time. You are not yet twenty-one, and the world is still before you."

"It is not study which has had the effect of which you speak. It is due to some other potent cause." Carlito glanced at Mary, and a tear stole down his cheek.

"Then what can you have weighing so heavily upon you? What else could it possibly be?"

Carlito endeavoured to turn aside the conversation.

But the Canon became rather apprehensive.

"Perhaps he has discovered a clue in connection with his identity," he thought; "and if this is so it is necessary for me to withhold no longer his history from him."

With this resolution he rose from the table.

One evening a short time afterward Carlito and Mary were reading together by lamplight. They were alone, and only the voice of the wind murmuring monotonously among the palm leaves now and then caught their attention.

"What is it which makes you appear so sad, my dear Carlito? My uncle noticed it in you, and I have myself seen you stand for moments as, if you were completely lost. Tell me what it is,—do not keep it from me."

"My darling, my only love,—say that you will forgive me if I tell you the truth which has caused me unutterable sorrow and anguish of soul from the moment I felt that you loved me. For this I had not dared to hope, though I know I would give my life to save you from the slightest suffering. When it so happened that fate had intertwined our hearts I felt that all the joys of earth had been combined together and laid at my feet. It was for me a realization of the highest pleasure which this world affords. I would not have exchanged the wealth of Golconda for that gentle smile or kind word which men have sought and have not received. O Mary, my love for you is greater than you can ever imagine. I have watched you tenderly at every possible opportunity and have yearned constantly for you, although I have pained you by my apparent slights. We are toys in the hands of Fate, whose caprice it is to mock hearts. O Mary, my short-lived day of brilliant joy has been suddenly turned into the black night of despair. I must tell you that I have pledged my word to a simple Spanish maiden whom I once thought I loved but whom, as I fully realize now, I did not. Forgive me, darling, that I did not tell you this before. How can I be false to that trusting heart which placed all confidence in my word, and how can I be true to myself if I fail to keep my plighted word? I cannot be less than a man, and to maintain my manhood I must make the eternal sacrifice that will forever embitter my life. I cannot be yours."

One would have thought that Mary Highfield would have succumbed to this severe shock which fell upon her with terrible effect, but she bore it with a superhuman strength not common to woman. Instead of being diminished, her love was strengthened, and her faith in Carlito became impregnable. He was before, in her eyes, as an ordinary man blest with genius and rare gifts; but now a heavenly halo seemed to surround him and she considered him almost a demigod.

"Carlito, you have saddened me beyond expression by your frank confession," she began steadily; but the firmness soon changed into a falter as she continued; "and although I, too, must feel the loss of that hope which had always given me pleasure, I must bend to the inevitable, since my unselfishness can picture the trusting creature relying on your word. You are the first man that I have ever loved, and you will be the last. There is no place left for another. In making the necessary sacrifice I do so with the cup not unmixed with some element of pleasure, that is to say, I shall retain and value the friendship of a true and honorable gentleman whose equal I have hitherto not found. It is now left for me to seclude myself from the world and give myself wholly to the lethean springs where I have often found a panacea for the discomforts that have menaced me from time to time. I mean a closer association with Virgil, Horace, Plutarch, and Dante, to say nothing of the Book of Books and our own immortal bard. The time for my departure will be to-morrow at midday. I shall endeavour strenuously to bury the recollection of this fated day. It is impossible for me to unburden my soul, but I shall struggle against the tide that threatens to overwhelm me."

"Noble type of womanhood!" cried Carlito. "Who would not die for such a being?"

"Noble type of manhood!" replied Mary; "and who would not die for a soul so beautiful and good?"

And they parted with hearts brimful of sorrow,— to meet again.

CHAPTER XXVII

> As are our hearts, our way is one
> And cannot be divided. Strong affection
> Contends with all things, and o'ercometh all things.
> *Joanna Baillie.*

Mary's departure from the rectory had immensely increased Carlito's struggle with himself against the terrible wave of passion which threatened to overwhelm him. Her presence had given him constant pleasure, and he pined for his only love. He knew the evil consequences that would result from a too near approach to the alluring flames, but like the doomed moth, it was beyond his will to resist such powerful attractions. Canon Highfield noticed that there was no appreciable change for the better in the young man's health, which was manifestly declining; nevertheless he did not carry out his resolution to enlighten him on certain important matters in connection with his history.

He, however, from a consideration of Carlito's movements reached certain conclusions. The young man had taken up the habit of visiting his old home. These visits had become more frequent of late, and often in the afternoon, when the cool and refreshing breeze invited the overworked frame and harassed mind to enjoy the luxury of the salubrious air, Carlito bestrode his little cream pony Mazeppa and wended his way to X, where he again met with Rita.

Canon Highfield knew that this was the period when

young men are apt to fall in love, and he took it for granted that Carlito had been seeking to win the hand of Rita, but had encountered serious obstacles which reacted on both his mind and body. As the reader knows, however, the thoughtful clergyman was entirely mistaken.

Carlito had renewed his vow to marry the girl to whom he had so solemnly given his troth, and as far as Rita was concerned there was no obstacle. She was no more the smiling, simple and talkative child who had won the Canon's admiration on the auspicious night of the beloric. She had developed into a stately woman with a countenance of beauty and dignity of expression, and a form as exquisite as any specimen of Spanish beauty. Her ideas had in a degree outgrown the crude mould in which they were once formed, but she lacked considerably that refinement and culture that can only be produced by the careful training and education of the mind. She was like a rare and beautiful flower whose virtues are unhappily pent up in the unwholesome environment of uncongenial soil. She had accustomed herself to hard work, and there were few men in the neighborhood who could put more energy in the felling of a tree, or toil more than she among the cocoa trees. Consequently she possessed physical strength to a great degree, and her complexion was of a healthy brown. She was fully alive to her own interest, and though Don Francisco Verde was nominally trustee to her properties, the whole duty of managing the estate devolved upon her, and she proved herself fully competent to perform this with entire satisfaction.

She looked with unspeakable delight toward Carlito's visits, and though at one time she had begun to think him unfaithful, she now felt convinced of the contrary, and cherished once more the hope that they would one day be united.

As she sat down on a chair near him one fine afternoon she observed that there was a melancholy air about him which considerably disturbed her mind.

"What's the matter, darling? Why are you so sad?" she asked.

"Nothing," was the laconic reply.

"I'm sure it is something. Maybe it is your ambition that still haunts you. I remember reading somewhere that there is no unhappier wretch than the man who is ambitious but disappointed,—who has the desire for fame but has lost the power to achieve it. You see, therefore, that ambition is an awful thing, and I am afraid it is that which makes you look so sad at times."

"Maybe it is ambition as you say, darling, because I have been duly considering my position of late. I shall be twenty-one early in September, and I have not yet seen my way clear to carry out my promise. I should certainly not dare to marry until I have secured a profession and a competency to support you properly. I must, under the circumstance, implore you to wait until Providence blesses me with the realization of my wishes, which ere long I hope to obtain."

"You astonish me really, Carlito. If it is merely a profession you want,—that can easily be provided for. I can give you money to cover all expenses in that direction, and I have wondered why you will drudge away at that old schoolkeeping, wearing out your lungs when you can do so much better."

"I thank you for your kind offer, sweet; but I would rather not accept it, since it does not harmonize with my principles."

"But all that is mine will be yours one day."

"Naturally; but I must then be in a position to give you something worth while in return."

"Will you not reconsider your decision, Carlito? Do you mean I must wait all these years? Had I not known you as I do I would have thought that you were vacillating, but I cannot do this because I know that you are honorable and true."

That evening, as Carlito was returning home, he noticed a dark shadow silhouetted against the evening sky. On a nearer approach he distinguished the form of Cyril Merton, who advanced toward him and laid his hand on the pommel of his saddle.

Carlito seemed surprised, but did not speak.

"Hello, de la Mar," said Cyril. "You have got so big, it seems, you hardly care to recognize me."

"Oh," replied Carlito somewhat sarcastically, "I would recognize Cyril Merton anywhere. I can never forget him."

The words were spoken in such a tone that Cyril at once felt their import.

"I am glad to see you, man. Since I quitted X I have not been back more than once, so I am anxious to know something about the folk. You see, I have grown quite a Robinson Crusoe, and am, as it were, isolated from my own circle."

"Ah, yes; your sudden disappearance from amongst us astonished a good many people. However, I indirectly learned that you had identified yourself with the Plantocracy and were managing some important estate in this quarter. Is that really so?" Carlito asked casually.

"That is really so. I have plenty of work to do, and I can spare little time to come down to the village. It is therefore my good fortune that has brought me in contact with you this evening."

"But my visits here are frequent, and it is strange that I have not met you before."

"For the simple reason that I have already explained. I observed your pony at a certain place this afternoon, but I thought it was some adventurer after that Spanish girl's money. I would not, however, imagine that of a high-souled being like you."

"Thank you for your compliment, Cyril. I am sorry I have not more time to spare. It is getting late, and I must be home before the Canon dines."

So saying Carlito parted from the man whom of all others he utterly abhorred, and on whom he had not laid his eyes since the day of the examination at the Canon's Grammar School.

When he reached home he found to his great dismay that the Canon was out, so he was obliged to take dinner alone. He ordered a cup of tea before he rose from the table, and as Ellen was bringing it in the waiter slipped and fell on the floor, spilling its contents. Carlito started.

"What's wrong with you, Ellen?" he said sternly. "This is a piece of downright carelessness on your part, and I shall expect you to exercise more care in the future. There is the carpet soiled by your slovenliness, and I am not pleased."

"I did not do this on purpose, Mr. de la Mar," replied Ellen, touched to the quick by this harsh and unexpected rebuke; and as the tears welled up in her eyes she continued: "My feet unfortunately stumbled, and in my effort to maintain my balance I allowed the waiter to fall."

"There is no use making excuses; this is an accident

THE SWORD OF NEMESIS 187

which could have been avoided if you had exercised greater care."

"I shall try not to allow it to happen again, but I am sure you are quite unlike yourself to-night, dear, gentle Mr. de la Mar, and have treated me more harshly than I ever thought you capable of doing. That I am a servant, sir, and in this position I owe to an unkind fate, or rather to the villainous plotting of a base usurper. I am not deserving such harsh treatment."

At these words the woman buried her face in her hands and wept violently.

Carlito felt for her and would gladly have recalled the words which in a moment of ill temper he has used.

"I am sorry that I have pained you, Ellen," he said with deep emotion; "the best of us are sometimes led away for a moment by evil influences to say or do unkind things. I offer you my sincere apologies for my harshness, which has wrung those tears from you."

He rose from his seat and patted the woman gently on the cheek, while his own eyes filled with tears. Ellen was satisfied with this manifestation of genuine regret, and concluded that there was certainly something serious at work to sour the gentle disposition of the young man for whom she always had had a warm corner in her heart.

"Can you say, Ellen," inquired Carlito when their differences were settled, "what has taken the Canon out?"

"Oh, sir; this you should have known before but for the accident. Mr. Highfield, Miss Mary's father, sent post-haste for his brother this afternoon as Miss Mary had been taken ill, and the doctor says there is a very grave strain on her nervous system. The poor young lady is suffering very much, and the servant hints there is a general opinion that something weighs heavily on her mind."

"Something on her mind!" ejaculated Carlito in some surprise. "What can it be?"

"Oh, I suppose, sir, it must be some love affair. You cannot imagine how this can affect the minds of young people."

"You are certainly joking, Ellen. Miss Highfield is too sensible to be thus influenced."

"Ah, dear master, education cannot stay the tide of human passion, and it is not strange to find the erudite and accomplished courtier sighing like a furnace and making woeful ballads to the eyebrows of his mistress. Such is the mystery of our incomprehensible humanity."

"You speak wisely, Ellen. I trust Miss Highfield will not be any worse by to-morrow. Were it not already late, I would have gone over to see how she is to-night. This must, however, be postponed now until to-morrow."

It was with a heart laden with sorrow that Carlito retired after the sad news of Mary's illness had reached his ears, but when in the midnight stillness he communed with himself, his unbounded sympathy for Mary made him feel miserable indeed. He listened anxiously for the footsteps of the Canon, and when eleven o'clock had arrived and he had not returned, he became exceedingly uneasy. It was not, however, long afterward that voices were heard a short distance off, and Carlito in pajamas and slippers ran down stairs. His suspense was at an end when the Canon, with an unusually troubled countenance, bade him good-night.

"Good-night, sir," answered Carlito. "What news? Is Miss Highfield any better?"

"Not better, nor yet worse," was the reply; "but I am afraid that she is in a very precarious condition."

Carlito stood awestruck, and he trembled in every limb. At this moment both Annie and Ellen were on the spot, anxious to learn what news the Canon had brought; and when they heard it they retired with sad faces and troubled hearts. They were fond of Miss Highfield, and were much concerned about her.

"I would be glad if you would come down to my study early to-morrow morning, Carlito," said the Canon; "I have something of importance to say to you. Meanwhile you had better retire."

"Very well, sir. Good-night," replied Carlito.

And they parted.

CHAPTER XXVIII

There is nothing in the wide world so like the voice of a spirit.
Gray.

There is laid a sword in thy father's tomb,
And its edge is frought with thy foeman's doom.
Mrs. Hemans.

CARLITO could not sleep. His efforts to do so were in vain. The wind began to howl monotonously among the trees, and a slight shower of rain, producing its rhythmic music as it pattered on the house-roof, had a soothing effect on him, but not sufficient to produce slumber. An unbearable heat pervaded the room,—which was unaccountable, since the weather was, on the whole, cool.

He had not much faith in supernatural apparitions; nevertheless a queer sensation seized him; his hair stood on end, and he began to fear the intrusion of some unwelcome visitor, and in this he was not far wrong. The light, dimly burning on the table, was suddenly extinguished. He got out of bed and relighted it. It was again put out. A form enveloped in white could be clearly discerned.

Carlito, though naturally brave, trembled as he saw the strange object approaching. He quickly rose and prepared to meet his visitor. The apparition threw off the white robe in which it had appeared to be wrapped and revealed the regular outlines of a man clad in deep black. Its face wore not the hue of earth, but upon it rested a solemn, sad, almost repulsive, expression. Carlito, filled with the impetuosity with which fear had imbued him, thundered:

"Goblin of hell, damned spirit, return to your resting place! What do I owe to you who thus disturb my rest?"

No answer was returned to his address.

"Speak!" cried Carlito, "or by the Powers of Heaven I will compel you to do so."

He advanced, bent upon touching the unwelcome visitor; but his hand passed through the form as if it had been ether. A slight laugh rang through the room, and the ghost spoke in a clear, firm and resolute tone.

"Fear not, child of earth," it said. "I am not come to injure a hair of your head. Long years have I waited for this hour! It has now arrived. My blood shall not be unavenged, nor virtue suffer longer. Go to Australia. Robert Heineman waits there to greet you. Adieu!"

With these words the spirit disappeared and left Carlito wrapped in amazement and wonder. The next morning as he left his apartment and came downstairs he met Ellen, who greeted him with a pleasant smile.

"You look haggard, Mr. de la Mar," she said. "Why is that? Have you not slept well?"

"I have had a strange adventure," he replied, "such as would have made an ordinary mortal mad,—a vision from the regions of the dead. You seem astonished, but nevertheless I am convinced that it was no illusion but an incontestable fact."

"I never thought that a place like the rectory was haunted, nor since I have been here have I heard any hint of such a thing."

"Nor have I, hence the significance of the phenomenon."

"And what did your visitor say to you?"

"I never thought a disembodied spirit could utter sounds until this was unmistakably illustrated to me last night, and I am still left wondering by what vehicle the impalpable shadow, through which my hand passed as through the air, spoke in so clear and coherent a manner. It is no fairy dream. I have never yet been victimized by illusions, I again repeat, and the words which so impressively fell upon my ears still cling tenaciously to my memory: 'The time has arrived,' said the ghost. 'My blood shall not be unavenged, nor virtue suffer longer. Go to Australia. Robert Heineman waits there to greet you.' What this means I cannot tell."

Ellen stood for some time like a sphinx, transfixed to the earth; dark shadows appeared to float before her, while a curious light shone in her eyes, and a deadly pallor fell upon her cheeks. Something in Carlito's words had undoubtedly struck her.

"Your hand a moment, sir,—your hand I would see."

She gasped as if her breath had suddenly stopped.

Carlito seemed astonished at this request, but stretched out his hand. Ellen nervously rolled up his sleeve as far as the elbow, while Carlito, with the essence of good nature, looked on with a smile. A pomegranate mark was exposed to view, and Ellen had not gazed upon it for a second when she fell upon Carlito's neck, with an impulse akin to frenzy, and kissed him eagerly, then fell upon the floor insensible. It was the work of a moment for Carlito to summon old Annie and the Canon.

"I always taut dis lady did have a secret," said old Annie. "Sometime she sit down wid her han' under her jaw an' begin to cry, and wen I ask her what's matter she say in a way dat bring tears from my eyes: 'Noting, Annie, I am de chile of misfortune, but I hope God will soon relieve me by tecking me to heself.' Las' night she come in my room an' begin to cry because she say Mr. Carlito say something rough to her and she lub him as her own chile. De ting went to her heart and perhaps dat is the matter. Poor ting! Mr. Carlito, you might not have hurt her so."

The tender-hearted dame at this moment fixed her eyes upon the unfortunate creature on the floor, and large tear-drops fell from her eyes.

Carlito was himself struck with remorse on seeing that the wound which he had created in Ellen's heart was not easy to heal.

The Canon ordered Ellen to be taken up and laid on her own bed, where she received the best attention possible. Carlito, with his own hands, administered restoratives and bathed the woman's heated brow with refreshing lotions. She did not remain long in an unconscious state, and as she opened her eyes and saw Carlito, Annie, and the clergyman looking at her with Christian solicitude she heaved a sigh of relief. A glass of brandy and water was administered, and the patient was left to enjoy the benefits of quietude.

A little later Canon Highfield sat in his study, and Carlito stood before him, ready to hear what he had to say. The Canon seemed disquieted, there was evidently something of much importance engaging his mind.

"Before commencing to speak to you on what I intended," he said, "I would like you to tell me, Carlito, what you think has so effected Ellen. She seems of a curious temperament, and I have acutely watched her movements of late and my pity has been aroused."

"So have I, sir, and I have come to the conclusion that she suffers from some nervous disorder."

He then related his adventures of the night, and said that he believed that it was the relation of this incident that caused Ellen to swoon. The Canon, too, was much moved by the narrative.

"Robert Heineman, you said, Carlito! Robert Heineman!" he repeated again. "Were I not accustomed to hear startling things,—an experience that has steeled my nerves,—I should have no doubt swooned like Ellen."

The Canon paused a while, and with a solemn, pensive air shook his head. Having fairly collected his thoughts, he looked at Carlito and said gravely:

"Who says that the affairs of men are not governed and directed by a superior intelligence? There is no such thing as chance, and the atomist and materialist must give us more tangible evidence of the correctness of their theory of fortuitous circumstances. The 'Inscrutable Force' behind the universe, as Kant designates God, with his excellent wisdom designs each separate link in the chain of circumstance connected with our being, and though man's incompetent cognition cannot foresee the connections, the links are suddenly united by one mystic touch and joined into a harmonious whole by the will of the Almighty Ruler of creation. Carlito, the time has indeed come when what I had hitherto withheld from you must be told."

Canon Highfield then began to relate those startling facts which transpired between the tragic death of Burleigh Woodhouse and the time when he discovered Carlito at the house of his late benefactor, where he had remained for the period of five years in a condition of complete idiocy. It is not necessary to repeat these details, as the reader is already acquainted with them. There were some portions of the Canon's narrative that appeared to Carlito like disconnected threads of an interesting dream, but they were not so indelibly fixed on his brain as to reproduce perfect memories.

"Do you see the hand of God pointing out your path, and do you not see your remarkable destiny? Surely there are few men who have such wonderful horoscopes cast for them."

Carlito sighed. He had listened with rapt attention, and his facial muscles had undergone several changes. He uttered, however, never a word. When the Canon told him that he had good reasons for believing that Ellen was no other than his long-lost mother, he glared wildly around him as if seized by consternation and ejaculated tremulously:

"Impossible! You have almost bewildered me by your tale. Do not madden me, sir, I pray, do not madden me. Ellen my mother! O God! Can this be so? Help me, sir, I am overcome."

And Carlito leaned heavily upon the Canon for support. His next impulse was to rush into Ellen's room and throw himself joyfully into her arms, but he had enough good sense to know that the emotions that such an action was likely to produce would be detrimental to her. He therefore stood for a while with his head bent on his breast, his hands extending downwards and clasped together, while the saddest pathos rested in his eyes, and the perpendicular lines on his brow became more distinct.

"Why is it, dear Canon, that you so suddenly conclude that Ellen is my mother?" he asked after a few moments had passed.

"Come with me and I will tell you my reason," said the Canon.

He conducted him to his own bedroom upstairs, and approaching a life-size picture draped in black he removed the drapery and revealed a beautiful ebony-hued woman whose evenly chiselled features impressed Carlito strongly.

"But who is this beautiful woman," he enquired of the Canon.

"It is your mother, Edith Woodhouse. That picture I took the liberty of taking from her baggage when she was thought to be lost forever."

"But how can you say then that you believe Ellen is the same person; there is certainly no resemblance between that picture and the wistful, broken, emaciated creature below."

"Scarcely, my boy. You are very right indeed, and up to a few moments before I spoke to you such apparent madness would not have entered my brain. No, I would not then have thought that Ellen was identical with the handsome Edith Woodhouse, although there was always something in her manner that seriously impressed me. It is you who have unconsciously furnished me with the invaluable key for discovering the identity. Why did your strange story so interest her, and why did she swoon when she saw the pomegranate on your arm? Do you not see any resemblance between Ellen and that picture now?"

Carlito did not reply, but gazed with rapt attention on the portrait.

"Well, I shall help you," said the Canon. "Observe that mole on the cheek and that gentle curve on the under lip, those thick-set arched eyebrows, and beautiful dark eyes. Sorrow and grief have almost re-cast the face, but there are those marks which have not wholly been stamped out. Let us go downstairs; the problem will find its solution soon."

Carlito, as if struck dumb, followed the Canon into the study.

"The first part of my story is ended," continued the Canon, when they were duly seated at the study table; "but there is something yet to follow which I know will pain you. My brother has been seriously disturbed by the failing health of Mary since her return from her visit to me. The doctor has been called in to her on several occasions and has not been able to discover what is wrong. It was concluded that, owing to her peculiar isolated habits her nerves have been affected, or that something rests on her mind. Under no circumstances would she tell her secret until she betrayed herself in sleep. She called your name several times, then clung to her pillow and pressed it, passionately uttering words which, however, were not quite audible. This continued at intervals for some time. On the last occasion her father determined to speak to her and obtain a confession. She absolutely refused to say anything and was so shocked at the probable discovery of her secret that she fell into hysterics. Though she has regained her equilibrium, she continues very weak, and the doctor recommends a change of air. My brother is of a naturally irate disposition, and has unjustly poured forth anathemas against you. He swears by all the powers of Heaven that he will have you shot if he hears anything further about the matter. I could not have imagined that there was any love affair between Mary and yourself, and if this be really so, I deeply regret it. This would be unsuitable attachment."

Carlito was naturally surprised at the Canon's words, and though he hung down his head in a somewhat bashful manner, the thought of Mr. Highfield's threat caused indignation to swell within his breast like a mighty river. Then as if seized with a sudden inspiration, he said:

"Canon Highfield, it is a fact that an irresistible attachment has sprung up between your niece and myself, for which neither of us is responsible; and I cannot but say that it is evidently a lack of good sense on the part of your brother to allow his prejudice to blind his reason. However, he need have no fear as to the issue. For Fate, and Fate alone, has set the boundary which cannot easily be overstepped."

"I have as much to regret in this unfortunate love affair as yourself, Carlito. To begin with, it is necessary that you should leave here at once in order to avoid any further complication. You will have to give up the school, and I shall seek somewhere else for a remunerative office, where you will no longer meet the dangers which now sternly menace you."

"This is another instance of your paternal sympathy, sir; but I do not think I shall avail myself of it, as I have other plans. Can you imagine why your brother's ire has been so much kindled against me? Is it my poverty?"

"I am afraid it is the question of color. The pigment,—yes, the pigment, and nothing more."

"But God has made of one blood all nations under heaven to dwell upon the face of the earth, and since the mind is the standard of human excellence, I do not see why the poor casket should be given pre-eminence. May God help me to illustrate the brotherhood of the human family; may God help me to show that virtue and integrity are far above the color of the skin or the facial characteristics of a man! And may John Highfield be thereby edified one day."

The bell rang for tea, and both men proceeded to the dining-room.

CHAPTER XXIX

> O that I had wings like a dove, for then
> Would I fly away and be at rest.

LET us leave Carlito surveying carefully the intricate labyrinths of mysterious circumstances he had passed, lifting his soul on high to the kind Providence that had guided him onward through the misty gloom of a hard and stormy fate, and placed him in view of the haven where he would secure Peace and Happiness, Rest and Hope; and glance at Rita, the charming Spanish girl, whose heart continues to beat with an unabating affection for him.

It is one of those delightful evenings when the air is laden with the sweet perfume of lilies and roses, and when the gentle zephyrs play wantonly among the trees, imparting a pleasant, bracing stimulus to the body. Fireflies in their silvery beauty illumine the grassy plots here and there with their phosphoric brilliance as they gaily flit from blade to blade. The monotonous croaking of the frogs hidden in the bushes blends with the music of the tiny crickets.

Rita had long ago returned from making her customary tour through the vast forest of cocoa trees over which she held absolute ownership and authority and before her modest home awaits her lover's accustomed visit. He is long in coming, and she begins to fear that something has happened to cause such unusual delay. The clock strikes seven, and his beloved footsteps have not yet sounded upon the pathway. It strikes eight, and with it the last lingering ray of hope dies; she concludes that he will not come. But, hark! —there is the sound of approaching footsteps. Her pulse throbs quicker and her heart leaps for joy. He is coming at last! She approaches the door, her face aflush with delight, but, alas! what disappointment! It is not he. It is, however, a well-known person who is on terms of friendship, and who evinces much solicitude for her welfare. It is Cyril Merton!

"I have rather gloomy news for you, Miss Cedeño," said Cyril, after the usual civilities had been gone through.

Rita manifested interest, and he continued.

"I all along have told you that Carlito was not sincere in his professions of attachment to you and had made up his mind to slip the cable as soon as possible and leave you in the lurch."

"Why do you say such unkind things of Carlito? He would never deceive me. He is too noble and good to stamp his name with perfidy. Do not wrong him, Mr. Merton."

"But he has sailed for Southampton," continued Cyril, with a haughty, overbearing ring in his voice.

"Impossible! That can never be. I would not believe it."

"Well, then, I shall convince you."

And Cyril drew a copy of the *Port of Spain Gazette* from his pocket and pointed out the name of Carlito de la Mar in the list of passengers who had sailed for Southampton on the previous day by the steamship *Barraconta*.

No pen can picture the feelings of poor Rita at this moment. She wished the earth would take tender pity of her and engulf her miserable self in its depths. The beauties and glory of life had now lost their charms for her, and in a moment she turned her eyes away from them and prayed for death. Her chivalrous spirit assumed all its wild ardor, and as her lofty pride felt the sharp darts of spurned, insulted, and abandoned love, her eyes glared with a fierce, unhallowed light. She stood and mused awhile, and then smiled an extraordinary smile. It was evident that she had resolved upon some desperate deed.

"So, he has really gone then!" she said turning to Cyril.

"Yes, undoubtedly gone," replied Cyril sympathetically. "He is smitten by Miss Highfield, who warmly reciprocates his affection, as I have confidently told you more than a hundred times; and if you had followed my advice you would have sent him about his business long ago, before you permitted yourself to suffer such base humiliation."

"It is only now I can truly recognize your honesty and your worth, as also the marks of sincere friendship, which you have always evinced towards me. Ah, Mr. Merton, had I remembered your advice when Carlito told me that he could not marry for some time, I would have understood his meaning,—but it is too late! All is irreparably lost, and I must pay for my ignorance and folly. Too late! Too late!"

Cyril Merton did not go away that night from Rita's home without securing the preliminaries for carrying out the monstrous schemes over which he had so long brooded in order to possess himself of the vast wealth that Rita possessed. He had the courage to ask her hand in marriage, and she did not refuse it. She no longer cared what happened to her. Though under ordinary circumstances she would never have thought of allying herself with Cyril, it now seemed a matter of small importance to her. Her love had been mocked,—cruelly mocked,—by an unfaithful and wicked heart, and she would now go blindly on, troubling not herself with the indiscretion or discretion of her actions. It was not necessary to take all this pain; there was no philosophy in gilding the road of shadows where she was now determinedly pursuing her course.

The next day Mr. Cox, the village schoolmaster, who had always been on intimate terms with her and who had taken much interest in her education, was summoned to an interview. He was a pleasant, fat-faced, elderly gentleman, who smiled gracefully and inspired much confidence in all those with whom he came in contact. To him was given the task of writing Rita's last will and testament, and when he had winked, knitted his brow and looked serious, he stared at Rita and said:

"What's matter, me darling, that you are going to do this now? You anticipate that you are going to die,—a healthy stripling like you."

"But, Mr. Cox, what are you saying?" she replied, assuming an air of innocence. "Do not the young die as well as the old?"

Cox did not reply to this. He might have thought much, but he would not run the risk of endangering the possibility of gaining a few dollars in performing a comparatively easy task. Rita placed him in possession of her wishes, which principally consisted in bequeathing all that she was worth to her betrothed, Cyril Merton. The schoolmaster was shocked, but did not venture to interfere further than was necessary. Rita observed his embarrassment, and by way of satisfying his curiosity, said:

"I know you think my action strange, but it's all right. Mr. Merton has promised to marry me. He has been very kind and gentlemanly toward me. The marriage may be delayed for some time, owing to unavoidable circumstances. I am to go for a sea voyage with him; this will be in a few days, and so I mean to take his advice and have my business arranged before incurring the perils of the sea."

That same day the document that made Cyril Merton heir of all the estates of Rita Cedeño was duly signed and sealed.

CHAPTER XXX

> Alas! for love,—for woman's breast,
> If woe like this must be!
>
> *Mrs. Hemans.*

Cyril Merton's plans were happily frustrated. He had really intended to take Rita across the sea and dispatch her by some foul means when he was certain that his heirship was well secured. But he was spared the pains of red-handed murder.

It was just seven days since Rita had received the shocking news of Carlito's flight. It was Friday afternoon, about the time when he usually came to see her, and her thoughts wandered restlessly until they alighted on him.

"O heartless Carlito!" she sobbed. "You have treated me so cruelly, yet I cannot hate you. And what have I done? Given another my heart, while you are still alive. Nay, I never meant it. Would that it were some dream, some harassing nightmare! But, alas! it is not so, and you have run away from me,—your little Spanish maid."

She took off the medallion that Carlito had hung around her neck and kissed it, then placed it in an envelope with a slip of paper, on which were written the following words:

"Unfaithful Heart, take back your tribute. I want nothing from you. I will rid myself of the pain which you have given me by dying like a true woman who cannot take back her love."

The envelope bore the address of Carlito de la Mar and was placed on a table in a conspicuous place.

She then went out bent upon the terrible deed which she had contemplated. Toward the serpentine stream, girdled in by a belt of cocoa trees, the unhappy girl wended her way. There she had spent many pleasant afternoons, sitting upon a stone, listening to the rush of the waters and watching the tiny mudfish playing therein, with a mirth and happiness which she did not envy them. Now toward a deep basin in that same stream she advanced with a firm and steady step, while a frightful, unearthly pallor sat upon her face. She looked up at the skies, with the gay clouds floating above, then down at the earth, where vegetation smiled under her feet. She listened to the sweet melody of the bright-hued birds whose notes had always pleased her, and seemed to find some music in the dreadful, deathly screech even of the horned owl. She sank upon her knees and exclaimed:

"*Dios mio! Dios mio! Ayuda me.* All, all is happiness, I am of all beings on earth the most miserable. Holy Mary, come to my assistance!"

She tried to say more, but could not pray. She rose from her knees with a sudden effort, and casting both hands forward, plunged into the water and sank from sight. She rose again, then sank, and her hair floated on the surface of the water. Another moment and she would be no more, but quick as lightning some one approaches the stream.

It is Carlito!

Without delaying a second, he plunged into the water, and ere Rita sank for the third time, with a firm and steady grasp he lifted her to the shore. She was almost exhausted, and Carlito did all in his power to

THE SWORD OF NEMESIS

restore respiration. His heart throbbed within him when he saw her open her eyes and gaze at him. He entertained strong hopes of her recovery, and when he had settled her in a favorable position he ran to the nearest house for help and sent for the doctor.

Doctor Grayson was a clever physician, and was able to afford Rita temporary relief from the effects of her submersion, but he confessed he had much greater difficulties to contend with, which increased his fears of ultimate recovery.

CHAPTER XXXI

> O Spartan dog,
> More fell than anguish, hunger, or the sea!
> Look on the tragic loading of this bed;
> This is thy work.
>
> *Shakespeare.*

A TERRIBLE fever seized Rita, and after a few days the symptoms of pleuro-pneumonia set in, which bore out the apprehensions of the physician. The patient soon became entirely prostrated, and a dry, painful cough continually disturbed her. *La vieja* Matilda, who was much concerned about her *hijita*, was unremitting in her attention, and her kindly disposition suggested every possible means to encourage Rita to take the nourishment which was unsparingly provided. But food was distasteful to the sick girl, and a great deal of coaxing had to be done before she would consent to swallow a mouthful of bovril or beef-tea. Her respiration was imperfect, hurried and painful, and the system soon became greatly debilitated. At times during the day her thoughts wandered, and she even became unconscious of all that went on around her. Don Francisco Verde walked to and fro in the room with gloomy brow, whispering to himself:

"No hay remedio, La Pobecita, no es mas por este mundo." [1]

Carlito had returned twice to see her, but she persistently objected to his entering her room. Every-

---

[1] It's no use, the poor girl cannot live.

body was astonished at this,—attributing it to the vagaries of her nervous derangement.

Dr. Grayson advised Carlito against attempting to intrude himself into her presence against her wish, and intimated that in his opinion she was suffering from some maniacal delusion from which she would in time recover and recognize him.

The good physician was right. It happened that a few days later Carlito was conversing with Don Francisco in a tone a little above a whisper when his voice seemed to be recognized by the invalid. She called him to her bedside. An unusual light beamed in her eyes, and she seemed imbued with extraordinary strngth. It was the first time since she had been laid on her couch that she had shown signs of returning reason.

"So you are here then, Carlito," she said. "I cannot understand this. It is heaven who has disappointed you and sent you back to see the result of your unfaithfulness. Ah, wretch! villain! monster! Why was I not allowed to die instead of looking upon you again."

"Rita! Rita!" cried Carlito, with indescribable emotion, "be careful what you say, or you will repent your words. What wretch has been filling your mind with falsehoods? You are not yourself! Think before you speak again such terrible words, Rita. Your excellent mind, your winning face, your womanly virtues will not shield you from my displeasure."

"Better the everlasting hate of an unfriendly viper than the poisoned stings of feigned sincerity," she replied, in all the eloquence of her native tongue.

"In what way have I been unfaithful to you, pray? Is this the reward for my honesty?"

"You think I do not know your aims; but you are mistaken. You have deceived me and are in love with

Mary Highfield, the niece of the Canon of St. Paul's. You have been deceiving me all the time. Tell me, how did your name come to be in the list of passengers booked for Southampton? Surely you had a purpose, and I believe you have met with disappointment."

"Then you accuse me of perfidy of the blackest kind, which my sense of manhood will not brook. Were you Aphrodite incarnate and beaming with the virtues of Lucretia this fact would not re-unite the links which you have now ruthlessly shattered by your unpardonable insults; and were you not armed with the strength of your womanly weakness I should have been unkind for once in my life and been goaded to desperation. Rita Cedeña," he continued with emotion, "I will tell you the story,—the incorrect version of which has caused you to place me in the category of deceivers; and then I shall leave your presence, and these eyes shall never again gaze upon the woman who dared to look into them and call their owner untrue."

Rita became nervous as she saw the resolution in Carlito's eyes, and for once the terrible thought occurred to her that she might have judged wrongfully, and that there might have been a misunderstanding somewhere.

Carlito continued:

"I had really booked to sail by the *Barraconta* for Grenada on some urgent business; thither I went and returned in a few days. If you had paid the same attention to the paper of the following day you would have seen that an error had unfortunately been made by the reporter, and I appeared as sailing for Southampton instead of Grenada. This, with my presence here at this moment, is sufficient guarantee of the truth of my story."

With these words he turned to leave the room.

Rita burst into a flood of tears. A few minutes before she was in great pain and suffering. Now, with an effort almost superhuman, she threw herself from the bed and clutched Carlito. He turned round and watched her, while tender pity came into his face.

"Carlito, Carlito, pity me!" she cried. "Forgive me for wronging you. You are still noble and good. Oh, it was Cyril Merton who made me do this. It was he who put these things into my head and heart against you. Forgive me, forgive me, my Carlito,—and I shall quit this world in peace."

She sank exhausted upon the floor.

At the mention of Cyril Merton's name Carlito's face assumed an awful frown; but how could he be so inhuman as to turn his back upon the prostrate girl, who looked into his eyes with all the penitence of keen remorse? He stooped over her and gently took her in his arms, and as he laid her upon the bed her pleading eyes once more sued for forgiveness. He imprinted a soft kiss upon her lips, and she gave a sigh of infinite relief.

"Poor girl," muttered Carlito. "I forgive you from my heart. That villain would overthrow a more subtle mind than yours. But he shall receive his deserts some day, if there be a God of vengence; and he shall be crushed by his own fall."

Before Carlito left Rita's bedside that day there was restored that complete harmony which had before existed between them, and Rita's confidence in his constancy and uprightness became firmer than ever.

As Carlito was going through the gate the clattering

of a horse's feet was heard, and Cyril soon appeared upon the scene. As they passed each other Cyril made a polite bow, which Carlito did not return.

"Something or other is up," mused Cyril to himself, as he dismounted from his pony and approached the house.

There was an abject fear within him, which made him tremble and spurred him on toward the end of his fatal tether,—an end that he was sensible enough to foresee. He spent a few moments in conversation with those who were present in the hall, and was, as usual, soon permitted to enter Rita's apartment. She was dozing when he went in, but was roused by the footsteps. Cyril approached the bed silently on his toes and peeped into her face. Rita endeavoured to raise herself, and as her eyes rested upon him she burst forth:

"Out of my presence! You have caused me to unjustly outrage a true gentleman by your lying tales. What you seek,—my wealth,—he shall receive; and that which he spurns,—villainy, deceit, and craftiness are yours and shall be yours."

The most notorious villain, whose constant atrocities shut out the light of conscience and who is prepared to commit the blackest crimes that a fiendish heart can suggest, finds that the very strength on which he depends suddenly deserts him at the moment when his schemes have been exposed. His true character then appears in the light of day. He becomes vulnerable to the darts of the weakest of mortals, and shrinks from the scene of exposure with the marks of ignominy written on his cowardly brow.

It was pitiful to see the wretched man, Cyril Merton, leave the presence of Rita, whose words had penetrated into his breast like a stiletto. One would have thought him demented. Perhaps such a conclusion would not have been far wrong, for that was the last moment that that degenerate specimen of the human race was to enjoy the light of reason. The symptoms of mania began to make themselves apparent ere he reached his home, only to develop into a more pronounced form of insanity,—which seemed to be a just punishment for his wickedness.

CHAPTER XXXII

> She gazed,—till thoughts that long had slept
>   Shook all her thrilling frame,—
> She fell upon his neck, and wept.
>
>   *Mrs. Hemans.*

THE reader will remember that in the course of Carlito's conversation with the Reverend Canon Highfield he had refused to accept the offer which the latter had made to procure him a lucrative berth elsewhere. After he had given due consideration to the circumstances by which his life was surrounded, he determined to leave for Australia, in accordance with the advice of his ghostly visitant, and seek out Robert Heineman, who, he had no doubt, would be able to furnish some valuable information and support in the gigantic task that now absorbed him,—the task of ferreting out the murderer of his father and avenging his mother's wrongs.

Canon Highfield was decidedly in favor of this step. Himself somewhat of a mystic, he did not despise a voice from the dead. He was naturally loth to part with Carlito, but being very much interested in the results of the adventure, he put every possible means within his power to assist Carlito in his undertaking.

Ellen had recovered from the effects of her swoon. The next day after the accident the Canon called her into his study with the firm determination to make all clear.

"Ellen," he said in a voice as friendly as it was kind, "from the day you came to the rectory I have noticed something mysterious about you. That wistful countenance you wear has more than once caused me to sympathize with you, and to imagine that you must have seen better days. Do not for a moment keep back your history from me. Speak outright. I feel confident that that face of yours, on which honesty and truth are plainly stamped, will not speak falsely. I have had my suspicions, and I think the event of yesterday has afforded some clue to a solution of enigma."

Ellen's face assumed a very anxious expression.

"Annie! Annie!" called the Canon.

The tidy old housemaid entered, attired in her smart cap and gay apron.

"Bring me some brandy and water," politely requested the Canon.

"Very well, Parson."

Annie rapidly retreated, and in an instant reappeared with a goblet of water, a bottle containing brandy, and a couple of glasses in a waiter. The clergyman poured out a good draught of the brandy, which he gave to Ellen, and continued:

"You will tell me all now, Ellen,—won't you?"

She demurred at first, after which she made an effort to speak, which was interrupted by a stifling cough.

"Have you known me or even seen me before you came to this place?" enquired the Canon.

The right chord was struck, and the answer came forth:

"I have."

"And do you remember where you met me first?"

Ellen paused a while, then in a faltering voice replied:

"In my own dear country, Canon."

"And which is that?"

"The Island of Montserrat."

"That is many years ago, isn't it?"

"A good many years certainly, sir."

"And you have seen much trouble since,—haven't you? That is quite evident."

"Oh, my troubles and sorrows are beyond expression! To speak of them would be probing afresh the wounds that have eaten away my life."

"You are a widow, I presume?"

"Yes, sir."

"And when did your husband die?"

"He did not die a natural death, but was murdered many years ago."

Ellen burst into a flood of tears.

"Do not weep so, my poor woman. 'Sorrow may endure for a night but joy cometh in the morning.' Have you ever had any children,"

"One, sir."

"And where is he? Is he alive?"

"Yes, sir. If I am not mistaken; if I am not mad; if I am not mocked by fate, I believe he yet lives."

Canon Highfield asked no further questions, but the words escaped his lips:

"Thank God there is no delusion; it is a reality!"

And at the words he fell upon his knees, a heavenly sweetness beaming upon his face, while he poured forth his thankfulness to Almighty God that his hopes had been truly realized. He rose from his reverent posture, and as Ellen watched him anxiously he seized her hand, while tears trickled down his cheeks, and then exclaimed:

"The ways of God are past finding out. Who enter into the secret place of the Most High? Edith Woodhouse, Hugh Highfield greets you. Providence decrees that you shall no longer pass disguised under my roof, and despite yourself, the veil has been torn aside and we meet no longer as master and servant but as friends. You, the wife of the unfortunate murdered Burleigh Woodhouse, shall henceforth have the respect that is your due."

Mrs. Woodhouse, for there was no longer any doubt of her identity, was awe-stricken when she found that her secret was discovered; the revelation had not been unexpected and had in a measure been prepared for unravelling. She, however, could not suppress the tide of emotion that overwhelmed her, and she threw herself into the Canon's arms and wept.

"Compose yourself, dear lady," he said. "With this discovery, the night has disappeared, and, behold! the morn with its glorious brightness is at hand."

But another scene equally touching was soon to follow. Carlito had just entered when this little drama was being enacted. The sobs from the study had attracted his attention, and he turned his steps in that direction.

The Canon thereupon took him by the hand and led him toward Mrs. Woodhouse, with the words:

"Madam, here is your son; Carl Woodhouse, here is your mother!"

Mrs. Woodhouse embraced her son with all the passionate ardour of a tender, loving mother, and the maternal affection that had been so long buried within her breast now burst forth with intense force.

Carlito was almost dazed when the reality of the presence of that mother of whom he had heard such tales of suffering and sorrow broke upon him.

Annie entered the room as Mrs. Woodhouse and her boy stood face to face, with their countenances eloquently expressing the feelings that permeated their hearts at that supreme moment, and which words were too feeble to express.

"Annie," said the Canon, breaking the solemn silence, "henceforth Mr. de la Mar becomes Mr. Carl Woodhouse. He is the son of this lady, and she whom you knew as plain Ellen must in future be known as Mrs. Edith Woodhouse, and respected as being a wellbred lady who was at the sunny period of her life an intimate friend of mine. An evil destiny has clouded her life, but the day of her troubles is now ended."

Annie stood spellbound when the Canon had finished his speech, and she opened her little eyes wider than she had ever done before, and placing her thumb in her mouth, shook her hand frantically. When she had recovered from her astonishment, she said:

"I do not grudge Ellen her good fortune; beg yo' pardon, milady, I mean Mrs. Woodhouse. I always used to think she was something, as I often tell you, sir. What is in de bones can' come out, and when a pusson is bring up a lady or a gentleman de real character will always shine 'bove de pot sut. Sometimes when she used to talk to me I couldn't understand she, an' I use to quarrel an' say she playing English lady, but afterward, when she watch me so an' smile wid such a heavenly smile 'pon he face, I had to say she can't help for she diction-necessary word, because she must have been well brought up. I am glad that de Lawd has help you in your trouble and bring you to dis moment, mistress. You have a precious chile, an he will be sure to make you mose well. God bless you two, ma'am."

She made a respectful courtesy and was about to leave the room when she was strictly warned by the

Canon not to mention to any one what had occurred.

In a few moments Mrs. Woodhouse related her remarkable history. We saw her last launched in a tiny boat on the broad ocean by merciless villains who had doomed her to a terrible end. Providence, however, frustrated their designs. The boat drifted on and on until it came under the lea of Martinique, where the frail occupant was rescued by some French fishermen, who took her ashore and extended her their hospitality. She continued in the island for some time, and did good work as governess in an English family.

She was, however, induced to leave her employment by a person who misled her into believing that he could find a more lucrative situation for her in Cayenne. Monsieur Gardier, for that was the name of this individual, was a general commission agent, and undertook a contract for supplying a number of immigrants to Cayenne. He was a man of no principle, though he endeavoured to force himself upon his credulous victims as a man of high moral qualities and sound religious principles. This was the cloak under which he had concealed his real infamy, and it was this which crowned his energy with unbounded success. Mrs. Woodhouse, like many others, had fallen a prey to his machinations. She agreed to put herself under his care as a passenger aboard his vessel to Cayenne. On the voyage she received every mark of respect, and it was only when the shores of Cayenne were sighted that the demeanour of Mr. Gardier became suspicious. Mrs. Woodhouse approached him with a view to obtaining some necessary advice and information from him, but received for her anxious enquiry a ringing, ironical laugh, followed by the startling words:

"You are to be indentured as an immigrant, madam,

and you will please give me no more of your nonsense. Get below! Boys, strike up the good old song."

And the well-known refrain, "I've reached the land of corn and wine," rent the air as it burst forth from scores of throats.

Mrs. Woodhouse now felt all the terrors of despair. She endeavoured to speak, but her tongue clave to the roof of her mouth. She had become temporarily speechless, and her eyes spoke utter bewilderment. It followed that she was indentured for a period of seven years as a domestic servant, where she endured the greatest physical and mental suffering. After her term of indenture had expired she went to Trinidad, where she was eking out a miserable existence in extreme poverty and complete obscurity in the malarial district of Chaquanas. It was from this place that she ventured out with a strong determination to improve her condition when the tide of Fortune turned.

It is needless to say that this story considerably impressed Carlito and the Canon.

On being informed by the latter that he had quite recently received news from Lindsay, who was taking a vacation in the beautiful Island of Grenada, Mrs. Woodhouse's heart beat with joy, and she immediately decided to communicate with her sincere friend who she felt certain would be filled with delight to see her once more in the flesh. It was arranged, therefore, that she should leave for Grenada that week.

CHAPTER XXXIII

> Vainly we offer each ample oblation,
>   Vainly with gifts would his favor secure:
> Richer by far is the heart's adoration;
>   Dearer to God are the prayers of the poor.
>
> *Heber.*

THERE was no extraordinary demonstration when Carlito Woodhouse, who had taken a short vacation, boarded the steamer with his mother, with the intention of accompanying her to Grenada. There were a few busybodies who wondered if the highly respected and learned young gentleman had lost his senses when he allowed himself to be seen in such close relations with a common domestic servant. However, their faith in Mr. de la Mar's unstained character was sufficient to imbue them with the idea that he was, despite ugly appearances, perfectly able to take care of himself and to maintain his dignity, *sans peur et sans reproche*. The trip across the channel was most delightful. A clear sky and placid sea increased the pleasure of the voyage, while the balmy breezes that swept over the waters produced a most exhilarating effect.

As the steamer sailed into the harbour of Grenada, the towering mountains in their vernal splendour, grey hills, and picturesque houses attracted the attention of mother and son, and they rose with light hearts to gaze upon them.

Mrs. Woodhouse stole from her stateroom, where

she had been indulging in reading "Plutarch's Lives," and went out to meet Carl. Her heart seemed to burst with inexplicable delight as she looked forward to her reunion with Maud after so many years of separation.

In about half an hour after the *Barraconta* had dropped anchor, Carl and his mother were on their way to Bellevue Cottage to be the guests of Mrs. Maud Lindsay.

It is not necessary to lift the curtain and reveal the touching scenes that were acted in that first half hour when the two long-separated friends were once more thrown together. The reader can but imagine the waves of sympathy and spontaneous human emotion that rose high and mighty during those moments, and submerged the soul in the very depths of tenderness and love.

Carlito was pleased to be introduced to the friend of his mother, and was much taken with her. He learned that Lindsay would join them as soon as he got an opportunity to do so.

Having been fairly satisfied that his mother was duly installed under the kind and hospitable roof of her hostess, he again sailed for the land of the humming bird.

Carl, for so we will now call him, took the earliest opportunity of calling upon his fiancée. The little note that Rita had written and placed in a conspicuous position on the table was the means of saving the rash girl from an untimely end. Carl had discovered it a few moments after it was written, and alarmed at its contents he had hastened to the river. The reader is already acquainted with the result.

Rita continued much prostrated, and anxious friends unceasingly enquired after her condition. She was a good, kind-hearted girl, and had won the esteem of every one round the village.

Carl had abandoned his school, to the deep regret of both parents and scholars, and was bent upon carrying out his resolution to sail to Australia in search of that important personage, Robert Heineman. He was obliged, however, to postpone his voyage and await the result of Rita's illness.

The Canon was in no great hurry to part with him, especially since his brother's ire had somewhat subsided. Mary had left her home and had gone elsewhere for a change, by the doctor's advice. Carl had never ventured to enquire about her movements, although he felt much interested in her. The fact was, the only person he would have cared to ask was the Canon, and he maintained strict reticence.

The young lover paid every attention to his betrothed, and whenever possible was found at her bedside.

It was a bright moonlight evening when a delicately-shaped figure, closely veiled, without ceremony entered Rita's bedroom, approached the couch whereon the sick girl lay, and throwing off her shawl and bonnet, laid her hand tenderly on the invalid.

"How are you this evening, Rita," said the visitor, —Mary,—"I have been anxious to learn how you were, and not hearing, I have stolen away from home to come and see you."

Rita, with a pleasant smile upon her pale, wan features, turned and looked up.

"So you are not afraid you might one day be trapped in coming to see me?"

"No, darling," was the reply. "Even though I know I am running a great risk, I am willing to take the consequences, since I feel there is something that links us together."

"Ah, how kind and good you are! Whenever you come to see me I always feel better, because I love you so much. And now that I feel I am making my journey homewards, I would like to see your kind loving face as often as possible. But, tell me,— why does the doctor prevent you from coming this way?"

"My father has strictly requested that Dr. Spencer should not allow me to come in this direction."

"Do tell me what reason he has for this. I am anxious to know. Are there traps hidden away to hold you?"

"No, no, Rita! But if you are so anxious to know I shall not hide it from you. In order to do this, I must begin at the beginning. Though I have never seen Mr. de la Mar here, I know that he comes to see you often. Well, he and I have met and loved. My father has discovered this and hates him. Some telltale has informed him that Mr. de la Mar is a constant visitor at your home, and he does not want us to meet under any circumstances whatever. Though I have clearly stated to papa the impossibility of anything arising out of such a meeting, he still insists on my not coming. But it is honor alone and not his veto that arrests the progress of our love; it is you, Rita, and not the voice of the multitude, who have fixed this gulf between Mr. de la Mar and myself."

"How?" questioned Rita, in a tone savouring of surprise.

"O Rita, I am no hypocrite; and my soul would rebuke me if I hid what you must hereafter know. If I touch a tender chord in your nature or arouse your jealousy, I hope you will be charitable enough to forgive me."

"When first I met Carlito de la Mar my heart went out to him. His brilliant intellect, his winning manners, his noble character, his ambition to scale the ladder that leads to the Temple of Fame,—all seriously impressed me; and when I examined my own heart I found that I loved him; yes, loved him passionately. I tried to keep it secret, but in vain. The impress had been too indelibly stamped upon me, and nothing could remove it. In an unguarded moment I betrayed my feelings, and I found that he loved me too. Rita, do not sigh. It was not his fault that he was exposed to the darts of love. It would have been his fault if he had sacrificed honor and principle. With his soul overflowing with emotion, he told me he had pledged his word to a simple Spanish maiden whom he could not forsake. That simple Spanish maid has now developed into the charming, lovable Rita, whom I think worthy of his noble heart. Ah! how I regarded him almost as a demigod at that moment when the dagger pierced my heart, when he bowed with heroic resignation like any son of Sparta, and with the tears streaming from his eyes said feelingly, 'I cannot be yours.' Since then I have always thought tenderly of you, and cannot but love any one who is allied to such an exalted being by any ties whatever."

"Ah, dear lady," replied Rita, "years of serious thought have entirely changed me, and I now see things differently from what I saw them in the days of childhood, when Carlito and I played together. Were it then I should have stabbed you for confessing that he loved you *really* and only *thought* he loved me; but since my reason has taught me some of the mysteries of love, I am wiser and less impulsive. There is, therefore, no room in my breast for foolish jealousy of such an angel as you are. Though I am bound to confess that when it came to my ears that Carlito loved you and intended to deceive me and to marry you, I despaired of life and sought to destroy myself. But it was all a lie, which was invented by a fortune-hunter. The All-wise Father spared me to see that my darling was as true as ever."

Before she had ended the door was thrown ajar and Carl appeared.

Rita looked anxious, and a ray of pleasure stole across her wan, pale face.

He advanced toward her, and bowed politely to the female figure standing in close proximity to the couch, then, leaning over Rita, he pressed her withered hands and imprinted a loving kiss on her parched lips.

"You do not know this person," said Rita in a half whispering tone.

Carl turned to scrutinize the face before him, then ejaculated:

"O Heavens! Miss Highfield, is it really you?"

"Yes, Carlito," replied Mary Highfield.

"Some startling events have happened of late, my dear Mary, and I have had to tax my brain to decide whether my senses are intact, or whether I have passed into dreamland. I knew you had been sent for a change of air somewhere, but never for a moment thought it was this way. What curious coincidences do really happen in life! I am very glad to meet you after such a long separation, and hope that your health has improved."

"Thank you, Carlito. I am very much better and hope soon to be quite well again."

Rita turned her face toward them both and smiled sweetly.

"Miss Highfield," she said, "were it possible for me to live and become Carlito's wife, I would have taken hope that, although he loved you more than me, he would have learned to give me his undivided affection; and now that the Angel of Death beckons me to the other land I leave him free to take you to his heart. I shall die happy when I know that he will become the husband of an unselfish pure-minded woman like you. I do not envy you your happiness; and in token that I do not—See! Carlito, give me your hand; Miss Highfield, yours."

She joined Mary's hand with Carl's and whispered solemnly:

"*Dios y la Virgen Santissima vos bendigan.*"

Having done this, she sank exhausted upon her pillows, while Mary and Carl stood with tears in their eyes, gazing at the emaciated face in which two lustrous orbs seemed to shine more brilliantly than ever.

Overwhelmed with emotion, Carl leaned over the dying girl and pressed his lips to hers. Mary followed his example, and Rita opened her eyes slightly and smiled; then closed them again.

A week passed, and it became evident from her sunken condition that she could not last much longer. Dr. Grayson, who continued unremitting in his attention, shook his head ominously whenever Don Francisco or *la vieja* Matilda enquired after Rita's condition, and said:

"I think all hope is lost now; it's no use hiding it from you. I expect the worst. The lungs are almost gone, and it is as evident as daylight that she cannot last long."

The services of Padre Domingo Sylvain were immediately requisitioned, and he administered to the spiritual wants of the dying girl.

Carl was in his study busily engaged in painting an interesting picture when some one rapped at the door. He laid down his brush and opened it in answer to the call.

He fell back in amazement as his eyes fell upon the distorted countenance of Cyril Merton. The man's eyes were bloodshot and seemed to be dropping out of their socket; his face was besmeared with dirt, and his once beautiful raven hair was almost gray and fell in a disordered mass on his neck. There were numerous bruises about his head, which told that that member had been subjected to extraordinary violence. He raved fiercely, and the expression in his eyes was frightful. In a moment the indignation which had been piling up in the breast of Carl against the underhanded and unprincipled Cyril Merton now gave way before the rushing stream of pity that rose within him as he contemplated the miserable specimen of manhood before him.

Cyril uttered in a loud voice words that startled Carlito.

"You are the king of the world," said he, "and the mighty Empires of Rome, Assyria, Carthage, and Phœnicia are now at your feet! Look at your brilliant white steed! Are you riding forth to battle? Yes, you are great indeed, Carlito de la Mar; but I have come to conquer you, and conquer you I will! Do you not see that Jupiter has sent me armed with power to hurl you from your mighty throne? I have her now in my possession, that glorious Queen, the lady whom you robbed me of. She is now in my castle on the Blue Mountains over there, and I shall carry her over to the domains of my master, who has sent me to reclaim her. Ha, ha! Carlito of destruction! You are defeated by a mightier hand than yours."

With those words he turned away, and left Carlito wrapped in pity and amazement.

"Poor fellow!" he said, as he shook his head sadly. "How has this man's infamy recoiled upon his own head!"

A few moments later a painful train of thoughts passed through his mind.

"After all," he mused, "there must be some method in this man's madness. I am afraid that something can be gathered from his ravings. What queen is it which he had taken away from me and borne to his blue mountains? Can it be that Rita has become worse and that this is the form of words which his madness allows his lips to employ to boast of his triumph? No! but this cannot be. The man is evidently too insane to show the least possible sign of reason. Ah, the foolish fears that will sometimes invade the breast of a rational man!"

A strange medley of thoughts continued to grow and trouble him; and in order to gain some respite, he ordered his pony and started for X to see how Rita fared. About two furlongs from her home he met the good Father Sylvain, from whom he ascertained that he had administered extreme unction to Rita, who was undoubtedly perfectly reconciled, and was prepared to meet her fate. With a heavy heart, the young man hastened his steps, and as he stepped upon the threshold of the door of that gloomy home wherein lay the prostrate form, the once beautiful casket that contained the bright, loving soul of Rita Cadeño that was now fleeting onwards to its eternal home, a picture filled with pleasant reminiscences and affectionate associations appeared before him, and his breast swelled with a deep tenderness almost womanly.

He had recovered somewhat when he entered Rita's bedroom. She looked at him with sunken eyes lit with a heavenly light, and her livid lips parted to utter her greeting.

"So you are come at last," she said. "I have been waiting so long for you. Will you prop me up that I may lean upon you for the last time. I have not many more hours to live."

Carl did as he was bid; and when he felt that she was resting comfortably, he looked at her sadly.

"Do not be sad," she murmured, placing her arms around his neck lovingly. "I am only going home, and you will meet me over there some day. May God forgive me the one rash act of my life, which has resulted in my untimely end. Two things I shall ask you ere I close my eyes upon this world. The first is that you will forgive the intrigues of Cyril Merton. His condition demands my sympathy and forgiveness. Only yesterday he raved outside the house and would not be appeased until he saw me. I have wept for him. My second request is that if you do not marry that sweet angel, Mary Highfield, promise me that you will marry no other woman!"

Carl was somewhat struck by this strange request. He had just discovered the cause of those expressions of the lunatic, Cyril Merton, and his mind was still dwelling upon the incident that had caused him to be at Rita's bedside at that moment, when he was again plunged into serious reflection. He could not for a moment resist the sad, sweet light in those dying eyes, and replied impulsively:

"Yes, darling; I shall promise you that."

"Then I shall die in peace, knowing that you will keep your word."

They were alone, and the golden streaks of sunset crept in gently through an open window.

"The time has now come when I must deliver to you what I can no longer keep."

Carl felt surpised, but his astonishment became more intense when she took from under her pillow a bunch of keys, and having selected one of them she directed him to open her chest of drawers and take therefrom a small box. Carl obeyed and handed to her a beautiful mahogany casket with rich engravings, and the initials "C. de la M." cut on the outside.

"This is yours, Carl. My father at his death asked me to keep it until you were about to be married." Her tone became weaker and her words less coherent. "I will not live to see that day, so you must take it now. Its contents I do not know, and since I have kept faith and curbed my curiosity, you must do likewise until that day arrives."

She had grown weaker, and her whole weight was thrown upon Carl, who tenderly brushed back the locks that covered her face.

"Put me down," she whispered. "Carlito, will you read for me that beautiful hymn that you taught me once?"

He began to read the inspiring verses of the hymn, "Let Saints on Earth in Concert Sing."

She smiled sweetly at him as he ended, and made an effort to draw him nearer to her, but the hand fell back heavily, and Carl realized that the end was approaching. He bent tenderly over her. She clasped his hand with the fervor of death.

"The angels are waiting," she whispered. "Good-night, darling."

The bar was crossed; the spirit had taken its wings, and had soared aloft to the everlasting mansions of the Blessed.

CHAPTER XXXIV

Where hath not woman stood
Strong in affection's might? a reed upborne
By an everlasting current!

Anon.

THE genius of love having contrived a meeting between Carl and Mary a few days after Rita's interment, they then pledged their hearts sincerely to each other, and vowed that though at present insurmountable obstacles stood in their way, they would spare no effort to remove them so that they might eventually secure the object that they both so earnestly desired.

The long wished-for day for his departure dawned, and Carl, amid the encouraging words of Canon Highfield and the kindly expressions of his most intimate friends, boarded the steamer *Solent*, bound for Australia.

Let us leave him enjoying the pleasures of his long trip across the ocean, and indulging in all kinds of fancies as to the possible result of his remarkable adventures, and follow the beautiful, erudite Mary Highfield, who has sufficiently convalesced to return from her temporary home amid the wild scenes of X to her father's house.

"Well, Mary," said her father one day in the paroxysm of gout. "Bring me my slippers. By Jove, I think I shall have to take some radical steps against these blooming feet if they won't let me alone. Ah,—

by the bye,—you are becoming yourself again, little dear. Another month would have made you as pink as a rose; but you see I couldn't burden Dr. Spencer any more with you. You must have the finishing touch here. I considered it was too much study that had turned your head and made you dream of the negrito *savant*. It's all right now, it's all right, I guess, and I won't apprise your bright soldier cousin of your mania."

Mary blushed. She read the purport of these words, but the change that came over her face was not perceived by her father, who in the same strain continued:

"Sooth my nerves, darling, sooth my nerves by playing one of those lovely pieces you know."

Mary went to the piano, and in her rich soprano voice sang that spirited song, "Les Italiens en Algiers," while her fingers moved gracefully over the keyboard. The old man was pleased, and as the music charmed him, he kept time with his head. It was the zenith of his happiness to sit on the balcony in the cool of the evening and hear Mary discourse sweet music. He loved her more than tongue can express, and in her all his hopes were centered. Imagine, therefore, the condition of mind in which his apprehensions concerning the clandestine affair between Carl and herself had thrown him.

There was to be a ball at the Brownes', the leading society folk of the district. Colonel Browne had been in the Army and had fought in several engagements, which had added glory and territory to the British Empire, and as old age approached, he retired on a decent pension and settled with his two handsome daughters,—children of a second marriage,—in an old-fashioned yet comfortable building in the suburbs of the town. These spoiled girls were attended by a governess who was also fond of amusement, and who encouraged them in their penchant for pleasure.

At this ball Mary was one of the honored guests.

Gathered in the spacious drawing-room was the élite of society.

Mary was the last guest to enter, and the grace with which she passed across the room, coupled with the rich beauty of her face, caused the attention of all present to be centred upon her. Beautiful faces there were,—many, too,—within that hall, but their light was eclipsed by the effulgence of a far greater luminary.

Little Violet Browne's heart suddenly leaped, as handsome young Gerald Chesters suddenly left off pressing her hand to gaze with open mouth upon Mary.

"Why do you stare so hard at Miss Highfield?" enquired Violet.

"That question ought not to be directed to me alone, Violet. I am not singular in this."

"But is she so pretty, do you think? She is already labeled 'engaged, none need apply.' "

"To whom?" enquired Chesters.

"Oh, all the world knows that her cousin Bertie Melville has won her hand. It is expected that he will marry her when he returns from the continent. I hear Mr. Highfield is much taken with the match, and I have it upon good authority that he intends to make over thirteen thousand pounds to her,—at least so he told Papa."

"Then poor Tommy Atkins will have a good unction to soothe the bullet wounds he must have received during his campaigns," said Chesters laughingly, and then, turning to a thick-set, pleasant-faced fellow who had just come up and overheard the latter part of the conversation:

"Have you not heard this, Leslie?" he said.

"I have not," said Leslie, with an air of the know-all personage. "Young Melville had better remain where he is and keep company with cold steel rather than expose himself to a snubbing and a broken heart. He will never get those thirteen thousand pounds, though the old Nick stands at the door. Don't you see poor Merton has gone stark mad? It was that enchantress that turned him, so the world believes. She has locked her affection against all others except the sable Plato who went to Australia some time ago."

"Do you really mean that? There was a rumour, I remember, about some love affair between de la Mar and Miss Highfield, but I thought it rubbish and gave it no place in my mind."

"That can certainly never be true, Mr. Leslie!" put in Violet. "Do you think Mary would be so foolish?"

"I beg your pardon, Miss Browne," replied Leslie in a suave yet impressive tone. "I am positive that what I assert is correct. Besides obtaining certain information from an authorative source, Holingsworth, who is the second clerk at the post office informs me that he has spotted de la Mar's writing on an envelope bearing the Australian postmark addressed to Miss Highfield.

"Ah, Mr. Leslie, you are telling tales out of school!" chided Violet, with a gentle rippling laugh.

"Then the post office is no longer an inviolable institution."

"Since there are powerful detectives there," put in Chesters with a sarcastic twitching of the lips.

"A rather unpleasant compliment for Mr. Holingsworth," remarked Violet.

"It does not matter what your opinion may be," said Leslie, unable to conceal his displeasure. "Since you take my remarks with so much irony, I will leave you to find out for yourself."

Mary continued to be the cynosure at which all gazes were directed that evening. Her courteous and gentle manners attracted and impressed all, and there were sincere hearts that would have given their life's blood to win that sweet child of Nature on whom that dear old Mother had lavished the most bewitching adornments.

That same night, after the party broke up, Colonel Browne and his daughters sat around a table in deep conversation. The old gentleman betrayed unusual excitement, and from the unpleasant look which Lily,— the younger of the two girls,—cast at Violet now and then, it was evident that the latter had aroused the Colonel's ire by some imprudent remark.

"Never mind, Papa," said Violet, tapping her father gently on the shoulder, "you must never believe such nonsense. I never took it seriously."

"Don't mind what you believe," thundered the old soldier. "I know a great deal more about this than you, and, by Jove, I shall put John upon the scent at once or hang me for a rogue! It's all nonsense; and though I break the chap's heart, the thing must be nipped in the bud ere it gets beyond control."

The colonel rose from his seat in a flurry, while the two girls stood up, astonished, and watched him disappear into his room.

"You were wrong, Violet, to have mentioned anything to Papa of such a nature," said Lily.

"Yes, darling; but I had never dreamt of such results."

And the opening act of a most pathetic drama commenced.

CHAPTER XXXV

How sublime a thing it is to suffer and be strong!
Longfellow.

Four months had passed since Carl bade *au revoir* to the shores of Trinidad, but they seemed like four years to the anxious, loving Mary, who more than ever prayed for his speedy return.

Since his departure she had received one letter from him, which reported his safe arrival at Melbourne. She had placed that letter in her bosom, near her heart, after having watered it with tears of love.

Of late she became distressed in consequence of the exhibition of a sudden coldness toward her by her once devoted father, and the elaborate formality that accompanied his intercourse with her.

John Highfield was a perfectly changed man toward his daughter, and though Mary sought by every means in her power to restore the old relationship that had become so mysteriously strained, nothing would induce the resolute old sire to breathe a familiar word of love, or to make one of those customary requests the performance of which always gave her so much pleasure. However, it was not long before she discovered the nature of the barrier that stood between them.

A few hours after the arrival of the English mails, one morning, Mr. Highfield, though suffering intensely from his old complaint, ordered his carriage to take him down to the post office.

Mary heard the order, and advancing towards her father, said, with a somewhat sad expression:

"Papa, why are you going out this ugly morning? I'm sure Joseph can bring up the mails as usual. You were so unwell last night, and I felt so much for you. Although you are so cold toward me, you cannot imagine the love of an affectionate daughter."

Mr. Highfield did not seem to listen to the sweet voice of the girl, and reiterated his command to the groom.

"Papa, dear Papa, why treat me thus? This will surely break my heart!"

And poor Mary turned away; and sitting down she burst into tears.

The trap was drawn up at the door, and as Mr. Highfield prepared to enter, by a sudden impulse she caught his hand, but he shook her off with disdain.

Half an hour had elapsed when Mr. Highfield alighted from his carriage and stepped into the house, with an expression of determination on his face. He went straight to his office, and placed upon the table a pile of newspapers and letters. But there was one letter, —opened,—that he still kept in his hand.

"Come here, Mary!" he called aloud. "Do you remember this writing?" he asked.

"I do," replied Mary, trembling in every limb.

"Well then, Miss Highfield, I hope I shall be excused for an infringement of the code of etiquette, if in exercising the prerogative of a father, I have broken the seal of your letter, which I now hand to you. I have indeed given you credit for a higher ambition than that of which this communication has convinced me. I can no longer feel myself justified in identifying myself with a daughter who seeks to bring disgrace on the honored name of Highfield; and much as I have loved you, I now spurn and despise you. Henceforth I shall extend to you no fatherly protection, and I expect that you will leave my house before the night closes. And may the just judgment of Heaven repay your disobedience!"

Mary listened with astonishment to these determined words, but having drawn herself up to her full height, she assumed an air of dignity, and returned slowly and impressively:

"Papa, I have not much to say in reply to your harsh expressions, for fear that I should for a moment be guilty of disrespect of using some word that may savour of unkindness to you who are responsible for my being. Nevertheless, it is necessary to tell you that, since you have deemed it proper to deprive me of your home and protection, I shall never, till my latest day, cease to remember that you were capable of turning me out upon the streets, and thereby giving the lie to the exalted opinion I have always held of you. Though I henceforth go through the world without your paternal smiles, this fact shall not prevent me from being a true woman and from maintaining the dignity of my sex. You spurn me because I have responded to my own natural feelings in loving a youth whose only crime is that he wears a darker skin. Ah, my Father, would that your blinding prejudices would allow you to see that the pigment is but the 'guinea stamp.' I had rather face your displeasure and be true to his noble soul than forsake him and be reinstated in your affection. Your daughter has spoken. Good-bye for ever, my once beloved Father, and if we meet no more in life, may our onward march toward the eternal home be directed in the same path."

She moved off with the grace of a duchess, while her

THE SWORD OF NEMESIS 241

father folded his arms before him and looked at her in bewilderment. As she disappeared from his view he clenched his fist, bit his lips, and stamped with anger.

Mary soon prepared to leave her home, and she determined also to leave the district altogether and cast in her lot with strangers. She would not entertain the idea of placing herself under the care of her uncle, for fear that she might cause the good man some pain by refusing to listen to his counsels,—which she anticipated,—to abandon her lover.

Four o'clock had just struck when a cab drew up at John Highfield's door and called for his daughter. Mary, without any hesitation, entered with her luggage, consisting of a large trunk and a basket, then bade the cabman drive to the railway station.

As the vehicle sped on at a rapid rate she lifted the curtain and gazed with tearful eyes upon her fast-receding home, which perhaps she might never again enter. As she sat in the train a terrible sensation crept upon her, and she was weak enough to wish herself once more revelling in the sunshine of her father's love.

She took up her handbag and drew therefrom a neatly bound copy of the New Testament, and turned over the leaves until she alighted on the story of the Prodigal Son. A few teardrops fell upon the leaves of the sacred volume, and the expression on the face of the unhappy girl was sadder than can possibly be told in words. But when the train arrived at St. Joseph, the conflict within her ceased. She drew from her bosom a letter and began to read it. The effect was marvellous. It was the glorious sunshine after the black and stormy night; it was the oil that calmed the troubled ocean into gentle sleep. The letter ran thus:

MELBOURNE, AUSTRALIA.

DEAREST MARY:

I am happy to tell you that I have been most fortunate in my peregrinations. Up to the present, brilliant success has attended my adventures. I shall be in Trinidad, accompanied by a most valued friend, before Christmas. How long the time seems since we parted! Verily, true love has the power of converting days into years. The loving thoughts of you, which constantly fill my breast, make me wish that man's genius might soon reach that stage when it shall render possible the annihilation of distances. I shall come back to you, my love, before long, Providence being my guide. Meanwhile you must pray for my speedy return.

With a heart overflowing with love,

I remain, yours fondly,

CARLITO.

Mary replaced the missive in her bosom just at the moment when the train steamed into Port of Spain. That same evening she entered *incognito* one of the hotels of the city under the assumed name of Gertrude Manners. Here she continued for some days awaiting the result of the following advertisement which she caused to be inserted in the daily papers:

A young lady conversant with Spanish, French, German, and Italian, besides possessing a thorough English education, is desirous of obtaining a position as governess in a family. Reply to "DUKE," office of this paper.

This advertisement continued to appear for a few weeks, without any satisfactory result to Mary. This was indeed most unfortunate for her. She had anticipated that her accomplishments would have attracted immediate attention, and she had not exercised much economy in spending the small amount that she had brought from home. With the diminution of her funds, it soon became necessary to avail herself of cheaper apartments, so she at once hired a small room in the beautiful and healthy environment of Belmont, where she cosily installed herself.

Day after day she scanned the papers with the hope that her advertisement might be answered, but she was doomed to be continually disappointed. She spent most of her time in manufacturing fancy articles, which she occasionally sold to the neighbors about, thus replenishing now and then her depleted exchequer.

One morning, however, she found herself actually penniless, and without any hope of obtaining a single meal for the day. She sat in a melancholy mood near a window, looking out upon the radiant sky; a little bird hopped upon a twig nearby and chiruped sweetly, and, as it glanced now and then at the pale face at the window, seemed to enquire what was the burden that hung so heavily upon her. Mary was interested in the pretty little thing and watched it eagerly and lovingly as it alighted on the ground and proceeded to pick up a few worms. She did not move from her seat until the bird had flown, when she burst into tears.

"What little faith have I," she said, "that I should have mistrusted Providence and rendered myself unhappy thereby, when that little creature, among the smallest that came from the Mighty Father's hand, is so happy and so well-cared for! Ah! I am a coward and cannot face adversity. Nay, worse,—I am a hypocrite. Why have I professed Christianity and pretended implicit faith in Christ when I tacitly ignore His divine direction in all things, Is the servant greater than his Lord? Can our vile hearts not consent to share a small portion of the tribulations of our great Leader who sacrificed himself upon the alter of an all-absorbing love? May God forgive me for my faithlessness!"

With these words she began to sing in a melodious and spirited tone the following lines of Miss Waring's beautiful hymn:

> "There are briars besetting every path
>   That call for patient care;
> There is a cross in every lot
>   And a constant need for prayer;
> Yet a lowly heart that leans on Thee
>   Is happy anywhere."

From that day forward, although Mary struggled against fearful odds,—sometimes going to bed hungry and tired,—she never lost confidence in Him who clothes the lilies of the field with magnificent splendour, and tempers the wind to the shorn lamb. She awaited patiently the day when her weeping would be turned into joy,—that most glorious day that should bring her face to face with him she loved. The remembrance of her sufferings would only sweeten their cup of love and draw closer the links that should ever after unite them.

She gave up all hope of receiving any reply to her advertisement, and one afternoon she wended her way into the city to see if she could get anything there to do. She was returning, much dispirited, having met with no success, when she turned her steps to the burial ground. It was a place to which she had often resorted since her residence in the city, a melancholy haunt for a melancholy soul. Within the precints of this vast enclosure she sat down and contemplated this fleeting life in all of its phases.

There was a grave-digger busy at work preparing a grave for one who had died a few hours before, and as the stalwart worker threw up spadefuls of heavy moist earth he whistled a lively air and seemed quite at home in his vocation. But Mary's heart grew sick, and a

THE SWORD OF NEMESIS

sensation of awe and curious fear struck her as she recollected that down there in that cold damp earth she would one day be laid to be the feast of worms.

"What is poor frail man after all!" she mused.

And, as if to accentuate her expressions, the grave digger's spade struck a hard substance, which proved to be a skull. This he threw up, without the least ceremony, and it fell with a thud at Mary's feet. She recoiled from the repulsive-looking object, and it was not until she had recovered her self-possession that she again drew near to it and scrutinized it.

"Were you not afraid to handle that thing, Quarmin?" she asked.

"No, ma'am. I's been use to dem for over thirty years now, and de Lawd knows I hab no hesitashun in handlin' it. To me is de same like tecking up a piece o' dirt."

"But it might have belonged to a great man, hence you ought to treat it with more reverence."

"Excuse me, ma'am; dis is only de paper in which de nice tings was wrap. If it was belong to a great and good soul dis don't matter anyting now. De real man is now living wid de Lawd."

"Yes, poor illiterate man!" mused Mary. "Simple demonstration of a marvellous truth. What does this earthly structure, which must soon dissolve into its proper elements, matter? The man lives! The energy, the ego, the soul, or call it what you will, that once enlivened the frail casket is indestructible; and these works, whether for good or evil, that were evolved from that silent, sad casement must leave their influence on mankind when the clay shall have been transformed into new creations. Pythagoras, Anaxagoras, Zeno, and you, sweet Hypatia,—illustrious beacons of classic philosophy; you who labored to dive into the deeper depths of human thought, to find those principles which should elevate your species and satisfy its moral, social, and religious instincts,—the shortcomings of your ethics are evident. Socrates, your splendid idealisms have failed. The voice that you heard is not the right voice. This poor ignorant grave-digger, in his simple faith, has within his grasp the everlasting keystone that you sought with all the ardour of your intellectual nature,—and did not find. The mysteries of mind have been solved, not according to pagan myth but according to the revelations of the Incarnate Son of God. Better the least in the kingdom of Paley than the greatest in the kingdom of Aristotle. Poor skull! What was once your complexion? Black, white, or yellow? Were you beautiful? What was the color of your eyes? Were they rich blue, hazel, brown, or black? Was your dome covered with glossy raven locks or coarse wool? Ah! you seem to frown at me as if to accuse me of folly. My blood thrills as I imagine what beauty might have adorned you. Where is all this? I fancy I hear you replying in plaintive, solemn tones, 'No more! No more!' Touching reality! Who therefore will be so supremely foolish as to worship poor frail flesh and ignore the powerful claims of the mind? Is the university professor particular about the physique of Euclid, Theon, Pythagoras, Galileo, or Newton? Who ever remembers the form or color of Hippocrates, Pasteur, or the illustrious Hervey, when associating their names with their gifts to humanity? The most superficial would not sink to such trifles. What Christian soul will ignore Cyrenian Simon bearing his Lord's cross, while he reveres the memory of tender Mary performing the work of love at her Master's feet? These noble minds have all left their 'footprints on the sand of time,' which are as indestructible as the source from which they emanated."

Mary's musings had quite startled old Quarmin, who concluded that "She had too much larnin' and that her head was a leetle crazy," and when she left the cemetery that afternoon the simple man leaned on his spade for a full quarter of an hour and considered, with pity in his eyes, the "Handsome leetle young lady with the sad eyes and mournful face," who, he expected, would one day be an inmate of a lunatic asylum.

CHAPTER XXXVI

Strong affection contends with all things and overcometh all things.

Joanna Baillie.

Great men are those who see that mental force is stronger than material force.

Emerson.

THERE is an old adage which says "it never rains but it pours," and it is a remarkable fact that one calamity treads upon the heels of another. So, likewise, it may be said that when the fountain of joy is once opened it flows delightfully on into streams of happiness. Such was the case with Mary Highfield. With her countenance beaming with pleasure she laid on the table near her a note she had just received from the editor of *The Port of Spain Gazette,* telling her that her services as governess were immediately required by a well-known French family who requested that she should call at the "Bee Hive" the next morning.

Glancing over the columns of the morning's paper she was filled with delight when her eyes fell upon de la Mar's name in the list of passengers who had arrived the day before from Southampton. It was with much difficulty that she controlled her feelings.

Her first act was to indite a letter to the good editor who had written to her and declare her inability to accept the position which she had but a few days before so eagerly sought. Having done this she wrote the following letter to Carl, who, she inferred, had gone to X——— on his arrival.

BELMONT, P. O., SPAIN.

MY DARLING CARLITO:

Imagine my surprise when I saw your arrival announced in this morning's paper. Can I give thanks enough to God for having brought you back again safely to me, your own true love! You are by this time aware of all the suffering and sorrow which I have endured for your sake: a father's anathemas; a life of privation, misery, and isolation; a heart almost broken with suspense. But the cloud has passed away, and now I think only of that happy moment when we shall meet again. I need not tell you that I shall suffer the pangs of suspense until I receive word from you.

I am still your darling,

MARY.

P. S. When you come, enquire at the post office for Miss Manners, and should you write, address your letter in that way.

M. H.

This letter was forwarded by the midday post to the country, and the next morning to Mary's intense delight three gentlemen were ushered into her humble apartments. They were her uncle the Canon, Carlito, and a dignified looking personage who was announced as Mr. Robert Heineman, merchant of Melbourne, Australia.

The scene that followed was extremely touching.

Carlito wept for joy as he again looked upon his beloved and thought of the power of that enduring affection which had weathered the roughest storms and never for a moment swerved in its course.

The Canon glanced around the room and sighed deeply. He took in the whole situation at a glance, and looked with tender pity at his frail niece whose whereabouts he had long wished to know.

Mr. Heineman seemed interested.

"What about my Father, Uncle?" enquired Mary, after the lapse of some moments.

"Ah, poor child," replied the clergyman, "since your

departure from home he has been experiencing calamitous times, which have completely submerged him. In trying to grasp everything he has lost all. He invested a large sum of money in a certain enterprise that failed completely after an extraordinarily short existence. This left him a sadder but a wiser man. Immediately after this, Messrs. Barton Bros., to whom he had heavily mortgaged his property, came down upon him and threatened to foreclose within six months. This will leave him a completely ruined man,—almost penniless. He recently received a letter from your cousin Bertie informing him that he had left the army and had amassed a considerable fortune in South America, where he is now settled comfortably. The fact that you could have been Bertie's wife has considerably exasperated him against you, and he swears that he will have nothing whatever to do with you."

"But, my dear Uncle, Father does not see that it is just probable that, had I consented to marry Bertie, the tide might have turned in the other direction instead of into the channel of immense wealth. It might have been immense sorrow." Then, her eyes filling with tears, she continued: "O Uncle,—dear good Uncle,—what do you think of me? Are you angry with me for what I have done? Oh, pity me! How else could I have rescued myself from the horns of a terrible dilemma? My poor Father, he does not care for me nor pity me, but my heart yearns for him. Would to God that we could be reconciled, that I could once more rejoice in his loving smiles, that I could again sit at his feet and with tender hands soothe his pain. Speak, Uncle, do not keep me in suspense. Do not tell me to abandon the only being I have ever loved or am capable of loving as my husband."

THE SWORD OF NEMESIS 251

The Canon's heart sank within him. He drew a deep breath and then briefly replied:

"Do not dwell upon this painful subject any more, Mary. You have my sympathy, and you may depend upon me for my assistance. Is this enough?"

"Thank you, Uncle," she replied. "I am satisfied."

"Now, Mary," continued the Canon, "since you have made up your mind to marry Carlito, I shall not object. Both my experience as a man and my personal convictions forbid interference between sweethearts. You shall accompany your cavalier to the island of Montserrat, whither I also am going this week to take my share in the solution of certain mysteries that have laid in the shades of obscurity for many years."

Mary felt her heart beat high with hopes, but still, a look of concern crept into her face.

Mr. Heineman, who was engaged in a deep conversation with Carlito, expressed a desire to retire to his hotel in the city, as he had important matters engaging his attention there. The Canon accompanied him, and Carlito and his fiancée sat together interchanging thoughts pregnant with the highest joy and happiness.

"I rather like Mr. Heineman's countenance," remarked Mary. "He has greatly impressed me."

"Rightly so," replied Carlito. "He is a man full of rich benevolence and a true sense of manhood. It is enough to say that in the interest of justice he has left his far-away home in Australia and has traveled all the way to the West Indies. This speaks volumes for his good nature, doesn't it?"

"What's all this about? It must be something very grave that caused him to come. Won't you give me a hint, darling?"

"You shall know all later. There is a pleasant surprise for you," naïvely replied Carlito.

"Very well; I shall not be overcurious," she said playfully, then continued, "I want you to accompany me to dear Rita's grave in the country. I may not have the opportunity of seeing it again since we are going away."

The next day, leaving Mr. Heineman to look after his business in the city, they took the train and, accompanied by the Canon, they arrived at X, where, having parted with Mr. Highfield at the rectory, they proceeded onwards to look at Rita's last resting-place.

It was a bright and lovely day when the two young lovers entered the "garden of God." It was a lonely place. Not a sound stirred the air, and it seemed as if the cold finger of Death had imprinted itself on everything else except a tiny humming bird that flitted from tree to tree, extracting honey from the flowers. The stone slabs and wooden crosses suggested forcibly the last dread end of human existence,—the tranquil and eternal sleep. Overhead heavy, dark clouds were floating, while the sun's beams kissed the grassy mounds reared above the remains of those who were sleeping their last sleep.

They approached Rita's grave. It was covered with sod, and two lovely lilies adorned it at either end, while a freshly-gathered garland of flowers had been placed in the middle by some loving hand. There was an elaborate marble stone at the head, on which were inscribed the following words:

A LA MEMORÍA DE
RITA CEDEÑO
QUIEN FALLECIO EL 28 DE OCTOBRE DE 19—
EN DESCANSO ESTE[1]

[1] To the memory of Rita Cedeño, who departed this life on the 28th October, 19—. May she rest in peace.

Carl broke off a piece of the smiling lily and held it in his hand. Mary began to remove some stray leaves that fell around the grave, and her eyes were moist with tears. As they prepared to leave the spot they observed some one coming towards them. It was soon discovered that it was none other than Mr. Cox, the village schoolmaster and hedge-lawyer.

"Good-morning to you, Mr. de la Mar," he said, extending his hand to Carl, and making a very polite bow to Mary. "I am indeed very glad to see you, sir, I heard you had gone to Australia. You did the trip very quickly, and I rejoice to see you are looking so well."

"I thank you sincerely, my dear Cox. I am now a regular bird of passage, and I shall be leaving here again soon. Not for Australia, but for an island nearer home."

"Is that so? Then I hope you are in quest of something important. You will, I presume, enter into possession of your property before you leave the island, won't you?"

Carl was startled.

"I do not understand you," said he. "Will you kindly make yourself more explicit?"

"Do you mean to say you are not yet aware that you have been made the sole heir of Miss Cadeño? I made two wills for her. The first she destroyed and the second has put you in possession of her entire estate."

Carl stood transfixed; and simultaneously the words "Poor Rita!" escaped the lips of both himself and Mary. No thought of this had ever entered the mind of either of these two high-souled beings. There was no rearing of any air castles, which they could well afford to do from the knowledge of such a lucky windfall.

No, it was only the thought of poor, dead Rita,—the sweet girl who had been taken away under such painful circumstances.

"What steps will you take, Mr. de la Mar?" enquired Cox, who was evidently struck by Carl's coolness.

"I have other business, Mr. Cox, which demands my immediate attention. I shall see Mr. Frost the solicitor, who will look after my interests."

Thus saying, he shook hands with the schoolmaster, and taking Mary on his arm, conducted her to her uncle's residence.

The next day he did not hesitate to call upon his solicitor as he had intimated to Cox,—after he had discovered the truth of his disclosures. Certain details were gone through, documents were signed, and important arrangements made in which the welfare of John Highfield formed a matter of primary consideration,—of which we shall hear further in this narrative.

CHAPTER XXXVII

Horror and doubt distract
His troubled thoughts, and from the bottom stir
The hell within him.

Milton.

ON shore, four hundred miles away from their home in Trinidad, where they had breakfasted just two days before, were to be seen a small party consisting of Canon Highfield and his niece, Carl Woodhouse, his mother, and the stranger from Australia, Mr. Robert Heineman, to whom we have been previously introduced. They were all being entertained under the hospitable roof of the famous barrister, Oscar Lindsay, whom we have met before.

Canon Highfield and his host were inseparable friends, as has been previously told, and though many years had passed since last they met, the same warmth and good-will remained.

There were frequent conferences of a private nature between Heineman, the Canon, and Lindsay, which had for their purpose the securing of evidence against the suspected murderer of Burleigh Woodhouse of Elmsdale.

Many years ago when plain Hugh Highfield, then the guest of Lindsay, had remarked in connection with the Elmsdale murder: "McIntyre is at the bottom of it, I'll wager my last dollar!" his shrewdness and perspicacity had convinced him of the correctness of his conclusion, and all through the years during which the mystery remained unsolved he never for a moment lost hope that it would one day be discovered to the satisfaction of all who loved justice.

McIntyre meanwhile enjoyed his prosperity, without the least idea that there was a terrible storm gradually collecting its most destructive powers that would fall and crush him with its terrible force. His estates were in a flourishing condition, and though he lived well and continued in his epicurean habits, they remained unencumbered. He had never thought of marrying. He spurned the idea. Flitting around him were gay and winsome ladies, but he was never attracted by any. Cupid had never touched his heart. The darling of society, he had gathered around him an extraordinary amount of interest. There was no sport considered of much consequence unless it was patronized by McIntyre. And if he did not happen to lend his beautiful tenor voice in an evening soirée half of the fun would be considered lost. His seat in the parish church was never vacant unless through illness or other unavoidable circumstances. Even the old rector, Father Fairley, had absolutely lost sight of the suspicion of murder with which the name of the popular McIntyre had at one time been associated, and admitted him to the companionship of his family circle without the slightest scruple. The cut of his coat, the shape of his collar, and the style of his walk were imitated by the street urchins, while the women of shadowy reputation found a pleasure in linking his name with their lewd songs, holding him up as the truest sample of the "man of life."

Seated in his portico one evening about half past six o'clock, enjoying a pleasant smoke and awaiting the calls of his usual visitors, a servant appeared and announced that lawyer Lindsay wished to see him. McIntyre experienced a strange feeling of anxiety, which he had scarcely known before. This was the first visit he had ever had from Lindsay.

"Conduct him to the drawing-room," said he to the servant, as he cleared his throat, which seemed all at once to have become parched.

A few moments later he greeted Lindsay, who in a stiff and distant manner said:

"Good-evening, Mr. McIntyre."

"Good-evening, Mr. Lindsay," returned McIntyre. "I'm indeed glad to see you. Will you take a seat?"

"Certainly, and with the greatest pleasure; but may I be permitted to introduce to you some particular friends who are in my carriage at the door?"

"Yes. You need not have asked such a question, Mr. Lindsay. My house is a house of good cheer. By the way, I have heard that you have a good many visitors from a neighboring island; but not thinking it likely that I should be acquainted with them I did not take the trouble to enquire who they were. I am really very much indebted to you for the honour you pay me in bringing over your guests to Elmsdale."

Lindsay strode across the room, to the door. Meanwhile McIntyre trembled with fear,—a premonitory symptom of impending ill had seized him. It was the work of a moment for Lindsay to return with a dusky dame on his arm and four other gentlemen bringing up the rear.

"Mr. McIntyre, Mrs. Woodhouse, late of Elmsdale. Mrs. Woodhouse, the distinguished Mr. McIntyre of Elmsdale," announced Lindsay.

This was a moment of the most terrible ordeal for the popular proprietor of Elmsdale. A veritable bolt from the blue had fallen! He wished all at once he had never lived to see that day. Despair, anguish, remorse, clouded his features, and his hands fell heavily by his side, while his knees shook nervously under him.

The others in their turn were introduced to him by Lindsay. A bystander cognizant of the circumstances that had placed McIntyre in the state of mental torture which he could hardly conceal, would have pitied him as well as admired the efforts that he made to hide his embarrassment under cover of a *laissez faire*.

When the party left that evening McIntyre closed his private apartment and communed with himself.

The night was pitch dark, and through a window that opened on the street he looked out and gazed earnestly at the few stars dimly shining in the heavens, silent witnesses of the struggle that he was undergoing. He closed the window suddenly, and his hands trembled nervously. It was evident he had shrunk from a desperate deed,—that of flinging himself from the window and thereby putting an end to his existence. With his hands behind his back he paced the room to and fro, while great drops of perspiration bathed his brow. In the agony of despair, he exclaimed:

"Great God! What shall I do? O Ambition, Ambition! Cursed be the moment when I encouraged you to enter my breast. See the recompense you have brought me, the stamp of Cain and the everlasting disgrace which stands at the door. Oh, that I had been satisfied with what God had given me, and made the best of life in a poor but honest way! But it is now too late, and the poorest would not envy the usurper and murderer, George McIntyre. Ah, how do those horrifying sounds distort my ears! O Father of Heaven, nay, can I, with these blood-stained hands, call

THE SWORD OF NEMESIS

Thee, source of purity and goodness, 'Father?' O thou Christ of mercy, whom I had forgotten in my prosperity, extend to me the clemency which thou didst show to the degraded thief upon the cross! Though sin has stained my life and has brought me face to face with the gallows, still can I look back to the time when on my mother's knee I lisped words of love gathered from the mine of God's Holy Book. I can remember how the story of the crucifixion impressed me and brought tears to my eyes. I can see now my mother's fair face bending down sweetly upon me as I repeated the simple lines:

> "Gentle Jesus, meek and mild,
> Look upon a little child;
> Pity my simplicity,
> Suffer me to come to Thee.
> Fain would I to Thee be brought,
> Gracious God, forbid it not!
> In the kingdom of Thy grace
> Give a little child a place.

"But for ambition, foul ambition, this moment had never come."

Here the strong, iron-framed man burst into piteous tears and threw himself headlong upon the floor. A few moments after his emotion had subsided an unusual sound caught his ears. He rose, and throwing back the window curtains, looked out and saw the light of a lantern and some people moving in the street. He closed the window and sat down, when he distinctly heard from a well-known voice the words which sent a fresh pang through his soul:

"When black clouds cover the sun at midday then shall begin the sorrows of Elmsdale, and when the white dove no longer sits upon the wall, the dark lantern will shine, to drag the fox from his hole, the bones from

the earth, and give back virtue and honour to Elmsdale."

"This surely points to me. But then I have no white dove accustomed to sit upon the wall whose flight must mark my downfall," mused McIntyre. "This is the only irreconcilable thing in the prophecy."

The next morning he rose from bed at an unusually early hour and took his accustomed route round his demesne. He examined the interesting menagerie of Elmsdale, which he had never neglected from the day he took possession of the premises. His pigeons, monkeys, parrots, guinea pigs, and other pets came in for their share of attention, and he seemed to have a few moments' respite from the terrible thoughts that were weighing heavily upon him as he fondled the gay little animals that greeted him with pleasant demonstrations of joy. His splendid brood of pigeons was the last thing he thought of, and as he wended his way toward the pigeon-house a gloomy picture met his gaze. The pigeonry was deserted, and not one of the favorite birds could be seen. They had all flown to seek new homes!

McIntyre was stunned, and the word "Ominous! Ominous!" involuntarily escaped his lips.

He returned to the house, scarcely conscious of what he was doing. As he entered the door one of the servants, wearing a look of dismay and horror met him with the words:

"Two policemen, sir, two policemen."

This was enough. McIntyre instantly solved the problem, and without further ado entered and met the officers of the law. As soon as they saw him, one of them produced a warrant signed by a magistrate, authorizing the arrest of McIntyre. This document the officer read in a stern voice, and then said:

"George McIntyre, in the name of the King, we arrest you for the murder of Burleigh Woodhouse, late of Elmsdale."

A deadly pallor came over the face of McIntyre, and he drew his breath painfully, but not a word escaped his lips. By this time all the servants had collected together in the room and were looking on with amazement. One of them, in livery, made bold to approach his master and asked him what was the meaning of this curious demonstration and what steps should be taken during his absence from home.

"It's nothing serious," replied McIntyre, "there is a mistake somewhere, which will soon be set right. My good Thomas, you will take charge of everything until this unfortunate situation is made clear; meanwhile *au revoir*. Don't neglect to see that everything is all right."

The two policemen, without further ado, then led the criminal away who, as he passed through the long streets, with dejected countenance, became an object of pity and wonder to all who beheld him.

CHAPTER XXXVIII

Pride and worse, ambition, threw me down.
Milton.

On Tuesday morning, two days before the examination of the accused, Lindsay sat in his office turning over some papers, and by his side the venerable Doctor Fane playfully swung round in an office chair and pored over the morning paper. Suddenly he looked up as if struck by some thought, and watching Lindsay steadfastly, said:

"By the way, old chap, as I have some moments to spare I may intimate to you that my report anent the exhumed remains of our deceased friend Woodhouse has already been sent to the authorities."

"Is that really so?" asked Lindsay, surprised. "Why, that's much sooner than I anticipated. I had no idea that the remains had been already exhumed. And what further conclusions have you arrived at? The same old story, I suppose,—a bullet?"

The doctor looked serious and gave a negative shake of the head.

"I'm afraid," he said, "that Canon Highfield's philosophy is superior to that of many of his confreres. He was always of the opinion that Woodhouse was not shot, and a note made in his pocketbook years ago to that effect has now been unmistakably confirmed by my examination."

"Great God!" ejaculated Lindsay, rising from his

seat. "Is it possible that that chap Hugh could have been so long-headed? I remember he did endeavour to force that conviction on me, but I did not think his inductions sufficiently weighty for my consideration. Go on with your explanation, Dr. Fane."

"In my evidence at the inquest touching Woodhouse's death I regret to say that my foregone conclusions prevented the due exercise of my professional acumen. My previous opinions have been greatly changed by my recent investigations. I am convinced beyond the least shadow of a doubt that the instrument that dealt the mortal blow was not a revolver. The orifice is much larger than any bullet would have made, and although the occipital bone is fractured, there is no evidence of a bullet having penetrated it. It is evident therefore that a blunt instrument about the size of a crowbar must have pierced the brain, and was apparently later used to batter the skull."

"This evidence is sufficient to hang him. We had depended mostly upon Heineman's testimony, not having imagined that your professional investigations had rendered us such valuable service."

"As far as I understand, Mr. Heineman's evidence is merely circumstantial, although he set the ball rolling."

"To the contrary,—quite direct. But in the face of yours, it will become now of secondary importance, as also a certain letter and manuscript which I was perusing when you came in."

"But is not Mr. Heineman an Australian merchant? What connection can he, therefore, have in this matter, and what about the manuscript and letter you speak of?"

"Let me say briefly: Mr. Heineman was once a resident of this island, and was employed many years ago on the staff of *The Daily Chronicle*."

Here Dr. Fane seemed startled, his countenance became more thoughtful, and he knitted his brow and gave an assenting nod.

Lindsay was continuing his speech when a commotion was heard at the door. He rose to see what it might be, and his eyes fell upon a very old negro, bent and crooked, who was approaching the office by the aid of a long staff, while a number of persons followed. Old age had not altogether robbed its victim of a certain amount of intelligence which seemed more evident as an expression of joy and extreme pleasure brightened the countenance.

"Well, Zac, what is it now?" queried Lindsay; for this individual was none other than our interesting acquaintance, Professor Zac.

"Ah, Marse Ossie," replied the Professor, "you know if you destroy the root of a tree the branches can't stay. No, sir; they must die. Well, sir, since you all have cut the root, a branch has fell. It couldn't remain a day longer. Praise to Jehovah, who hath delivered the Philistines into our hands!"

"What do you mean?" enquired Lindsay impatiently, nervously toying with the lappet of his coat, and forcing a smile. "You are always talking in parables, Zac. Pray what is it?"

"Well, sir; Dick Ray has been imitating Judas."

"Oh, to the point. Do not beat about the bush. Will you please explain yourself?"

"Well, sir; I shall make it as plain as I can. Dick Ray has hanged himself."

"Hanged himself!" reiterated Lindsay, "and cheated the hands of the law."

"Better so, poor fellow!" remarked the Professor. "He has left the world for the world's good, and this is the kindest thing he has ever done."

The people had now dispersed, and after a few moments spent in answering some questions put by Lindsay, the Professor retired with these words on his lips:

"I told you, Marse Ossie, that I would live to see honour and virtue come back to Elmsdale."

"What a queer chap that fellow is!" remarked Dr. Fane as the old man disappeared.

"Yes, a remarkably queer one," replied Lindsay. "How lightly indeed does he take that rogue's death! I, for my part, am sorry, since we were on the eve of arresting him."

"I am anxious to hear the story of that interesting manuscript you hold and which purports to supply valuable information," said Dr. Fane, after a few moments, breaking the spell of silence which had lasted for some time. "I do not believe that the news of the tragedy has altogether upset you."

"No, my dear Doctor," continued Lindsay, producing the manuscript in question. "I shall soon satisfy your anxiety, and you will be surprised to know what schemes a rogue can resort to to accomplish his ends. To begin with, I discovered the manuscript in Woodhouse's study after his death, but by a strange fate I never glanced at the pages, as events of much greater importance occupied my attention at the time. I threw it among some old volumes in my library, whence it was not long ago unearthed by old Zac. You will observe, doctor, that this is an unfinished drama by poor Woodhouse. Literature had always been his hobby, poor chap! If you can read just here," pointing to a particular point of the manuscript, "you will observe from the prologue of this speech, which Ralph Gordon pours forth against his wife Ethel, that an interesting part of the context is missing, which would just harmonize with the contents of this letter that implicated Mrs. Woodhouse, and which, according to my custom, I took pains to preserve. Now, you see, Doctor, that not only do the words fit in, but also the slip of paper, which was clipped from the manuscript."

"That is possible," said Dr. Fane, interested by this very important explanation. "But what about the difference between the names Edith and Ethel?"

"I shall satisfy you upon that point in a moment," said Lindsay, as he got up from his seat and opened a large drawer, whence he withdrew a powerful magnifying glass, handing it to the doctor with the request that he should look at the writing through the glass. Dr. Fane did so, and, with a smile on his lips, ejaculated:

"Well done, Mr. McIntyre! This would have deceived the devil himself. I can see that the name 'Ethel,' occurring in two places, has been carefully erased and the name 'Edith' inserted instead."

"Very well, Dr. Fane. You now have as near a solution of this intricate problem as it is possible to obtain."

At this stage a tall slender person, with a very intellectual face and bright blue eyes, entered, and Dr. Fane withdrew.

This last visitor was Mr. Henry Berkley, barrister-at-law, who had won the implicit confidence of the community since his *début* in the law courts of the colony when he concluded an interesting and important case, and the masterly manner in which he defended his client surprised not a few of the learned members of the bar, and inspired the hope that at no distant date he would reach the zenith of fame. It was therefore with the greatest pleasure that Lindsay consulted him in this case.

"I learn that you will not consent to defend the criminal, Berkley," began Lindsay.

"Under no circumstances whatever," was the emphatic reply. "I do not think there is a jury in the world who would think of acquitting McIntyre of murder, in the light of recent discoveries. I have decided not to associate myself with the case."

"So you are of opinion he will be condemned."

"Decidedly. I am so convinced. There will be much interest taken in the examination on Friday. The affair is on everybody's lips. I have been to see the unfortunate fellow in prison, having had a special call from him. He implored me to defend him, but when I told him I found it impossible to do so he utterly broke down and seemed to lose all hope. I think he means to try Foster, whom he thinks he will secure. I left him in a most pitiable condition, weeping like a woman. Despite his base crimes, I could hardly help feeling sympathy for him."

"I shall, if I be permitted, call to see him to-morrow," said Lindsay; "he may have something to say to me as the representative of young Woodhouse, and this may relieve his mind."

"That would not be a bad plan," replied Berkley.

And the interview terminated.

CHAPTER XXXIX

> All nature is but art unknown,
> All chance direction which thou canst not see,
> All discord harmony not understood,
> All partial evil universal good.
>
> *Pope.*

MARY HIGHFIELD was enjoying herself in the pleasant home of Mrs. Lindsay, where every possible care and attention were lavished upon her. There were certain enigmas which daily presented themselves to her for solution, arising out of the peculiar sayings and doings of her companions. She was altogether isolated from the rest in their movements and serious conversations. It is true she had a strong suspicion that there was something important engaging the minds of Carlito and the Canon, from the hints that had been thrown out by them, but of the real import of these hints she never dreamed. She had left her home in Trinidad with a simple, childlike faith in the man whom, above all others, she thought most excellent, and she felt that she was perfectly secure under his protection. Dreaming not of ill, she believed that her barque would move smoothly on, manned, as it was, by a pilot of exemplary virtues. More than once she attempted to obtain some information from Carl as to his suspicious movements, but he always gave her the same old reply:

"I have a pleasant surprise in store for you, darling."

Mrs. Woodhouse was on excellent terms with Mary, who had deeply impressed her by her endearing charms and her utter devotion to Carl; and she longed for that happy day when the clouds should roll away and they should recognize each other as mother and daughter.

It was a delightful evening when Mrs. Lindsay, the Canon, Carl, and Mary were sitting around a card table enjoying a pleasant game. Lindsay had not yet come in, and Heineman and Mrs. Woodhouse, in a corner of the room, were conversing together on the merits of Tennyson's "Enoch Arden." Carl and Mary were partners at the game against the Canon and Mrs. Lindsay.

The last round of the cards was being played. Mary threw down the queen of hearts (trumps), on which the Canon placed the king with a smart snap of the thumb, saying triumphantly at the same time:

"I've caught that jack, Master Carl. Put it down."

Carl, with a pleasant smile, laid down the ace of trumps, to the entire discomfiture of the minister, whose chagrin was augmented a thousand-fold when his partner, with a vanquished air, placed the knave upon the winning card.

"I've broken his neck," ejaculated Carl.

And all joined in a right hearty laugh.

"Yes, his neck is surely broken, poor fellow!" sounded a voice from the corridor, and in another moment Lindsay entered, wearing a look of utter amazement.

Everybody turned round to hear what news he had brought, and after he had seated himself he announced without further hesitation that Dick Ray had hanged himself.

The assembly was startled by the unexpected news, and Mary felt as if she was living in a world of enchantments, with dark, mysterious shadows gradually enveloping her. It was not so with the others, who received the announcement with some measure of regret that the notorious culprit did not get his deserts at the hands of the law.

"This is the second piece on the programme," said Lindsay, as he strode toward the door and lit a cigar.

He was immediately followed by the Canon, who seemed to lose all interest in the game in which he had become so much absorbed, begging for a postponement on the ground that he had something of importance to communicate to his friend Lindsay.

"I am afraid you have been arousing considerably Mary's suspicions," said he, as he stood with Lindsay in the large airy gallery overlooking the street.

"Do you really think so?"

"I am certain; for she exhibited an air of concern, or rather of excitement, when you spoke of the tragedy."

"Poor, trusting girl, I hope that the climax will soon be reached and these mysteries solved, when she will be amply repaid for the patience that she has exhibited under these very trying circumstances."

"I hope so," breathed the Canon with a sigh.

"There will, I suppose, be unusual public interest at the trial, and I imagine half the town will be present to listen to the examination. Berkley has refused to plead for him, I understand."

"Yes, and I think he deserves credit for refusing to associate himself with the defence. He would ruin his hitherto untarnished reputation were he to meddle with it. I shall go to the prison to-morrow and see how McIntyre fares."

"I fancy that would be striking below the belt. Your presence would only increase his misery, and you have no right to rejoice over a fallen foe."

"Ah, you are exhibiting the elements of Christianity for once in this matter. Well done, Canon Highfield, you can afford to be charitable now."

And Lindsay could not repress a hearty laugh.

"The fun is over when the game is caught. I have sought all these years to expose this man for his villainy and perfidy against me, and now that he is pinned to the ground I almost pity his condition."

"By the way, how memories of the distant past can be revived in an instant. My mind reverts now to that horse-whipping affair. It is certainly not my intention to visit him in the depth of his degradation to increase his misery, but as the inevitable consequences must follow it may be my privilege to be of some service to him."

At this moment they were startled by the melodious strains of the piano as Mary struck up with her usual fascinating touch the prelude of the grand old song, "Home, Sweet Home." Her voice then rang out in sweetest harmony with the soul-stirring notes, and all eyes were riveted upon her. Her whole being seemed merged in the song. As she reached the last verse her feelings became more intense, and she sang more passionately, while her touch became livelier. Carl had been turning the pages for her, but he seemed all at once carried away by the torrent of the thrilling music that fell like a charm upon his ears, and when he collected himself and realized that he had been a moment dilatory in his duty, he looked tenderly into Mary's eyes. They were sad and filled with tears; but before he could ask himself why those sweet, sparkling orbs were bedimmed, the last note of the song had died away, and Mary suddenly fell upon the floor as if dead. Her face was ashen pale, and her hands had become icy cold.

Carl, mad with excitement and fear, caught her up

in his arms with superhuman strength; the ardour of his passion found itself unchecked by his hitherto unfailing discretion, and he imprinted a score of kisses, mingled with tears, upon the cold lips.

The panic fortunately did not last long, for after suitable remedies had been applied, there was a speedy recovery. Carl lingered by the girl's side as she reclined on a couch, and pressing his hand gently upon her brow, said:

"Do you feel better, sweet?"

"Yes, much, darling," was the reply. "But oh! my heart is overburdened with sadness. Why do you keep me in suspense? Ah, Carlito! though your presence ensures my protection, I do not like such mysteries. There seems to be some doleful secret that you are hiding from me."

"Do you trust me, love?" said Carl.

"I do sincerely. How could it be otherwise?"

"Then, continue to trust me, and all will be right."

She looked at him, her heart beating with emotion, and a gentle reassuring smile lit up her face as she said:

"Your love alone, Carl, serves as an invaluable solace for the sad thoughts that sometimes overwhelm me. Do you remember having read in your first Latin book *Si naturam expellas semper recurret?* Although my Father so strenuously locks his heart against me, my affection for him remains unchanged. His tender smiles, his words of devotion, his trustfulness, and the confidence he once reposed in me are all pictured in my memory, and sometimes my heart feels as if it would burst when I realize the great gulf that divides us. O my Father, my Father, could you but know your daughter's grief! But, ah! the die is cast."

"And all this for me," groaned Carl, deeply affected,

as he turned aside and paced the room. "How can I ever repay such unparalleled devotion, such sweet, self-sacrificing love? How wonderful this mysterious linking of souls by the Divine Power. Is not this a process as sublime and marvellous as those laws regulating the natural affection between the child and its parents? 'Therefore shall a man leave father and mother and cleave unto his wife.' This is the Divine mandate, and this reversed must apply to thee, my angel, and exonerate thee from the charge of ingratitude which the world will not hesitate to charge thee with. Even Schopenhauer, in the fury of his pessimism, would have hailed such a one as thee as a beaming light! And I, how shall I call thee,—by what name under heaven shall I classify those inestimable qualities which make thee so dear to my heart?"

When Carl parted from Mary that night he began to consider whether it would be wise to still prolong her suspense or reveal to her the whole secret which had been so long kept from her.

The morrow, however, decided.

CHAPTER XL

> No action, whether foul or fair,
> Is ever done but it leaves somewhere
> A record written by fingers ghostly
> As a blessing or a curse, or mostly
> In the greater weakness or greater strength
> Of the acts which follow it; till at length
> The wrongs of ages are redress'd,
> And the justice of God made manifest.
>
> *Anon.*

PRISON life is far from being a pleasant one. It is a time for sad reflections, and the criminal unaccustomed to such an atmosphere must, if he possesses a spark of manhood, feel a keen sense of humiliation as he broods over his environment and the associations which force themselves upon him.

McIntyre had been only four days in confinement in the Royal Gaol, and the total change of his appearance was as remarkable as it had been rapid. He had aged considerably. His face became gaunt, and his eyes sunken. Whenever he paced the narrow apartment in which he was confined, his knees shook and appeared hardly able to sustain him. His once raven locks were now a snowy white. In fact, he was a miserable figure on whom the marks of complete distraction and despair were plainly visible.

The unfortunate prisoner endeavoured to obtain some respite from the desperate thoughts that pursued him, by tracing geometrical lines in chalk upon the floor, and giving his imagination play by drawing flowers, trees and animals upon the walls. At other times he would gaze fixedly and intently through the prison bars upon the streams of passers-by carried away in the roaring, rapid tide of the city's traffic. The noise of carriage wheels and the hum of the town were truly companions in his solitude and misery. The sweet cadence of the evening bells was falling upon the twilight air, summoning the faithful to prayer at St. Mary's Church. McIntyre could see the good people passing by in the moonlight, and his heart began to fail him and he sighed mournfully. His accustomed seat, one of the uppermost in the church, was now vacant. He placed his hands upon his ears to shut out the sound of those "sweet evening bells," but their persistent peals seemed to haunt him more and more; and he wished he might have been struck with instant deafness so as not to hear the horrifying sounds.

The large town clock pealed out the hour of seven, and instantly the church bell ceased. The silence was a relief to the miserable man, who threw himself heavily upon the floor and sobbed violently; then, composing himself, he murmured:

"Never will I face this terrible crisis. It is surely more than I can bear. I am a murderer; my hand is red with the blood of Burleigh Woodhouse, and the laws of the realm would have me expiate this. There is obviously no use of my seeking to ward off the inevitable consequences by means of lying and hypocrisy. The gallows,—the gallows menaces me, but I will cheat it." And he beat the floor violently with his fist. "Ah!" he continued, "if I were allowed the chance to escape would I not repent of my crimes and by my acts of humiliation and self-crucifixion labour to erase this most fatal blot from my name. But alas! blood has been shed, and my own blood must pay the penalty. O human persecutors, have a little of God's mercy and spare a forlorn villain who may yet live to some good purpose in the world, and die reclaimed! But if they condemn me thus, I shall defy the destructive powers of my kind, and these very hands shall extinguish the spark of life, and that portion of my being which is beyond human control must go forth to meet its destiny. But I must make a sacrifice which will lighten my passage through the vale that I soon must enter. That sacrifice must be a complete confession of my crimes."

His face had become deathly pale, and he clenched his teeth after reaching this resolution. He lay, therefore, quietly and dreamily upon his pallet, but with the despair of a self-condemned man. His thoughts dwelt upon the various circumstances of his life, and he gathered together the principle incidents, associated with his crimes, with the intention of committing them to writing on the morrow.

At ten o'clock the next morning he had just completed the task and was enclosing his confession in an envelope, when an unexpected visitor was ushered in.

It was Lindsay.

"Good-morning, Mr. McIntyre," said he.

McIntyre looked up suddenly and seemed half frightened.

"I know it all," he groaned, his wan features presenting quite a woeful appearance. "You need not taunt me with 'good-morning.' I shall not give you much trouble. My agony will not be much prolonged. I have something of the greatest importance to communicate to you, and if you will return to this cell in half an hour, with Mrs. Woodhouse and her son, I shall explain what I have to say."

The change in McIntyre's appearance and in his demeanour quite startled Lindsay. He encountered a scene which he had hardly expected, he did not anticipate seeing the lion crouching so readily, and, with a feeling of pity mixed with abhorrence, he walked rapidly out of the prison to summon Mrs. Woodhouse and Carl.

In exactly half an hour he returned with them. Mrs. Woodhouse was nervous and trembling from head to foot; but this was the result of a great anxiety. She had prepared herself for something unusual.

McIntyre was lying prostrate on the floor when the three made their appearance. He seemed to be suffering, but the cause of this was not imagined by them. On a nearer approach, however, it was discovered that he was in a semi-conscious condition. His eyes were half closed and his face was cadaverous. Mrs. Woodhouse drew back terrified at the sight, exclaiming:

"My God, what is this?"

The cry roused the wretched man, and he looked up with glazing eyes at the visitors.

"One word from you, madam, that speaks of forgiveness," he murmured weakly, "and my burden will become lighter. That I have wronged you a thousand times and dragged your name in the dust by nefarious and devilish chicanery I must confess. The climax has now been reached, and I can never face the just penalty that awaits me. Rather would I tear my heart from its place than submit to the awful ordeal. I have invited you here to see the last of a monster's career, and if you will but mix your exultation, in this your signal triumph, with one drop of pity for the wretch who lies vanquished at your feet, you will help him to die in peace."

He paused awhile and hung his head to await an answer, but none was forthcoming.

"I should have liked to make a confession with my own lips, but I could never face your honest gaze, so I have written a confession that all the world will see."

His face was becoming more ghastly, and his voice grew feebler. With an effort he raised himself and put his hand into his bosom. When he withdrew it it was besmeared with blood.

Lindsay, fearing the worst, approached him, and laying open the murderer's bosom, discovered that a pocket knife was sunk almost to the hilt in McIntyre's breast. He drew back with alarm, the idea not even occurring to him to withdraw the fatal instrument.

"Drive it down deep, my avenger," gurgled McIntyre as the pains of death seized him. "This has been reserved for you."

And he looked painfully into Carl's face and expected to see him plunge the knife up to the hilt into the flesh, but he was astonished when he saw Carl watching him with pity.

Mrs. Woodhouse murmured with unbridled emotion:

"Poor soul, may God forgive you!"

These words fell like a charm upon the ears of the dying man. He sighed deeply, and lifting from under his pillow the confession he had written, handed it to Mrs. Woodhouse.

At this stage his breathing became rapid and his voice sunk to a mere whisper.

"The Sword of Nemesis has fallen," he ejaculated. "The last scene of the act is played. I——"

He could not complete the sentence—the end came so rapidly.

McIntyre was in the presence of his Maker.

CHAPTER XLI

*All yet seems well; and if it ends so meet,
The bitter past more welcome is the sweet.*
    "*All's Well That Ends Well.*"

The curtain had fallen over the last tragic scene in connection with the Elmsdale mystery, and a new and brighter scene was opened, to the extreme gratification of all who were interested.

"Poor wretch!" fell from Canon Highfield's lips as he learned of the painful manner in which McIntyre had escaped the gallows.

Heineman, however, seemed somewhat disappointed, as he did not entertain much sympathy for the murderer, but he shrugged his shoulders and said platonically:

"Whatever is, is right."

Carl took a favorable opportunity to explain everything to Mary, ending with the awful tragedy, and her interest in the remarkable narrative was visibly expressed in her luminous eyes as she took in each word that fell from Carl's lips.

"So you have thought fit to keep me in the dark all this time, love," she said, when she had assured herself that Carl had completed his tale. "Indeed you have fulfilled your promise and given me a most pleasant surprise. Not that I give the smallest place in my heart to any consideration of the worldly advantages that you are so soon to gain,—advantages that I had never for a moment anticipated,—but because there is once more the hope of a reconciliation between myself and my Father, when his haughty pride will gratify itself in the fact that you were not what you seemed to him, but a noble scion of a noble sire."

"Thank you, sweet, for your compliment. I only hope that the significant and forceful words with which you completed your sentence may never, never be found false. The mysteries are all over now, and we enter the ordinary world and will mark our entrance therein by—," and he paused, while his lips trembled nervously,—"by casting our lot together."

At these words Mary could not suppress the emotions that rose within her, which were indicated by the tears which fell down her rosy cheeks. She could have cried for joy at the happy words that she had so long expected and wished to hear.

For some days nothing occurred to disturb the ordinary course of events at "The Grove." The company enjoyed themselves by riding and driving, and playing whist and lawn tennis.

Mr. Heineman, who was thoroughly satisfied with the gradual unravelling of the Elmsdale mystery, waited to see the celebration of Carl and Mary's nuptials before returning to Australia.

One morning while the inmates of "The Grove" were wrapped in quiet sleep a visitor appeared, throwing the entire household into surprise and consternation. It was none other than Mr. John Highfield, Mary's father. When the name of this gentleman was announced the entire household donned their garments and rushed down-stairs with incredible rapidity to satisfy themselves that they were not victimised by some gigantic hoax.

Mary stood awe-stricken, but Carl's face shone with unmistakable marks of pleasure as he faced her with the equanimity of the most ardent disciple of Zeno. The young girl did not dare to face her offended father, and so lingered behind, while Carl and the others went forward to meet him. He looked somewhat careworn, and his face was much thinner than it was wont to be; and yet the pleasant smile which hung upon his lips indicated that the bitterness of his heart had somewhat softened.

Mary had secured a coign of vantage, whence she could observe the scenes which were about to transpire. Her heart throbbed violently within her as she looked upon the face of her father, and her extremities became icy cold.

"A hearty welcome to you, Mr. Highfield," was the greeting that Carl extended to the newcomer in a clear, manly voice, at the same time holding out his hand, which John Highfield grasped eagerly.

"May God bless you, my son!" was the affectionate reply, while further efforts to speak were stifled by sobs.

"And your baggage, Mr. Highfield?" enquired Carl, in a manner that showed the warmth of his welcome.

"The porter is at the door," replied Mr. Highfield.

Carl immediately turned his attention to the impedimenta of the new guest, who meanwhile was undergoing the closest scrutiny by those present. Indeed, John Highfield proved an object of much curiosity to the household at "The Grove."

The Reverend Canon Highfield, although a far-seeing man, never anticipated such a rapid,—and to say the least,—melodramatic reconciliation between Carl and his quondam antagonist. Lindsay's happiness knew no bounds, but still he was puzzled to know what had caused this visit.

"And my daughter, how does she fare?" enquired the interesting old gentleman, as Carl returned and sat by his side.

"Oh, as well as possible," put in the Canon, who was just recovering from his astonishment.

But what were the feelings of poor Mary at this supreme moment? Well-nigh indescribable. She was experiencing one of those remarkable moods when the mind drinks in the honey of pleasant emotions in which cruel drops of gall, springing from painful recollections, suddenly fall with evil effect. Ah, how memory recalled that last outburst of her irascible parent, when he mercilessly drove her from under his roof! From that moment the iron had entered her soul and had continued to crush her down to the earth. "May the just judgment of Heaven repay your disobedience!" These were the words that had doomed her to a life of gloom, —and they had never been effaced from her memory. And was this the crisis of the just judgment of heaven? Then, truly she needed no more weighty evidence to convince her of the righteousness of her cause, if Heaven dispenses its punishments commensurate with the gravity of the sins committed by mortals!

And it was this thought that ultimately took possession of Mary and caused her to rush boldly into her father's arms. She could not account for his presence there at that moment, nor could she imagine what was the cause of the change in his disposition, but she feared not the consequence of her impulsive action.

The old man pressed his child to his heart. There was something awe-inspiring in the deep, impressive silence,—a silence that seemed to suggest the hallowed presence of some smiling angel registering the reconciliation of paternal and filial love.

As days wore on, old Highfield found himself quite at home among his new circle of friends.

Carl took the first opportunity to intimate to his curious and anxious companions that before leaving Trinidad he had made arrangements with his solicitor to call upon Mr. Highfield with a view of offering to assist him in his unenviable pecuniary embarrassment by winding up affairs with his creditors.

There is truth in the old saying, "Any port in a storm." The haughty old patrician had stooped to earth in order to gather strength and so avoid inevitable disgrace, and probable suicide. The estates that Rita had generously bequeathed to Carl were mortgaged for eleven thousand pounds. This amount was handed over to Mr. Highfield, without security, which entirely released him from his creditors and started him afresh with his valuable properties untrammelled.

And now the old man's heart swelled and was ready to burst with gratitude and love for his generous benefactor. His visit to "The Grove" had a dual purpose, —to enjoy the satisfaction of seeing his daughter united to the man who had saved him, and to settle for good all business relationships between them. But there were other surprises awaiting him, which he little anticipated. When Carl was reproved by his friends for his extreme reticence in the matter, with a smile he quoted the scriptural text:

" 'A man full of words shall not prosper upon the earth.' "

CHAPTER XLII

*Can comeliness of form or shape or air
With comeliness of words or deeds compare?*

Mr. Highfield and Carl were sitting together one afternoon in a cool spot in the beautiful gardens which surrounded "The Grove," when Carl took the opportunity to introduce the subject of their business relationship.

"I was greatly gratified," said he, "to gather from your correspondence that you had no difficulty in settling your affairs, my dear Mr. Highfield."

"Yes, indeed; and how generous it was of you to come to my rescue just at the time when I was on the brink of a most dangerous precipice! Those villainous money grabbers seemed to have steeled their hearts and would not listen to reason. They were bent upon sacrificing my estates at just one-fifth of their value. I assure you, my dear young man, that had my properties been thus confiscated I do not think I would have had the courage to live on. There is a divinity which shapes our end. Never for a moment could I have imagined that my deliverance would have come from this direction. The shock was too much for me, and I was almost overcome with joy and amazement."

"Oh, do not refer to that, my dear sir! You will sufficiently compliment me and repay me if you will but permit me to think that I only did my duty."

"Never mind, I shall never cease to thank you as my saviour; if I pay you compliments, they are sincere though feeble expressions of my gratitude. But, to business! As you are aware, according to your suggestions Mr. Frost secured eleven thousand pounds, at eight per cent, on your properties. This has entirely liquidated my debts. Now, as you have appointed me your attorney, and placed entire confidence in me to the extent of declining to take any securities, I propose to make the following suggestions. I shall manage your properties to the best of my ability without exacting a single farthing from you. They are in a position to pay for their care, and the handsome proceeds realized will be banked in your favor. My own properties will be worked with every possible care and economy so as to pay the interest on the loan and secure the principal, which I have calculated to pay off in half the allotted time, providing for contingencies and the fall of prices. I do not know what your future movements may be, but you will be in a position to live like a real Monte Cristo from the proceeds of your lucky windfall and still accumulate a handsome fortune. I cannot refrain from complimenting you on your remarkable career. Heaven has been most lavish to you in its gifts, and from your humble position has raised you to the seat of princes. But this has been your destiny.

"There must, after all, be some truth in the ancient doctrine of transmigration. Your exalted character has been apparent to all who have known you, and though I once pretended to ignore it, I must now confess it. I don't want to play the philosopher, but your ego, for aught I know, may have once animated the clay of a Plato who spurned the munificent gifts of

Denis and begged for books, or that of Xenocrates who refused to accept Alexander's gold because the royal donor had greater need of it.

"Charles V stooped to pick up the brush of Titian, Francis de Medici uncovered his head to the immortal Michaelangelo, and I, John Highfield, make way for the low-born youth whose genius and magnanimity overpower me; and my daughter's hand I confer upon him with the fervour of my heart, and consider that in accepting her he does me honour."

The expression "low-born" caused a smile to flit across Carlito's face. He remembered Béranger's verses bearing that title, and some striking reflections passed through his mind. The time had come for him to convince Mr. Highfield that he was not altogether as low-born as the old man thought, and drawing from his pocket a copy of *The Chronicle*, which was still extant, he handed it to his companion, with the request that he would read a somewhat lengthy article that was marked with blue pencil.

This important article embraced the whole history of the Elmsdale affair. It began with personal reminiscences of the Woodhouse family, which were flattering and almost panegyric; then dealt with the entire details, from the night of the fatal ball up to the arrest of Mr. McIntyre. Nothing was forgotten, no incident was omitted that would enhance the interest of the extraordinary chain of romantic mysteries. The whole of McIntyre's confession was there, and Mr. Highfield's astonishment was overwhelming as he read the following, which we produce to gratify the reader's curiosity:

THE CONFESSION OF GEORGE McINTYRE, THE ATROCIOUS MURDERER AND USURPER

Standing as I do upon the threshold of the eternal world, whence I shall not return, I, George McIntyre, prompted by a sense of regret for my mortal crimes which blacken my soul and blot out even the last vestige of manhood, do make these revelations, with the hope that the consciousness of having done some good, by exposing to the world of the unwary my life of crime and its just consequences, may produce some calm in the stormy state of my mind.

It was I who put an end to the useful, benevolent, inoffensive life of my cousin, Burleigh Woodhouse; these blood-stained hands were urged by craft and envy to lift themselves against the man who was my best friend. He had always loved me, and I in turn hated him for his love, and meditated destruction. A most favourable opportunity occurred on the fatal night of the ball, a night contemplated by my cousin in which to make me and others happy, but which I hailed with inexpressible delight, because I knew it would be favourable to my scheme, when reason would be clouded by champagne. My impatience ran high when others were enjoying themselves. I feigned illness, and so appealed to the sympathetic nature of poor Woodhouse. He accompanied me outside the ball room with the intention of giving me remedies, but I induced him to go with me to a dark spot under a lime tree, and there, with an iron stake, which now lies in a wooden chest in my private room at Elmsdale, where not a living soul has entered since I took possession of the property, I performed the heinous deed which stamps me a foul murderer. The revolver which was discovered near my cousin's corpse and which everybody thought was the instrument of suicidal death, was as innocent as heaven;—it was only a ruse that worked splendidly. It only occurred to the far-seeing Hugh Highfield that no report of firearms was heard on the fatal night. This was a thought which unnerved me at the time of the tragedy, since suspicion pointed to me. If this key had been utilized, the consequences might have been different, and retribution less tardy.

I had collected all materials which Satanic artifice could devise to make it appear suicide through the infidelity of his wife with young Highfield. (Ah monstrous, diabolic lie!) The innocent victim was thus deprived of all claim on her husband's estates. I forged a document making myself the sole beneficiary of the deceased and placed it in his pocket after I had killed him, with the famous letter to his widow leaving no doubt of her guilt. This letter was another masterpiece of iniquity. The sensation it caused at the inquest was marvellous. And after all, what was it?

A simple paragraph cut out from a manuscript of dramatic excellence which Woodhouse had written. The name of the prominent female character was neatly erased and "Edith," Mrs. Woodhouse's Christian name, inserted instead. I had thoughtlessly and injudiciously imparted information of my cousin's suicide to young Robert Heineman of the *Chronicle* quite early, and while in a state of excitement. This afterwards greatly obstructed my plans; but I managed to wriggle through. I sent the unsuspecting youth to Melbourne, to an imaginary firm with whom I was supposed to be connected, after giving him valuable pecuniary assistance. I had foreseen that he would have been honest enough to confess that I had supplied him with the matter for the sensational article which appeared in the *Chronicle,* and my plans would have been subverted, and I perhaps ruined. I had long forgotten him when he reappeared with the rest of my pursuers to hound me to the death.

After I came into possession of my ill-gotten gains, my next thought was to put mother and son out of my way. I asked Mrs. Woodhouse to permit me to send the boy Carl to Mr. Kuhner's Grammar School, and enlisted the Rev. Mr. Fairley's mediation to induce her to do so. The suggestion had the effect of a red rag before an enraged bull. It was well she did not give her consent, for I had been preparing a scheme to capture the child and strangle him. I hired two brigands and paid them in gold, bright tempting gold, for this purpose. Failing this, the resourceful villains, who were none other than Hawkie and Dick Ray (who lately took his own life), hit upon another plan. Providence seemed to have specially guarded the victims of my vengeance, and I trembled when I knew they were soon to leave for Trinidad under the protection of the smart young student, Hugh Highfield, and thus thwart my designs.

Hawkie and Dick Ray made a raid on the schooner, although I was at the time unaware of their schemes. They succeeded in capturing both mother and son. They brought me a massive gold ring which I knew belonged to Mrs. Woodhouse, and in this I recognized the token of the success of their adventure. I wanted no further proof to assure me that they had perished, and I gave the brigands another handsome sum.

The shock which Carraciolo's corpse caused to Nelson's crew was as nothing compared to my dismay and indescribable agony when I became convinced that my intended victims had been preserved through all vicissitudes to take vengeance on me. How it is, or by what miracle they still continue to live, I do not know.

May the good man whom I wronged and accused of adultery with one of the purest of women forgive me as he expects to be forgiven. It was I who impressed upon Rev. Fairley that Hugh

Highfield was guilty of this misdemeanor, and Mr. Fairley, having sternly censured him for the offense in his indignation, I got my deserts in a good horse-whipping. This humiliation, which I suffered, people do not generally know.

Long years ago I threw away the key to the private room I have spoken of. I could not bear to come near it, much less to enter it, for it contains that cruel instrument which made me a murderer. You must break the door to effect an entrance.

And now all is finished. Nemesis has pronounced judgment, and I go to reap my reward. Farewell!

Mr. Highfield's astonishment after the reading of this document can better be imagined than described. He now felt thoroughly satisfied of the wisdom of consenting to the marriage of his daughter and Carl. His interest in his prospective son-in-law became more intense as he thought of his remarkable career, and he felt pierced to the heart that he had so bitterly opposed him. Henceforth he vowed to do all in his power to promote his happiness and thus atone for his past uncharitableness by unabating evidences of kindly devotion and paternal solicitude.

CHAPTER XLIII

Be slow to judge, and slower to despise.
Oliver Wendell Holmes.

THE heir of Elmsdale had come into possession of his own. High and low, rich and poor, hailed with delight the installation of this hero whose checkered and adventurous career appeared more mythical than real. They had all seen the victory of virtue over vice, the triumph of right over wrong. Carl was the central figure of the day, and while he was greeted on all sides with sincere congratulations, George McIntyre's memory was clouded with curses and condemnations.

Carl was very happy. His conscience was pure, his mind was ever turning toward the sublime, the beautiful, and the good, and his generous heart was full of the milk of human kindness. The glowing sympathy that he received from his friends and acquaintances enhanced his delight, and to crown all, he was looking eagerly toward that day when Mary Highfield and he should be united.

It was not known outside of his immediate circle of friends who accompanied him to Montserrat that Miss Highfield was his chosen bride. The announcement of the banns was deferred for at least a couple of months until all should have regained their equilibrium and the excitement should have subsided.

Mary and Mrs. Woodhouse were the guests of Mrs.

THE SWORD OF NEMESIS

Lindsay, while the rest of the party enjoyed themselves at Elmsdale Mansion.

The old conservative mode of life and manners was again resumed by the genial host, and this was manifest to all. The Rev. Mr. Fairley, though much advanced in years, still continued his ministrations, and it was with evident joy that he congratulated Carl on the satisfactory turn that events had taken.

Judge Mapleton, an old aristocrat, who had retired with honor from a judicial career extending over thirty years, and who had been a warm friend of the Woodhouse family, manifested his appreciation of Carl's homecoming by proposing a picnic on one of his estates in honor of his interesting young friend. The scheme was taken up with animation, and several distinguished persons were invited.

Judge Mapleton was a widower. His wife had died several years ago, leaving him a pretty little daughter who had developed into a charming young girl on whom he doted. He was immensely rich, and this fact had induced many a courtly cavalier to pay his respects to Daphne Mapleton and sue for her heart and hand, but with no success.

The day of Judge Mapleton's picnic arrived. Mrs. Lindsay and Canon Highfield had the honor of driving with the Judge in his stately carriage, while winsome ladies and gay young cavaliers on finely caparisoned horses enjoyed the journey to the picturesque Broderick plantation.

Miss Highfield was accompanied by Mr. Dyett, a gallant youth, who had already distinguished himself by winning the enviable position of first treasury officer in the island. Dyett was lavish in his attention to the handsome young girl by whose side he rode, and did all in his power to contribute to her happiness.

Daphne Mapleton was accompanied by the young heir of Elmsdale, and it was manifest that she was experiencing great pleasure in Carl's company.

The journey to Broderick's was most delightful. Away from the hustle and bustle of the town, the party now looked upon scenes that charmed and impressed all. They were riding over a sandy beach; below lay the sapphire ocean, gilded by the rays of the morning sun which appeared magnificent as it encircled in its friendly arms the cosy little emerald island. The playful breakers at intervals lashed the shore, bringing with them sea-shells and marine animals which lay calmly and peacefully upon the sand, scintillating with the glory with which the sunlight so gorgeously bedecked them. Cocoanut trees lined the route, while at a certain point branches of the poisonous manchineel formed a high arch above. Passing through varied scenes, which more and more interested them, they at last arrived at their destination. After an hour's rest, followed by a sumptuous lunch, a ramble was made over the plantation.

Judge Mapleton was intoxicated with delight; his large heart was full to overflowing as he observed the young people heartily enjoying themselves.

But Mary Highfield and Carl Woodhouse were ill at ease, although both labored strenuously to conceal their mental torture. Carl, who was the very soul of gallantry, seemed to grow more attentive to Miss Mapleton. Even though he went to extremes which were likely to give birth to some wrong impressions in Daphne's heart and to arouse suspicion of his love for her, he nevertheless considered himself justified in doing this so as to avoid a betrayal of the unhappiness he was experiencing. Dyett did not know that Carl had any special claims upon Mary, nor had Daphne the least suspicion that her companion was deeply in love with another as they strode arm in arm around the plantation.

It was merely incidental that Miss Highfield and Carl were separated on the journey, but they both thought that on arriving at Broderick's they would have been reunited and so enter with high hopes into the pleasures and enjoyment of the day. Instead of this, however, Dyett became distinctly infatuated with Mary and was bent upon monopolizing all her time, while Daphne's manifest preference for Carl placed him in a quandary from which he could not easily extricate himself. Whenever Carl came in contact with his affianced he endeavoured to reassure her of his constancy by saying some tender and pretty things that he thought would interest her, while the smile of love hung on his lips. His discomfort was not occasioned by the thought that he would be dethroned by Dyett from the place he held in Mary's heart. No, for his faith in his love was unshaken. It was the longing he had to be by her side that made him miserable. He felt anxious to renew his vows of affection amidst these wild and charming scenes. Oh, how he wished that, hand in hand, and with heart and pulses beating with the rapture of love, they could drink in together the marvellous beauty above, beneath, and around them. On mountain heights were heard the wood-doves' cooing notes of love; in the sloping valleys the picturesque canefields were being wafted by the kindly breezes of perpetual summer, as they chanted their mysterious music that fell like a sweet lullaby upon the ear.

As the day wore on, Carl's disappointment became more intense, and a sudden revelation seemed to dawn upon him. It was on an occasion when Daphne and he were standing by a beautiful pond in which glittering fish were darting to and fro. The golden rays of sunshine fell upon the surface of the shimmering water and reflected the images of the pair as they stood upon the bank. Daphne had never before looked so charming as she did at that moment. Carl glanced from the gilded surface of the water into the face of the young girl standing before him. She was tall and slender, with a figure as graceful as it was faultless. Her complexion was of that beautiful brown which is so characteristic of Eastern people, but not uncommonly seen in the West Indies,—a result of miscegenation. Her eyes were as dark as midnight and shaded by delicately pencilled eyebrows; her nose and lips were so well proportioned and moulded in such exquisite forms that they not only imparted beauty to the face, but gave it an expression of dignity and sweetness. Her hair was tastefully arranged in the latest fashion and held together by a jewelled comb, while a broad clear brow added strength and vigor to the already fascinating beauty.

"What a fairy queen indeed!" mused Carl. "But I am proof against her charms, since my heart belongs to Mary Highfield and to her alone. Were it otherwise, I should scarcely have been able to resist them. How I wish she were my sister, my own dear little sister."

"What are you thinking of, Carl?" said Daphne, as she recognized his preoccupation.

"I am wishing you were my sister,—if I must confess."

"Only your sister?" said Daphne suggestively. "Then I shall consent to be that and enjoy the advantages which a sister can claim at the hands of a dear brother like you."

She drew nearer to Carl and placed her hand in his. Carl drew her toward him and put his arm around her.

"Dear sweet sister," he said, "do not forget the pledge we have made this afternoon. I shall always expect to have the privileges and the confidence of a brother."

He had just withdrawn his arm when he discovered that this little innocent act of his was observed by Mary, who was approaching with Dyett. As she drew near, Carl became convinced that the green-eyed monster had intruded upon the scene, for he observed in Mary's eyes an expression that startled him and chilled his very life blood. He had rated her high above the mean and unwholesome sentiment of jealousy, and as far as he was concerned was he not justified in doing so, since her experiences of him were enough to warrant the conviction of his profound stability in love? Could it be possible, he thought, that this erudite young girl, —whose brilliant intellect had fed upon the very best pabulum which the labours of philosophers and *savants* of ancient and modern times could afford,—should fall a prey to jealousy? Surely she has by this time learned to probe deeper into human nature than the ordinary illiterate woman, and to discriminate between the hypocrisy of a spurious love and that enduring affection which springs from the heart.

Poor Carl! his ideas of the nature of a woman's love were sadly defective. He did not realize that the instincts which draw together the opposite sexes are closely interwoven with the physical phenomena of their constitution and will always seek to gain the mastery, even though the higher self may strive to temper and subjugate them. Jealousy, selfishness, and suspicion seem to be dominant principles of our animal nature, and Carl's philosophy had not yet taught him this.

Dyett was looking at the arms of the old windmill, performing their continual revolutions as the strong wind from the hillsides struck them, while the massive rollers mercilessly devoured one after the other the fagots of sugar cane with which they were fed by the labourers. Mary, too, was viewing the same sight, but her thoughts were far away.

"You seem to love the old windmill," said Daphne, placing her arms lovingly around Mary's waist, as girls are wont to do. "Mr. Woodhouse also is very much interested in the quaint old structure. The wild and beautiful scenes of Broderick have quite fascinated him, and he would like to live among them all his life, he says. Did you not say so, Mr. Woodhouse?" turning to Carl. "What do you think of this, Mary? Are you, likewise, charmed?"

Carl had not replied to Daphne and was awaiting with some anxiety Mary's answer.

The latter did not speak for some moments. She was making an effort to control the choking sensations in her throat, and to subdue the beating of her heart. Having somewhat regained her self-control, she said:

"I do not doubt the possibility of Mr. Woodhouse's making Broderick his future home. That seems to depend upon himself."

Carl looked at her with amazement, a thrilling sensation passing through his entire frame. He was hurt to the quick as he considered the purport of these words. These were the fruit of his indiscretion and impulsiveness, and he actually scorned himself at that moment. He gave another puzzled glance at Mary, who seemed to realize the pain she had caused him, for a cloud of regret fell over her face.

It was evident that the meaning of Mary's words was not apparent to Daphne. She understood that her friend had implied a purchase of her father's estate, by Carl, and so replied:

"My father would not part with Broderick for a million pounds. It is the best of his properties, and is intimately associated with his family history."

Mary tried to look pleased as they strolled some distance away.

"I agree," she said, "that Broderick is a delightful place, and I, too, think I would be happy in making my home here in this fairyland."

It was toward sunset, and they were standing on a hillock whence they could view the landscape stretching far away toward the sea. The air was redolent of the scent of mignonette and geranium. The cattle, from whose necks the yoke had just been removed after their day of toil, were lying down lazily in the fields. Flocks of sheep were browsing upon the hillsides, and the toil-worn labourers were preparing to be gone.

"It's time we, too, were going," said Dyett. "We do not wish that darkness should overtake us on the way! We shall carry away with us pleasant reminiscences of this happy day we have spent together; shan't we, Miss Highfield?"

Mary looked up confusedly, then glanced at Carl, who was not less perplexed. The situation became still more critical as Daphne, with an air of womanly sweetness, her eyes beaming with liquid fire, which at that moment seemed to burn more intensely than ever, pinned a nosegay to the lapel of Carl's coat.

"Won't you wear this, Carl," she said, "in memory of this enjoyable day. You will remember me whenever you look at it, I am sure."

An indescribable, magnetic influence shot through Carl's frame. He felt the deft fingers resting upon his bosom, and he wondered why such marvellous sensations should have seized him. He had some experience in the various phenomena of human passions, but this was altogether novel.

"That's right, de la Mar," said Dyett tauntingly, after Daphne had finished her pleasant task. "I knew the boy Cupid has been very busy to-day. I am a very acute observer, don't you know. I know, too, that 'love and murder will out.'"

"What do you mean, Mr. Dyett, by your sarcasm?" put in Daphne, the hot, red blood rushing to her cheeks and betraying her embarrassment. "Can I not perform the duty which is peculiar to my sex,—namely, to increase the pleasure and happiness of another by some little evidence of appreciation springing from our natural inclination to please?"

"This is one of Cupid's little tricks, of course, Miss Mapleton. Your peculiar appreciation on this occasion seems to me the more suggestive in that, although there are flowers in profusion at Broderick, I have not been the recipient of any such marked token of regard."

And he laughed a meaning and suggestive laugh, looking meanwhile from Daphne towards Mary.

"I have seen Miss Mapleton present flowers to other gentlemen besides myself," said Carl, to whom the position was becoming embarrassing.

THE SWORD OF NEMESIS 299

"But not with such grace and evident delight," replied the sarcastic Dyett.

Jealousy was gnawing spitefully at the very centre of Mary's heart, while Carl was wishing that the situation, so unpleasant and undesirable for him, would change and relieve him of the cruel tortures that he was undergoing.

Providence happily declared in his favor, for in another moment there appeared on the scene Canon Highfield and the Judge.

"Why, we have hunted in every corner for the ramblers this whole afternoon without success," said Judge Mapleton, "and now that we have found you, we will stick to our prisoners. You have had enough of these woodlands and of these girls' company, my gallant knights-errant, and you will now leave it to the older chaps to entertain them with a drink good enough for the immortal gods. We would recommend for each of you young gentlemen a stimulating cocktail, which would give you courage to resume the journey homeward."

The two elder gentlemen accompanied the girls into the boiling-house where the sugar was being manufactured, and treated them with the delightful beverage known to the natives as "hot liquor," which was drawn from the steaming cauldron by an obsequious old plantation hand.

The journey homeward was without adventure. Some went home to dream about the pleasant intercourse they had held with wild nature and of their new experiences; others thought with delight of the convivial manners of their host and of his incessant desire to enhance their enjoyment; but there were two women and two men around whom some wicked fairy had woven a terrible spell of delusion which was only to be unravelled after a period of pain and suffering.

Carl took every opportunity to dislodge from Mary's mind the terrible suspicion that rested there. He was ever constant in his visits, and his devotion and attentions lacked nothing. But it is no easy task to reëstablish that confidence which fills the breast of a pure, trusting woman for the man whom she adored,—nay, actually worshipped and paid the dearest homage of her life,—when once she has had the slightest reason (rightly or wrongly), to entertain some suspicion of her hero's divided affection.

"You are cold toward me of late," said Carl one day to Mary, as they sat together on the airy balcony of "The Grove." "Do you not love me in the same old way? Since Judge Mapleton's picnic my life has been unhappy, for the warm and serene light of love that once burned in your eyes and set me in rapture, has faded away. Why is this? Can you not remember me as your only beloved, who vowed to love no other woman save you?"

Mary sighed, and Carl drew near and pressed her warm, glowing, vermilion lips with his own, then drew her to his bosom.

"Why do you think I do not care for you?" she said. "I shall always love you; but I cannot rid myself of the nightmare that continues to disturb me, even though I may believe that you are as pure and true as the sunbeams. I cannot help thinking of that unhallowed day that I saw you with your arms around Daphne Mapleton's waist, when I observed the gleam of delight that flushed her face with pride, nor can I easily forget the picture of that moment when she stood before you arrayed in all the power and charms of that rich beauty with which nature has so lavishly crowned her. I must confess that she is lovely,—we are as much alive to the beauty of our sex as members of the opposite sex. I hated her at that instant when I saw her fastening a nosegay to your coat, and I have since wondered from what unknown depth of my nature such a manifestation of savage instincts could have sprung. But we are human, Carl,—intensely human."

"Would it were possible for me to obliterate that unhappy incident from your memory, my angel! Let me once more implore your pardon. It was a thoughtless act, and had not its origin in such love as ours."

"Then, whence did it come?" And Mary's face assumed an appearance of pain that quite startled Carl. "I saw you looking into Daphne's eyes with that burning intensity, that exquisite tenderness, which I once thought was exclusively reserved for me."

"That may have been so. I will not deny a truth so evident to you, yet it was nothing more than the endeavour to reciprocate with the sympathy of a brother the innocent, hallowed, and childlike affection which I saw was in Daphne's heart for me. It was under this influence of sympathy that I acted so indiscreetly."

At this juncture Carl's breast was throbbing with emotion, and intuitively Mary discerned the storm that was raging within him.

"My darling," she said, "I believe you with all my heart! Your very candour has shamed me; and I now repay you with a thousand kisses for allowing an unnecessary thought against you to enter my breast. But take care, my only Carl, take care of what men are pleased to call a 'Platonic love.' This pretty idol, set up in the heart and worshipped by the most lofty souls, has often been mercilessly shattered into a thousand fragments by the batteries of that mysterious force within us for which nature alone is responsible. Beware of the Platonic love!"

She fell upon Carl and kissed him with that passionate love for which he had pined for many days,—and happiness reëntered their lives.

Carl then proposed that the risk of any possible misunderstandings again occuring should be prevented by an early solemnization of their marriage. Mary willingly agreed, and that same evening Carl instructed the Rev. Mr. Fairley to publish the banns of marriage on the following Sunday in the parish Church.

CHAPTER XLIV

> Alas! things are not what they seem,
> Despite their golden glimmer;
> All my fancies were a dream,
> I've seen their dying shimmer.
> *Mrs. N. E. Nelson.*

It was as though a bolt from the blue had suddenly fallen upon the head of Edgar Dyett when for the first time he learned the unwelcome news that Mary Highfield was to become Carl's wife. Life to him seemed suddenly to lose all its charms. In Mary he thought that he had discovered his soul's choice, and upon her his every thought was becoming centered.

In his constant visits to "The Grove" he had noticed Mary's reserved manner and the formal demeanour that she had observed towards him, and though this sometimes made him feel that his task to gain her love, on which he had set his mind, was by no means an easy one, yet being a youth of indomitable courage and perseverance, he had determined to woo and win her. He had seen nothing to indicate a special intimacy between her and Carl, and the way appeared quite open; but now he found that the towering air-castle which he had so ambitiously reared, was ruthlessly undermined and came crashing to the ground with a terrible effect.

In his deep disappointment Dyett became intensely jealous, and this jealousy took the ascendancy of clear, dispassionate reason. It ran riot within him. He accused Carl of dishonor to him, of unnecessary secretiveness, and of other questionable qualities of which he alone seemed to be cognizant. It occurred to him that it was Carl's business to have declared his relationship with Miss Highfield and thus to have saved him the pain of making himself ridiculous. Unfortunate, love-lorn lad. Blame him not, dear reader; such are the fallacies of human reason when our spirits are crushed to earth, when we find ourselves unhappily thrown into conditions whereby our haughty, human pride is made to suffer humiliation, and to drain the bitter cup of disappointment!

One afternoon Carl called at the Treasury to have a chat with Dyett, as he had done previously on several occasions. He was surprised at the reception given him by his friend.

"I will be glad if you cease coming to annoy me in my work, sir. This is the King's duty, and I will not be interrupted."

Carl laughed at this outburst, which he interpreted as a strenuous effort on the part of Dyett to be ultra-humorous.

"You cannot scare me, Edgar; try another ruse," said he.

"I am really not joking, my dear sir. If you have any business to settle, do so at once, or I will put you through the window."

Carl at this juncture saw an unusual flash of wicked fire in the determined eyes of Dyett, and his mind intuitively told him that things were really looking serious. He stood for a moment silent, his limbs trembling and his heart beating rapidly. He was not precipitate in either word or deed, and always waited to justify himself in any procedure he might think it necessary to adopt.

The silence was broken by Dyett.

"I wish to know, sir, whether you have any business at the office," he reiterated imperatively, approaching Carl, with venom in his eye.

"I have no business, Mr. Dyett. I am, however, surprised at your conduct. I thought you were joking at first, but I now see you are in earnest. You have always posed as a man of candour, and it seems to me a pity that you have not given me the opportunity of knowing what offense I have given you. It must be something very grave that has led you to play the part of an untutored savage."

"I had rather be an untutored savage than a civilized hypocrite; you who have been coming here and speaking to me as a confidential friend might have been honest enough to say that you were in love with Miss Highfield. We have spoken about this young lady on several occasions. I hinted to you my deep regard for her, and you never gave me the simplest notion that you have been all the time getting ready to be married. Is there anything manly or friendly in such covert action?"

"My dear sir," said Carl in a tone of evident anger, and with fixed determination on his lips; "I had given you credit for much more common sense. Let me begin by saying that, although I once thought myself justified in accepting you as a friend, I never for a moment imagined that there was that bond between us that would entitle you to a knowledge of my private affairs. If I thought to keep my espousal to Miss Highfield secret for reasons best known to us both, I cannot see that I have in any way offended the ethics of casual acquaintanceship. And, further, such talk as yours is nonsense,—simply puerile in a man of your age. I should have expected this from a boy of ten or twelve. You are simply making yourself ridiculous."

Thereupon Carl turned away from his aggressive friend. As he was going down the flight of steps that led to the street, he looked back upon the youth, who had retired to a corner, where he was leaning over a desk, with his hand sustaining his chin and a look of utter desperation upon his face.

Carl was disturbed over this unhappy conflict, and made his way to the house of his friend Zac, where he hoped to find in the old man's wit and pleasantries an effectual antidote for the present condition of his mind.

Zac had been provided with a comfortable home at Elmsdale, where he got the very best that could be provided for him. He had passed the three-score-years-and-ten span allotted to mankind, and was looking toward joining the great majority. The residents of Elmsdale treated him with marked kindness, and his liberty was not circumscribed. Mrs. Lindsay and her husband were unfailing in their solicitude for his comfort.

As Carl was approaching the door he saw at some distance before him little Dora, the five-year-old daughter of Mrs. Lindsay, carrying a basket containing the dainty dinner which came from "The Grove" every day for the old man. The delicate cherub voice of the child, with its ringing music of lisping monosyllables, the charming mellowed inflections peculiar to that tender period of life, fell delightfully upon Zac's ears.

"Tumming with Zac's dinner," said the little one.

The old man arose from his chair and approached the door with manifest joy. A bright light came over his face as he saw the child, and her pretty little voice again enriched the air with its melody. A thrill of delight went through Zac's frame. His heart was centred in this little blossom of humanity whose presence semed to rekindle the vital sparks that were fast ebbing away in him, and his love and complete devotion to her was as beautiful as it was pathetic.

"Do you still love your old Zac?" he asked of the child.

"Oh, yes!" she said. "Zac is so dood; I am going to bring my doll to play with you to-morrow."

"Yes, you must come with the doll, and come oftener, —every day,—because Zac won't be here with you much longer. He is going to Heaven soon."

"No, dear Zac. You must not do 'way from Dora. If you do I will go too."

And the child put up her pretty pink lips against the ebony face, then tightly threw her arms about the old man's neck.

Carl, who from without was witnessing this pretty scene, was so charmed that his mind was completely diverted from his recent quarrel. On entering the room, he said:

"Hello, Zac. I guess you want to steal Dora from her parents. She never seems so happy as when she is perched upon your knee."

"Thank the Lord, Mars Carl! For this dear little life I would give my own were it worth anything. Of course you know my mortal coil is only good enough now to fertilize the earth, and nothing else; so if I made the sacrifice it would be nothing. But when I was like you, sir, I would have thought it an honor to die for this little angel."

"Zac, would you give your life for this little white child?" asked Carl.

"Why not, Mars Carl? I cannot understand that a

gentleman of your education would ask such a question. When I was young they used to teach sense at school, but now I think they must be teaching the other thing."

"What other thing, Zac? Surely you do not mean to insinuate that I am talking nonsense?"

And Carl laughed in his accustomed good-natured way. He had come to measure swords with Zac, and he knew that he would be fairly matched.

Zac cleared his throat naïvely, then said:

"Mars Carl, will you have a drink?"

"No, thank you, Zac. Since Dora has such influence over you, I shall tell her to advise you to give up drinking. Dora, will you please ask your friend not to drink?"

The child looked spitefully at Carl, then petulantly blurted out:

"I won't do it. Zac can do what he wants."

"Mars Carl, do you really mean that I must stop drinking? The very angel in this little babe rebukes you."

"Yes, I mean it," replied Carl.

"Then, sir, I must say you are more cruel than I thought. Men in these days are thinking themselves greater than God who made them. If the Almighty say to them walk, they run; if He says stand still, they jump high up in the air; if He says to them drink, and gives for the purpose rivers, wells and streams, the great philosophers like you say 'don't drink!' Well, what must I do? Follow you or my Maker? When you meet old Dives down yonder and he gives you his experience, you will be sorry you ever despised a drink."

"But you are all the time referring to water,—pure,

harmless, water. You did not offer me water,—when I spoke I had alcoholic beverages in mind."

"And because you had your alcoholic beverages in mind you assume that I had them in mind too, don't you? Well, Mars Carl, if I could speak common words and if you were not dear old Massa's son, I would surely tell you what I have in my mind,—and that is that you only want little longer ears and two more feet, to be a pretty specimen. I had thought you were getting choked a while ago and that a glass of water would have done you good."

"Very good, Zac; but you called me an ass!"

"Such a word never escaped my lips this day, I am sure."

"But then you insinuated it."

"I will not swear that you are wrong. Your conscience knows better what you are yourself, and if you think my insinuation is correct, then it's all right."

"But it is not correct."

"I don't know, but I have great faith in the voice of conscience. Two more legs and a little longer ears would have made you a lamb in my mind, for you are indeed a fine young fellow, but as you consider yourself an ass, I have no criticisms to make whatever."

"Very well, Zac; I accept your apology. We are friends once more, aren't we?"

"Always so, Mars Carl."

"I am sure there is something strong in that basket, though."

"Evidently so, as little Dora brings my dinner, and the little angel might chance to fall and break the ware. Mrs. Lindsay does not send over her china, but enamel dishes, which are very strong, I tell you."

Carl went to the basket and mischievously drew out a flask of brandy.

"Aha! Zac, here's brandy! That's what I was talking about all the time. This will harden your arteries and make them become chalky."

"Well, sir, I am glad you have told me that, for even though I were foolish enough to give up my little grog to please foolish people, with this splendid information I get from you at this moment, I am resolved more than ever that I won't give it up. I am so glad that when this mortal coil is put under the earth it will furnish some material with which conscientious schoolmasters, I hope, will write on blackboards for your children and grandchildren better things than fell to your lot."

At this juncture Dora interrupted and called Zac's attention to the savoury dinner on the table.

"Eat your dinner, Zac, and don't bother with Carl. He is too bad."

Zac acquiesced in the demands of his little friend, and turned his attention towards his dinner.

Carl retired, leaving the Professor with the child.

The publication of the banns of marriage between Carl and Mary took the town by surprise. It was a severe blow to Daphne Mapleton, who was deeply in love with Carl, and who had entertained hopes that their close friendship might ultimately have developed into Carl's proposing marriage to her. When the news reached her ears she retired to her room and wept bitterly.

It was at the Judge's dining-table that Carl first met her after the publication of the banns. On that occasion few words were interchanged between them, but there was a pathos in Daphne's eyes, an expression on her countenance which seemed eloquently to rebuke Carl, and to interpret her inward pain.

Carl hardly dared to look into the pleading eyes of the girl; his soul seemed to accuse him of cruelty. He had undoubtedly known that Daphne loved him ardently, and it now appeared to him that he should have taken her into his confidence and let her know his real position. He, however, sought to justify the voice of conscience by the consideration that he had never spoken to her of love or given any encouragement to her overtures. As he bade good-night to Daphne she turned sweetly and, with ringing pathos in her voice, said:

"Won't you come and spend the evening with me, Carl? It may be, perhaps, for the last time. Father and I are going away for an extended holiday. I have something to say to you. I'm sure Miss Highfield will not issue any veto against my request."

Carl could not refuse the invitation. Those dark liquid eyes, so tender and sweet, that shone like two brilliant jewels in the face of the graceful girl, completely magnetized him.

"Yes, certainly, Daphne," he replied; "I will come. At what hour to-morrow evening?"

"I cannot say now, but will write to let you know. We must be alone for a while, and I must take time to consider when that will be most convenient."

Carl pressed her hand tenderly and they parted.

The next day Carl anxiously awaited Daphne's note, but it was not forthcoming. A curious thing, however, happened. One of Judge Mapleton's servants handed him a letter addressed to him in Daphne's writing, but on opening it it was found to be intended for Mary. The letter was as follows:

My dear Mary:

I have to congratulate you on your intended departure from the society of your spinster sisters. I am, however, surprised that you had the heart to keep this secret from me who loved you so much. Come and spend to-morrow with me, and tell me all about it.

Yours,
Daphne.

Carl had foregone the pleasure of accompanying Mary and her father on a visit to one of his plantations that afternoon, in order to keep his appointment with Daphne, and now it seemed as if she did not care to see him, and had perhaps closed her heart against him. Suddenly, however, like a flash of lightning, the thought struck him. Had Daphne made the unfortunate mistake of addressing his note to Mary and hers to him? This seemed a probable solution, but he hoped that it might not be so. With his mind weighted with anxious thoughts he hastened to the Judge's home at eight o'clock that evening. As he approached the gate he suddenly met Daphne, who was impatiently walking up and down the pathway.

"Is that the way you keep your appointment?" she said. "I have been expecting you since seven o'clock."

Carl's heart sank within him.

"I do not understand you," he replied. "I have been waiting all day for your letter, which I have not yet received; so I took it into my head to walk over and see what is the matter. I thought perhaps you had suddenly turned against me and did not wish to have me intrude into your august presence again."

"Fie, Carl! There is certainly a mistake somewhere. I sent two letters off by our groom to Elmsdale this afternoon, one for you and the other for your intended wife."

"Is that so? Then you have made a mess of it.

Oh, horror! You addressed my note to Mary and Mary's to me. This is Mary's; I have it here."

And he took the communication from his pocket and handed it to Daphne.

"O Carl," she exclaimed, "what a fool I have made of myself! I was worried when I wrote and scarcely knew what I was doing. I hope, however, Mary will not think I want to usurp her rights."

"I regret very much this occurrence," replied Carl, "for although there may be nothing savouring of usurpation or direct dishonour in the communication, it may be a means of raising a hornets' nest about my ears. You know very well that women are awfully jealous, and when blinded by this instinct are apt to become unreasonable. Pray, what did you write?"

"It was a very hurried note asking you to meet me under the flamboyant tree in the garden at seven o'clock, when I would tell you what I had to say."

"Enough in itself to arouse suspicion. I, however, hope that Mary knows me too well to lose her faith in me, and will content herself in believing that 'things are not always what they seem.'"

Daphne's face flushed with disappointment and suppressed annoyance. It was evident that Carl's apprehensions and tender appreciation of the feelings of his fiancée so candidly expressed had pierced her heart. Her jealousy began to burn with an overpowering flame, and her womanly pride was hurt. She had known that Carl loved Mary exceedingly well, but that hauteur, that peculiar egoism incidental to the woman who loves, would not allow her mind to dwell upon that thought. She could not fancy herself relegated to a secondary place in the heart of one whom she really loved, although the evidences that pointed to the fact that Mary had the precedence of her were as clear as daylight. She assumed a mask by which she voluntarily blinded herself, and drank in the delightful dreams that spring from unvanquished hope.

"Miss Highfield, it is true," she said, "is your prospective wife, and may at some later day be granted by you the privilege of reading your communications, but I think it is rather early for her to begin. It would have been both honorable and womanly had she given you the letter immediately after she discovered it was not intended for her."

"Be charitable, Daphne. It was not her fault. She had just got into the carriage to go with her father when the servant handed her the letter. It is, therefore, quite possible that she did not open it until she was some distance away from the 'Grove,' for she was deeply engaged in conversation with Mr. Highfield. I saw that she put the letter on the seat beside her, without opening it. I do not think they have returned yet from the country, as they were expected to dinner at nine o'clock. I shall go over to the 'Grove' and see if there be any sign of an impending storm."

"And suppose there be a storm, you would not mind it, eh? Carl, dear, would you?"

They were standing, facing each other, beneath the spreading branches of the lovely flamboyant. The rays of the silver moon shone down upon them through the sea of green and vermilion, and revealed the handsome face of the girl upturned to Carl. The black, lustrous eyes, with the mischievous light of love, seemed to mock with their alluring flame the mild serene beauty of their sister stars twinkling high above them in their milky way.

"I am sure you will not mind the storm, dear Carl,"

reiterated the girl, for her companion had not broken the silence that had followed her words. "If Mary becomes jealous and forsakes you, there are more fish in the sea than ever were caught, are there not? Is not your sister Daphne's love as good as hers?"

"It is quite true that I love you, Daphne; but Mary and I have met and loved under the most peculiar circumstances. I am bound to her by inseparable ties, and it would be terrible indeed if anything should occur to disturb the course of our affection. I would never feel happy after. The obligations that I owe her for her fortitude and implicit faith in me I shall never be able to repay."

"I thought as much, since you have waived the glaring inconsistency of marrying out of your own race. I had hoped that you would have reconsidered this step and looked nearer home; but I am now convinced that nothing in this world will hinder you from carrying out your determination. I summoned you here this evening to unburden my soul to you, and I know your kind heart will forgive my weakness. I at first admired, loved, then adored you,—and my life will henceforth be a dreary blank when I know you must marry another. Since I must abandon my fondest hopes, let me feel that you do not despise me, that you will still keep a warm corner in your heart for me, and I shall be content. One kiss, the first and last from you, dear Carl, shall leave its sweet impress on my lips, and the memory of it shall never be erased from my brain. Even though the fount of your love be reserved for another, I shall always think fondly of you."

Carl was mystified and awe-stricken by the pathos of the girl's words. The melting, faltering voice, so eloquent of her deep feelings, quite unnerved him.

Daphne stood before him like some alluring Venus, whose flaming passion appealed with irresistible power to his virile masculinity. He presented a spectacle of manly beauty. The symmetry of his stalwart frame was unequalled. With broad, well-proportioned shoulders, beautifully rounded, brown neck that supported like an elegant column his finely shaped head, he might have been taken for a statue of Apollo carved out of ebony. Daphne could hardly have escaped the fascination.

It was a supreme moment of struggle to stem the tide of overmastering human passion that came rushing with a mighty irrepressible force through the channels of the flushed senses. The higher self for some moments was entirely submerged. With animation akin to frenzy, Carl placed his arm around Daphne's neck and drew her face toward him. He was in the act of kissing her, but ere their lips met, a mysterious voice seemed instantaneously to reach his ears and to vibrate through his soul. It was the stern voice of conscience, of manhood, of honour, that had suddenly burst its bonds and appeared to utter the words: "Is it thus that you would maintain your honour, Carl? The bridge that you would now so ruthlessly destroy is but the beginning of disaster!"

It was not too late to receive the warning which his good angel brought to him from the eternal heights. Suddenly he turned away his face, and Daphne, with a deathly pallor, placed her arms on his shoulders and leaned on his breast as a support against the tide of emotions that threatened to overwhelm her.

Some moments afterward, on turning away from the garden, their eyes fell upon Mary Highfield retreating with rapid steps through the gate. Suspicion now

THE SWORD OF NEMESIS

seized them both and they wondered if fate had been so unpropitious as to have revealed this little episode of romance to eyes for which they were least intended.

Carl took leave of Daphne and walked rapidly home.

CHAPTER XLV

> Then wedding bells ring out for joy,
> And haste ye sluggard weary hours,
> Ye are the steeds that bear my life
> From barren wastes to blooming bowers.
> *Thos. Bailey Aldrich.*

CARL did not feel in an attitude of mind to meet his fiancée that same evening as he had intended. His equanimity was upset when he left Daphne, and he entertained a premonition of ill. He did not go down to breakfast until late the next morning, and as he entered the dining-room one of the servants handed him on a silver tray a letter, which he opened with great anxiety. Impatiently his eyes ran over the contents, and a painful expression came over his face.

"Gracious goodness!" he exclaimed, "can this be possible? Yet, alas! I am to blame."

He put the missive in his pocket and left the room without tasting the food that awaited him on the table, and went back upstairs to his room. He sat down heavily upon a chair and sighed deeply and sorrowfully, as if some terrible calamity had overtaken him. He once more took the letter from his pocket and read it over and over. It ran thus:

MY DEAR CARL:
  When this comes to your hand you will kindly consider our engagement at an end, and give immediate notice to the Rev. Mr. Fairley to stay the further publication of our banns. I know that this is a very serious step I am taking, but it is not without due

THE SWORD OF NEMESIS 319

deliberation that I have come to the conclusion that the severance of our connection will result to our mutual advantage. I have been an eyewitness to a scene in which you and another woman, —for whom I had entertained a high regard,—were the actors; and I do not know that I could ever again place implicit confidence in any mortal. My unsuspected presence near the place of your love episode was not premeditated, but simply accidental. I say this lest you should accuse me of the vulgarity of eavesdropping. If I had a thousand tongues I could never express the disappointment, pain and wretchedness which burst upon me when I realized that you, whom I regarded as the ideal of true manhood, had so unmistakably revealed your duplicity. I thought I had wronged you a little while ago when I became jealous of her on whom you seemed to be lavishing at least a portion of your affection, but perhaps I was not so far wrong. Do not think me impetuous or cruel, my dear Carl. This step has caused me much pain. Even now, while I write, my soul is steeped in bitterness, but I have no alternative.

You will remember that we had been drawn together by the irresistible influences born of pure devotion and lofty ideals. This sweet dream has now vanished. My idol has turned to clay. You may seek extenuation for your improprieties by pleading frailty and sudden passion. I could not, however, bear to think that you would voluntarily allow yourself to be blinded by such a fallacy. I grant, of course, that we are all human, but I had placed you upon a pedestal so high that it seemed impossible to me you could have made such an unfortunate *détour* from your standard. I think indiscriminate and promiscuous love directly clashes with lofty moral ideas. The one man is the complement of the one woman when they have left the merely carnal stage and risen to life's true plane. The action of diffused rays of light can never be as potent as when these are focused upon one object.

Now that I know you have only half a love for me, which may yet be divided into further fractions, I must emphatically refuse to enter into a contract which in my estimation is too grand and sacred to be made a farce of.

In order to save you the trouble of an explanation, which I deem quite unnecessary, I have decided that I shall not be able to grant you an interview, and believe that this will be kindest for both of us.

MARY HIGHFIELD.

This was a trying time for Carl. His characteristic Spartan philosophy, which had rendered him imperturbable under other serious circumstances, now entirely forsook him. It had taken him some time fully to realize the force and meaning of that decisive communication; and now that all his hopes were shattered and his dreams of happiness with Mary were vanished, a sensation of excruciating agony swept over him, and his very brain and heart seemed crushed by some terrible instrument of torture. Scarcely knowing what he did he rushed out of the house and went over to the "Grove," with a determination of seeing Mary. He discovered that that same indomitable will which had been once exercised on his behalf was now reasserted against him; for, like an impregnable rock, she kept her word and refused to see him. This deepened his misery.

With a candour that left nothing untold, he explained to Lindsay and his wife the circumstances that had resulted in this unfortunate *dénouement*. They offered him their sympathy and promised to exert their influence to bring about a reconciliation which was so essential to complete the joys of the new life upon which he had just entered.

Mr. Highfield was much troubled when his daughter told him of her decision, nevertheless he did not lose his confidence in Carl, and vainly advised Mary not to rush precipitately to conclusions that she might have reason to regret. When Carl learned this it cheered him greatly, as he was anxious to know Mr. Highfield's opinion in the matter. He now felt more confident in approaching this gentleman, whose sympathy he had reason to believe he would be able to secure. He walked into Mr. Highfield's room, and a cordial welcome was extended to him.

A lengthy conversation ensued on the recent unhappy events. Carl took the opportunity completely to unburden his mind. His steady, clear voice manfully expressing the feelings of his heart; his bright eyes glowing with the honest light that told that their owner could not possibly be false; his candour that endeavoured neither to hide his mistakes nor palliate his errors; the strong expressions with which he strenuously defended his honour and sought to establish his innocence, all appealed to Mr. Highfield's sympathy and large experience of the underlying currents of human nature.

"I am convinced more strongly than ever, my dear Carl," said he, "that you are perfectly innocent of the charges that Mary has made against you, and I hope to see a perfect reconciliation brought about, which will make us all happy once more. I shall use all my influence to disabuse Mary's mind of her false conceptions of you."

Carl found himself day after day growing more sad and morose. He drew away entirely from his friends and became painfully taciturn. A picture of Mary hung in his room, and he often stood gazing upon it and sighing from the depths of his bruised heart. She had refused to see him in person, and her picture therefore became dearer and dearer to him. Weeks had passed, and although he had visited the "Grove" frequently, he could never get a glimpse of his unrelenting love.

One afternoon, however, he saw Mr. Dyett and Mary walking across the grounds. They seemed deeply engaged in conversation, and Mary now and then laughed in a melancholy way. It was not that hearty, rich laugh that he was once accustomed to hear with so much pleasure,—merely an apology for it. This, however, did not impress Carl so strongly as did the fact that she should be in such close companionship with the man who had become his open enemy. The warm blood rushed to his brain. His heart throbbed angrily against his chest, and if he had given way to his desperate feelings, he would have rushed upon Dyett and throttled him on the spot. He knew well that this young coxcomb had now secured the opportunity he had long and earnestly sought for, and so could now have everything his own way. The thought simply maddened him.

Carl observed, to his further chagrin, that the intimacy between these two became closer each day. They indulged in afternoon rides together, and together they played lawn tennis and croquet. Matters assumed such a suspicious appearance that it was soon rumoured about that young Dyett had won the heart that Carl prized so dearly.

Carl had now reached a depth of misery that baffles description. He left Elmsdale early each morning and worked among the managers and overseers of his plantations, returning late at night. This did not, however, help him to escape from his burdened thoughts. One night as he stood before Mary's picture, gazing at it with burning, anxious eyes, he indulged in musings such as this:

"My dearest girl, perhaps if it were possible for me to hate you I could then determine to live on in this world and find my Eden in another woman's love, but, alas! I cannot hate you. O my God, it is true,—I cannot hate her! I must therefore face death and be released from the trammels which weigh down my every moment. I do not blame you, my high-souled girl, for your conception of virtue and honour, but I blame you for so cruelly locking your heart against me, without giving me a chance to establish my innocence. If you would but let me explain, all would be right."

He went to his iron safe that stood in a corner, opened it and took out a loaded revolver, which he held for some moments in his hand. The cold steel glistened fiercely. Its withering aspect excited fear and horror.

"Shall I do it now?" said the half-maddened youth, as his eyes glared with an unearthly light. He stood for a moment seeming to halt between two opinions. Then, as if a sudden inspiration had taken possession of him, he exclaimed:

"Great Heavens! what a fool I am making of myself. Has my Christian fortitude forsaken me? It would be cowardice in me to die. I shall live and fight manfully against this terrible ordeal, and time will heal my wounds, for God is just and good. 'Bettter bear the ills we have than fly to others that we know not of.' "

He therefore carefully unloaded the instrument of death, went downstairs, and threw it into the fire. He gave up all thought of marrying Mary Highfield, and with the banishment of this hope he gradually became more cheerful and once more entered the society of his friends, to find soon that the kind hand of time was healing his wounded heart.

Whenever he met Mary and Mr. Dyett together he found that his anger and jealousy had become greatly modified, and he lifted his hat with grace and apparent good will. On these occasions he noticed that Mary's face always wore a pained expression, which he interpreted as an index of some inward disquiet.

One day after he had been entertained with the rich fund of comedy and wit which profusely sprung from Zac's versatile brain, they both went toward the Elmsdale gate that opened upon the street. At the side of the road stood a huge tamarind tree, and between it and St. Alban's Church there was the path which immediately led from the highway to the rectory. A runaway horse, ridden by a lady, was speeding down the road toward this spot. As the animal drew nearer they saw that the rider was Miss Highfield, who was making desperate efforts to control it, but with little effort, and it seemed evident that she would be dashed to pieces against the tree.

Just at this moment little Dora Lindsay, who had not seen the runaway horse, appeared on the road, with Zac's basket on her tiny arm. Her life was imperilled; yet many who saw her position thought only of their own safety and fled with all their might to places of refuge, while Dyett, who was on his way to the rectory, joined the fleeing crowd. The bent, aged form of Zac, inspired with almost superhuman strength for one so advanced in years, recked not the danger. The life of his little friend, the darling of his declining years, was in imminent peril, and he must save her though he perish in the attempt. He ran into the road and caught up the child in his arms. Dora had now realized her position, for the horse was but a few yards away. Another moment's delay and she would have lain a trampled, bleeding corpse upon the ground. The faithful old man achieved his purpose, but as he placed the child down in safety he fell exhausted upon the pavement.

Mary's life was evidently jeopardized, for the horse was about to bolt into the rectory. One of two things seemed imminent,—either that the horse would run against the tree and dash her to pieces, or fling her upon the ground in making the sudden turn.

But so unhappy an event was averted.

Carl ran into the road to save the girl whom he still loved. Like Hercules of old, he stood undaunted, imperturbable, a hero of heroes. His dark, handsome face was set as if in granite; his rigorous heart beat anxiously within him, and the stout muscles of his stalwart frame stood boldly out to support him.

The horse, with its terrified rider, dashed fiercely along and was about to make the sudden turn when Carl threw up his brawny arms, and with a vigorous display of strength and agility caught the reins, suddenly arresting the progress of the recalcitrant steed.

A breathless silence ensued; for those who had been looking at the scene were overcome with fright. This was, however, followed by a loud hurrah in honour of Carl's manly act. He stood for some moments holding the reins, when Mr. Dyett, among others, came up and tendered his congratulations.

Mary could hardly utter a word, so overcome was she with terror. Carl led the now quieted animal into the rectory grounds, and with the grace of a polished cavalier, helped Mary to dismount. The dignity of his demeanour and the quiet formality that he observed were crushing to the young girl, whose heart smote her bitterly for her obduracy. One of Mr. Fairley's servants came forward and led the horse away, whereupon Carl courteously bowed to Mary and turned away without a word.

"But you have not waited for me to thank you, Carl. You are really so good to have thus jeopardized your life for me."

"Oh, don't mention it, Miss Highfield. It was simply a duty."

He looked back upon the pale, lovely face and smiled, then continued on his way to the gate.

As Mary stood transfixed on the curbstone where she had alighted, she presented an interesting picture. The complex expressions that sat upon her countenance would have furnished a fascinating study for an artist. There were the evidences of terror mingled with penitence and remorse, and she might have passed for some *Mater Dolorosa* of the middle ages, on whose ears some mystic voice had sounded, had not her form been relieved by the closely-fitting, elegant riding-habit that she wore and her head,—her pretty little round head, with its wealth of golden hair,—been covered by the shapely terai hat.

"Yes, he loved me,—I am sure," she mused. "I am afraid I was too rash in reaching my conclusions."

She threw up her veil, and gazing steadily at Carl's moving form, continued:

"I will, like the prodigal, return to the arms of my wronged lover, even though he should cast me from him. It is only the love that springs from the fountain of *our moral ideal* that could brave such danger for me."

Carl had almost reached the gate when she ran toward him and grasped his arm.

"Carl, can you forgive me?" stammered the girl, with quivering lips. "I know that I have wronged you,—how much I alone can tell. After your noble effort to save me at the hazard of your own life, the veil has been drawn from my eyes and I can now see you once more in your true light. It is I who am not worthy of your love."

With a glad cry Carl turned, his face illuminated with pride and joy.

"Then you think I have regained my *lost moral ideal?*"

"Nay, Carl; you had never lost it, I am sure. I

now accept fully my father's explanation of the occurrence that resulted in our estrangement."

"Do you really believe, Mary, that you are the only woman that I have ever loved with that love that many waters cannot quench, neither can the floods drown it?"

"With all my heart I do, my hero, my life, my only love."

"And are you prepared to take me again to your heart as of yore and believe me to be ever true?"

"Yes, Carl; and nothing in this world shall again separate us. What are we poor mortals that we should judge each other?"

Carl caught her in his arms, and rained kisses on her flushed face.

Freeing herself from his tender embrace, Mary, with a shy upward glance, said sweetly:

"Let us go at once to Mr. Fairley, and tell him to publish the banns again."

THE END